THE DEVIL'S DEAL

RAINE STOCKTON DOG MYSTERY #13

BY DONNA BALL

ISBN: 978-0-9965610-7-5

Published by Blue Merle Publishing
Drawer H
Mountain City Georgia 30562

www.bluemerlepublishing.com

First published November 2018

Cover art **www.bigstock.com**

Chapel Hill, North Carolina

ONE

Jason Broderick was not a criminal. He knew nothing about stolen key cards or bypassed security codes. He didn't own a gun. He'd never even failed to pay a parking ticket or thrown away a jury summons. He was a solid citizen, a good neighbor, a devoted father. He was not a criminal.

Nonetheless, he used a fake gate pass to get onto the Hartwell Labs property, and an altered key card to open the door of the employee entrance in the back of the building. It was one o'clock in the morning, and Hartwell did not run a third shift, so the building should have been deserted. It should have been. There was always a chance that some dedicated researcher was working late, or that the cleaning crew had come in early, or that someone had had a fight with his wife and was sleeping in his office, or... a thousand things. A thousand things could go wrong, and he couldn't even think of half of them, because he wasn't a criminal.

The building certainly looked deserted. Its spotless white walls and gleaming linoleum floors were softly lit by security lighting, like a hospital at midnight. He had seen enough of those to know. There was a digital log-in station—the high-tech equivalent of a time clock—where hourly employees scanned their thumbprints to register their arrival and departure. There were safety posters on the wall. There was a wooden door with a glass window, behind which was the employee lounge, and another door marked "changing room" where those who worked in biological areas could shower and change out of their scrubs. There were men's and women's restrooms. And there was an elevator.

Jason moved toward the gray steel doors, his steps echoing. The building *felt* deserted. He could hear his own breath. There was a camera over his shoulder and one pointed at the elevator, but he was careful to keep his face out of its range. He wore a baseball cap with a long bill, which helped, and a dark windbreaker and jeans. Nondescript. The kind of outfit a criminal would wear.

He swiped the key card to access the elevator, but his hand was shaking so badly he had to do it twice. Once the card was read, the door opened immediately, the sharp dinging of the bell making him jump. He stepped inside with his head down, turning away from the camera inside, and he pushed the button for the third floor.

Gloves. He should have worn gloves. He was leaving his fingerprints everywhere. But he wasn't a criminal. He was just retrieving what was his.

He was so distracted by the gloves that he forgot, for just an instant, about the camera. He moved to step back into the corner of the elevator and accidentally turned his face in that direction for a moment, glancing up at the dark, silent eye. That was when he noticed. It *was* dark. The little red light that had been blinking every other time he'd been in this elevator was off. The camera wasn't on. Had the others been on? He hadn't noticed. This wasn't a high-security area of the building; administrative offices and low-level processing, mostly. Those trying to access the research labs would've been subjected to three levels of security scans and a sterile shower, at the least. Maybe they turned off the elevator camera in this part of the building at night. Maybe it was broken. Maybe it didn't matter and Jason should thank whatever gods looked after people like him that the camera was off and he hadn't already screwed up.

The bell dinged again as the doors slid open, and his heart jumped in his chest. Even before he stepped out he heard the barking of a dog, muffled behind a closed door, but steady and determined—also a little hoarse, as though he had been barking for a while. Jason hurried toward the sound, his breathing shallow and his throat dry.

The same nighttime security lights that had been in effect downstairs illuminated the corridor, a long row of recessed lights just above the baseboards that cast weird shadows on the walls and across the white tiled floor.   After about thirty feet, the corridor branched left and right at a wall marred by a ten-foot-tall painting of nothing but red and orange blobs. Jason turned right. And he stopped.

"Christ!" The word exploded out of him in a hiss, forced through his lips by the slamming of his heart against his rib cage. He took a single step backward. "Martin?" he managed, almost in a croak. "Martin, what are you doing here?"

But even as he spoke he knew it was over. Jason Broderick was not a criminal. And that was exactly why he was going to get caught.

Hansonville, North Carolina

TWO

Hansonville was established in 1832 by—you guessed it—a man named Hanson; George Hanson to be precise. He came down from Virginia, thinking to cross the Cumberland Gap and claim some of the rich farmland in the Tennessee Valley for himself. He missed the Gap by a few hundred miles and ended up settling in this pretty little valley in the heart of the Smoky Mountains, where he eventually died of gangrene after shooting himself in the foot while hunting rabbits. No one said you have to be smart to have a town named after you.

Nonetheless, every year we, the long-term beneficiaries of George Hanson's inability to read a map, celebrate the founding of our little piece of paradise with fried pies, clown cars, cloggers, balloon animals, arts and crafts, and just about every other form of merriment known to man, at least in this part of the country. Main Street is shut down from Valley to Courthouse Square, and every civic organization, church group and club has a booth. There are demonstrations of soap making and wood carving, and the Historical Society sets up a display of a working moonshine still which they say was confiscated in 1923. I happen to know, however, being a long-time resident of Hanover County and the daughter of the judge who put its operators in jail, that that particular piece of illegal equipment was taken into evidence by my own Uncle Ro, sheriff of Hanover County at the time, in 1992. The Branson boys served eighteen months in state prison for their crime and set up a meth lab as soon as they got out. There is a lot to be said for the lesser of two evils.

Every year as part of the celebration, the Fire Department brings out its pumper truck and the Riding Club does a dressage demo, with the horses all decked out in harnesses decorated with silk flowers and the riders dressed up in glittering rodeo outfits, right in the middle of Courthouse Square. Members of the Quilter's Club hang their works of art on a long clothesline down the middle of Main Street, and bids are taken all day on each one, with the proceeds going to benefit the hospital auxiliary. A bluegrass band sets up in Courthouse Square, and the whole town smells like barbecue. The Humane Society always has a booth, and usually there's a demonstration by Search and Rescue Dogs. That's where I come in. Usually.

I've often thought that George Hanson would feel right at home wandering the streets of his namesake during Hansonville Day, so little has it changed over the years. But today, joining the crowd that had gathered to watch our newly elected sheriff show off the newest advances in crime-solving technology, I felt about as relevant as old George himself, and, frankly, just about as out of touch.

The crowd, however, was fascinated—probably as much by the presentation as by the technology it was demonstrating. Somewhere in the deserted, 1.5-acre field behind the courthouse, between the ball field and the creek that ran next to the hardware store, Sheriff Marshall Becker had hidden a gun. Overhead, a drone buzzed against the blue April sky. In his hands, the sheriff held a small computerized control box with a view screen, and behind him was a large video screen. He had somehow managed to hook up the control box to a projector, so that everyone in the crowd could see what he saw. He even had one of those headset microphones like they use in concerts, which amplified his voice to his audience.

"You see I can take it up or down," he explained as we watched the terrain on the screen grow closer and then farther away. "And once I get something of interest in my sights, I can magnify it up to twenty times." On the screen the picture zoomed in on a blackberry copse, on a leaf cluster, and then, surprisingly, on a baby bunny looking at us with big almond eyes, unperturbed. "Oops," said Marshall, "not my target."

A genial laugh went through the crowd.

"What do you think, Stockton?" The voice belonged to Chief Deputy Jolene Smith, who had come to watch the demonstration along with a handful of other deputies, all of them grinning like kids on Christmas morning. "Is this little berg ready for twenty-first century law enforcement?"

In addition to being Sheriff Becker's number one deputy, Jolene and her Malinois Nike were the county's only official K-9 team, which meant that emergency services relied heavily on volunteers like me to fill in the gaps. I was one half of the county's only canine search and rescue team; the other half, my golden retriever Cisco, was in a down-stay at my feet, his leash fastened around my waist. He had found a stick concealed in the tangled spring undergrowth and was contentedly munching on it, his plumy tale swishing lazily in the grass. While Nike was busy sniffing out guns and drugs during traffic stops or taking down perpetrators who made the mistake of trying to run from a trained attack dog, Cisco and I could be combing the woods looking for that lost hiker or the child who'd wandered off during a family picnic. Sometimes we do upward of twenty searches a season. Most of them are false alarms, sure, but when you live on the edge of the wilderness, there's no such thing as being too prepared.

I wrinkled my nose in disdain. "That's thing's a toy," I scoffed. "I could knock it out of the air with a rock."

"You do and you'll be guilty of a felony," she replied, watching the screen.

I muttered, "It might be worth it."

Jolene and I were not friends, and she never lost an opportunity to point that out to me. She was relatively new in town, the only African American on the force, and currently the only woman as well. The average person in that situation wouldn't have been that picky about who she chose to hang out with. But despite my repeated overtures in that direction—and despite my indisputably charming personality—she had never quite warmed to me. Go figure.

The sheriff said, "This particular model has thermal imaging capability. It can pick up the heat signature of any living thing..." He hit a key on the controller and the screen became a kaleidoscope of blues, greens and reds. "Even something as small as a rabbit." He zoomed in on the small pulsing red blob at the bottom of the screen, and pushed another button to transform the blob into a bunny again. "This greatly enhances our ability to track a subject over rough terrain, even at night."

There were appreciative murmurs and nods, but I said loudly enough to be heard, "Any good tracking dog can do that."

Marshall glanced at me and smiled, but said nothing. The drone buzzed away from the rabbit.

Beside me, Jolene chuckled. "You know what a troglodyte is, Stockton?"

I scowled at her. "Of course I do." It occurred to me that the only time I ever heard her laugh was when she was laughing at me.

It wasn't that I had anything in particular against Marshall Becker. In fact, he had adopted a rescue golden retriever from me—a gorgeous English Cream named Cameo with whom Cisco had fallen instantly in love—which meant he was basically a good guy, at least in my book. But he and I had different ways of looking at things, and this expensive toy of his was only one example. He was a by-the-book, up-to-the-minute, all-systems-firing kind of law officer; a lot like Jolene in that respect. I wasn't sure either one of them would ever entirely understand the way things were done in a small, isolated mountain community like this.

Also, if I have to get down to the bare naked truth, a member of my family has been the law in this county for well over thirty years. Uncle Ro was sheriff when I was born, and I married his successor, Buck Lawson. It's hard to get used to an outsider, no matter how qualified he is.

"Whoa, ladies and gentlemen, what is this?" Marshall's voice came through the amplifier. "I believe we have our target."

On the screen, the ground grew closer as the drone turned and dived and then hovered above what was clearly a gun lying in the weeds a half mile or so away.

"As you can see," Marshall said, "the coordinates are clearly displayed on my screen. If this were a genuine search for evidence, I'd be able to send my deputies right to the site."

When the applause died down, I raised my hand and called, "Excuse me, Sheriff, but don't you already have a munitions-sniffing dog on the force? Nike could have *taken* your deputies to the weapon. You wouldn't have to send them."

Again he smiled at me. "Not this one, she couldn't. It's plastic. I bought it at the Dollar Store for two bucks."

Everyone laughed, but I was merely annoyed. I raised my voice again, "What if the gun had been under a bush instead of out in the open? Could the drone have found it then? Can drones fly in tunnels or caves? Because we have a lot of them around here."

"Drones do have limitations," admitted Marshall. "However, the controller on these things can program a search grid much faster and tighter than we could ever do by hand, which increases the find rate immensely even when you do factor in the limitations. As a matter of fact..." There was mischief in his eyes now, and I knew I should have seen this coming. "How would you like to put it to the test?" He turned back to the audience. "Ladies and gentlemen, what do you say? Raine and Cisco versus modern technology? Before this demo began, one of my deputies concealed himself somewhere in this field. I have no idea where. Let's see who can find him first—the experienced search dog or the inexperienced drone."

Everyone clapped and cheered their approval, and Jolene murmured, clearly enjoying this, "Stockton, you should've kept your mouth shut. As usual."

I ignored her, reaching down to take the stick from Cisco's mouth. He looked hurt at first, but when I pulled his orange SAR vest from my day bag, he sprang to his feet, eyes bright and tail fanning a breeze behind him. Cisco doesn't know the difference between a demo, a training exercise, and a real search. It's all the same game to him, and there's nothing he loves more than a good game.

I strapped Cisco into his vest and harness, attached the long tracking lead, and walked over to Marshall, stopping only twice to speak sharply to Cisco as he tried to bounce into the crowd to greet a friend or a friend-to-be. Anyone who's ever met a golden retriever knows what I'm talking about. No matter how important the task at hand, there are always two things more important to a golden: food and love. Come to think of it, maybe they've got the right idea.

"How old is the trail?" I asked Marshall.

He moved the microphone away from his mouth. "About half an hour."

I regarded him skeptically. "Is this on the up-and-up? You're sure you don't know where the target is?"

"On my honor." He held up two fingers in a semblance of the Boy Scout salute, his expression sincere.

I believed him, not only because he was, as far as I could tell, an honest man and an officer of the law, but because to someone like Marshall the victory would mean nothing unless the contest was fair.

"So, what?" I said, maintaining my skepticism. "You just fly that thing around until you happen to see something?"

He shook his head. "In search mode, it uses an algorithm to project a search grid, then scans the ground until it spots a human. At that point it switches over to track mode and stays on the target until I tell it otherwise. It can go up to thirty miles an hour in search mode, faster when tracking."

I gave a noncommittal, "Huh," making sure to sound unimpressed. Actually the whole thing was pretty interesting, and I wouldn't mind hearing more about it. But right now I had a challenge to win.

I said, "Scent object?"

He took a plastic bag with a work glove zipped inside from the nearby folding table that held his equipment. The object of the search would have worn the glove long enough to permeate it with his scent. He handed me the bag and said, "Ready when you are. Say the word."

I glanced over at Cisco, who was happily licking an ice cream cone from a little boy's hand. "Cisco!" I shouted and jerked him back to my side—but not before he took advantage of the split-second opportunity and snatched the entire scoop of ice cream from the top of the cone. The little boy squealed a protest and his mother swept him up, glaring at me. "I'll pay for it!" I called back apologetically. She took her kid and stalked away.

Okay, score one for the drone.

I could tell Marshall was having a hard time keeping a straight face, but I didn't see anything funny about it. I waited until Cisco finished licking his lips and then took the glove out of the bag. I said, "Cisco, watch me." I've found it's always best to wait to give a command until you're pretty sure your dog will obey. And to his credit—and mine—Cisco's gaze snapped to my face, waiting eagerly for what I might do next. He was probably hoping I had more ice cream.

I offered him the glove and he sniffed it with interest. I tucked the glove into my day pack and knelt down to sweep the ground with my fingers. "Track," I told Cisco.

Marshall released the drone. Cisco started sweeping the grass with his nose, bounding off when he caught the scent. I trotted to keep up with him at the end of the long line. The game was on.

Cisco and I compete in a lot of dog sports: agility, rally, obedience, to name a few. Some we're better at than others, but all of them have one thing in common—we like to win. Okay, maybe I like to win a little more than Cisco does, but don't tell me that big grin on his face when I hold up his blue ribbon and present him with his hard-earned stuffed toy doesn't mean he's proud of himself.

Cisco is a good tracking dog. This doesn't mean he's infallible; no dog is. No human is infallible either. The weather, the scent pattern, the age of the trail and the amount of cross-contamination with other human scents all will affect Cisco's performance. He uses a combination of ground tracking and air-scenting to find his target, and when he does not have a specific scent item to tell him who he's looking for, he's trained to track any human in the vicinity. Of course, in this particular situation he knew exactly who he was tracking. Nonetheless, there were a lot of humans in the vicinity with the potential to contaminate the trail, so I had to make sure to keep his attention on the trail that had been made across the field by the missing deputy, and not on the parking lot where there were children with ice cream cones.

Under normal circumstances it would take Cisco ten or fifteen minutes to cover the ground and find the hidden deputy. I'd done this demo before and knew that the "victim" never went too far away; we wanted the crowd to be able to see and appreciate the find. But as good as he was, the one thing Cisco could not do was fly through the air at thirty miles per hour. We were barely five minutes into the search when I saw the drone stop and hover over a kudzu-covered copse a few hundred yards to my east, and a man rose to his feet, waving his arms, as applause broke out from the parking lot.

We had lost.

But the important thing about training a tracking dog is to make sure every exercise—or at least as many as physically possible—ends in a reward. This was easier today than it might otherwise have been because the grinning deputy who was coming toward us at a jog was only Cisco's favorite person in the world, my ex-husband, Buck Lawson.

The minute Buck rose from cover, Cisco started to dash toward him, then acknowledged my sharp "*Ank!*" by running quickly back to me, sitting, and giving a single sharp bark. This was his alert signal, meaning he had found his target. Of course, his butt barely touched the ground before he was up again and running toward his best friend, but I called him back and tossed him his rope toy, which he caught midair and gave a happy, dutiful shake. It's important to keep the routine of success and reward consistent, even though the exercise had not exactly been successful and the reward that was coming across the field toward him was much more significant in Cisco's mind than the rope toy. So I unsnapped the lead and let him have at it. Cisco took off like a shot, leaping into Buck's open arms like a child who hasn't seen his dad in weeks. Come to think of it, that's probably pretty much how Cisco felt.

Buck carried Cisco a few yards, laughing while Cisco grinned and licked his face, then set him on the ground. Cisco bounced merrily along beside Buck as they continued toward me, and I trudged toward them, not nearly as happy about the situation as the two of them were.

"Sorry about that," Buck greeted me when we met up midway across the field. He bent to ruffle Cisco's ears, and Cisco grinned up at him adoringly. "Done out of your job by a machine, huh, old boy? What a way to go."

I frowned, snapping on Cisco's lead. The worst part was I couldn't even complain about an unfair challenge; Cisco had been tracking someone he not only knew, but was highly motivated to find, and Buck knew as well as I did that we had lost fair and square. But that did not mean I wouldn't be doing some complaining to Marshall later.

I said, "I didn't know you were working today."

He was dressed in jeans and tee shirt, which I suppose wasn't technically out of uniform for someone in his job. His official title with the sheriff's office was Chief Investigator, and his job wasn't exactly nine-to-five these days. I hadn't seen him in a uniform since he lost the election to Marshall. As a matter of fact, I hadn't seen him much at all.

He shrugged and tucked his fingers into his jeans pockets as we walked back toward the parking lot, Cisco between us. "Just volunteering. It was either this or wear the padded suit while Jolene and Nike demonstrate the take-down. That damn thing is hot."

I said, "Slow crime day, huh?"

"Never a slow crime day in the big city," he replied easily. "I've got plenty of complaints about phone scams and missing pets waiting on my desk when I get back to work Monday."

We walked in silence for a while, but the only one who seemed comfortable with the situation was Cisco. It's never easy with exes, of course, but Buck and I had more than a little history. Now he was married to someone else. I was about to be. We never seemed to know what to say to each other anymore.

After a while, Buck said, "So what do you hear from Ro?"

He was referring to my uncle, his former boss, who was on a once-a-year solo trip to a retired sheriff's convention in Las Vegas. "Aunt Mart said he won fifty dollars at a slot machine in the hotel lobby."

Buck chuckled. "I'm surprised he told her. He probably spent seventy-five to win it."

"I wouldn't be surprised."

Silence fell again. We had almost reached the parking lot when he said, "So listen…"

I said at the same time, "How's Wyn?"

Wyn was his wife. She was currently living in Asheville. No one—at least no one who would share the information with me—knew why.

Buck gave a small, automatic smile that came nowhere close to reaching his eyes. "She's good. Started school last month. Three more credits and she'll have her teaching degree."

"That's good." I, too, gave one of those quick, automatic smiles that strangers exchange when they don't know what else to do.

We had almost reached the parking lot. "Well," he said, nodding toward the building, "guess I'll go in and return some phone calls. See you, Raine."

"Yeah," I replied. "See you."

He bent down and gave Cisco's ear an affectionate tug, and we branched off in different directions. I hate being an ex.

By the time I reached him, Marshall was putting away his equipment and the crowd had mostly dispersed. I took the glove out of my pack, slapped it on the table, and said, "I call foul. Flat terrain, contained search grid, of course your drone is faster. That wasn't a fair contest."

"You're probably right," he admitted, packing away electrical cords into molded-foam containers. "But the taxpayers are paying for this equipment. They deserve to see what it can do. Thanks for your help with that, by the way."

He was such a politician. "Yeah, well, if this had been a real search," I began.

"Then the drone wouldn't be only one tool in our toolbox," he said, cutting off my argument. "There's no substitute for boots on the ground."

Or paws, I thought, reaching down to scratch Cisco's ear absently. He grinned up at me, tail wagging.

"On the other hand," he went on, carefully fitting the drone into its case, "technology saves lives. Who had you rather send in to disarm a bomb—a man or a robot? I know what I would choose."

He called out, "Aikins! Roberts! How about squaring away this sound equipment, will you? And get the video screen back into the training room."

As the two deputies trotted over to comply, he turned back to me. "Times are changing, Raine, and like it or not we've got to keep up. See you later."

He turned to go back to the courthouse, carrying the drone in its case, and I went in the opposite direction with my dog. He was right, of course. Times were changing.

That didn't mean I had to like it.

THREE

On my way back to the Humane Society booth, I texted Melanie, the only ten-year-old I knew: *What's a troglodyte?* I misspelled it, of course, but thanks to auto-correct, she got my meaning. A moment later she texted back a quote from the Merriam-Webster dictionary:

> **Definition** of *troglodyte*. 1: a member of any of various peoples (as in antiquity) who lived or were reputed to live chiefly in caves. 2: a person characterized by reclusive habits or outmoded or reactionary attitudes.

She had added, *3: You*—and softened it with a smiley face emoji.

My expression soured. *Smart aleck,* I typed. She sent back an emoji that had its fingers in its ears and its eyes rolled up. I had absolutely no idea what that meant, proving, I suppose, that I was a troglodyte.

Melanie was the daughter of my boyfriend, Miles Young, who had recently become my fiancé, though we weren't officially telling people yet. She was currently on a class trip to Montana, searching for dinosaur bones. Two weeks ago she'd wanted to train drug dogs for the FBI when she grew up; now she was leaning toward being an archaeologist who trained dogs to sniff out phony antiquities. How, exactly, she was going to do that had been the subject of many a long-distance conversation since she'd been gone. She really is the most amazing kid I've ever known.

The Humane Society booth is usually nothing more than a shade canopy over a table with some brochures and a donation jar. If we have enough volunteers and the weather isn't too hot, we'll bring out some of our best puppies and kittens for adoption, which always draws a crowd but hardly ever proves to be worth the trouble. This year we'd gone in a different direction. For a $20 donation you could have a fifteen-minute session with our resident "pet psychic," my good friend and personal attorney, Sonny Brightwell. By the time I'd left for the drone demonstration, we had already raised $200, and there was a line of people outside the booth, waiting to hear what their pets thought of them. I have to admit, it was a brilliant idea. Exactly the kind of thing tourists love.

I put Cisco in the ex-pen with Mystery, Sonny's brilliant border collie, and after some bouncy play bows and ear tugs, they settled down on the rubber matting with chew toys, which they occasionally converted to tug toys. The great thing about having two such beautiful, well-behaved dogs (in Mystery's case, at least) was that it was impossible to pass their pen without stopping to admire them. Admiration inevitably led to fantasizing about how wonderful it would be to have a dog like this of your own, and since neither one of these great dogs were available for adoption, voila—another deserving shelter dog finds a home.

Sonny's service dog, Hero, lay alertly beneath the table at which she sat, watching the people come and go and waiting for his next command. Sonny has a degenerative joint disease that sometimes makes it difficult for her to get around without a wheelchair, but even when she was feeling good, like today, Hero went everywhere with her. Today his job was to come to the registration table whenever someone came up, take their $20 bills, and deposit them in the cash box we held open for him. That was another reason we were the most popular booth at the fair.

I relieved Casey, one of our volunteers, at the front table and waved to Sonny, who was just finishing up with a labradoodle and her blond-haired, well-dressed owner. Funny how that happens: designer dog finds designer human and they live happily ever after.

"How's it going?" I asked after the couple left the tent.

"Great," replied Sonny. "Lots of chatty dogs today. How was the demo?"

I shrugged. "It was rigged."

"Cisco says he won," she replied.

That made me grin. "Cisco always thinks he won."

So here's the thing about Sonny: Even though we were selling the whole "pet psychic" thing as a game, there is the slightest possibility that Sonny may actually be able to talk to animals. On more than one occasion she's claimed to have gotten information from a dog that she couldn't possibly have learned any other way—my own dogs included. Once my collie, Majesty, had gone missing in a rain storm, and Sonny dreamed that Majesty was sitting in front of a fire with pink ribbons in her hair, eating chicken. The next day my aunt called to say she'd found her, and when I went to pick Majesty up she was sitting in front of the fire, having just finished a chicken pot pie for dinner. My aunt had taken her to a groomer because she was such a mess from the rain, and Majesty had a pink bow behind her ear. I don't entirely believe the pet psychic claim, but I can't exactly explain it either.

And that, by the way, was when I knew that my aunt needed Majesty more than I did, and Majesty moved uptown. She eats a lot more chicken these days.

For the next hour I held the cash box for Hero as he retrieved people's twenty-dollar bills, and listened while Sonny told them how much their dog loved them, and what his favorite toy was, and what kind of food he preferred. The people, in turn, would exclaim things like, "I knew it!" and, sometimes, "That's right! How could you know that?" Whether Sonny really knew what the dog was thinking or whether she was making it up as she went didn't really matter. People left with expressions of delight and awe on their faces and a new respect for their canine companions and that, in my book, was a sign of money well spent.

We saw the last person standing in line a little after noon, and I took advantage of the lull to say, "I'm going to go grab us a couple of barbecue plates. Do you want coleslaw or potato salad?"

"I'm a vegetarian," she reminded me.

"Oh," I said, crestfallen. "I forgot."

Sonny was in her fifties and dressed like a hippie when she wasn't in the courtroom, with flowered skirts and a long gray braid worn down her back. She also ran an animal sanctuary on her mountaintop property which welcomed chickens, pigs, goats, sheep, cats, birds, ducks, geese, horses, cows and one very special border collie who kept them all in line. All of this should have served as a reminder to me that her philosophy did not include making a meal out of the animals she sheltered, but it didn't.

She chuckled at my chagrin. "It's a lifestyle choice, not a prison sentence," she said, and reached into the tote at her feet. "I brought a veggie wrap from home. But you can get me a sweet tea, if you want. I'll keep an eye on the dogs."

"Sure." I found a piece of paper and printed in bold marker, *Next appointment at 1:00.* I was about to pin it to the outside of the canopy when I saw a little girl approaching us, tugging a man behind her. "Daddy, please? I want to have Bongo's fortune told! Please, can we, please?"

The man held the leash of a glossy-coated, bright-eyed black Labrador retriever who was taking in all the sights and sounds with avid interest. His ears went up when he saw Cisco and Mystery, and both dogs came to the gate of the pen to check him out, their tails wagging. The Lab, however, gave them no more than a cursory glance before he found something of greater interest and swiveled his head in that direction, assessing a woman who was pushing a stroller and talking on her phone. I like a curious dog; it means he's eager to learn. And this one clearly had some training under his collar. For all the distractions that pulled at his attention, he never once broke heel position or tightened the leash, which hung in a perfect loop between himself and his handler's knee. I was impressed.

The man said, "Honey, look, they're getting ready to close for lunch. We'll come back later." He looked tired and rumpled, with the kind of pallor that comes from working in an office and the faint stubble of a pale beard on his cheeks. The denim shirt he wore open over a black tee shirt was creased and wrinkled in a way that only comes from long hours behind the wheel, and I figured him for a guy who was wishing he'd reconsidered that family road trip right about now.

I glanced over my shoulder at Sonny, who shrugged good-naturedly and put her sandwich back in her tote. I turned back to the man. "That's okay," I said. "Come on in."

The little girl's face broke into a wide grin. "Can we, Daddy, can we? They're not going to lunch, see? Can we? Bongo wants his fortune told, don't you, Bongo? Can we?"

The man looked at his daughter and a tenderness came into his eyes that showed exactly who owned his heart. With a smile of resignation that I had seen a hundred times on Miles's face—and on my own father's face— he took out his wallet. "How much?"

"Twenty dollars," I said. "It all goes to find homes for abandoned dogs and cats."

He thumbed through the bills in his wallet until he found a twenty while his daughter looked up at him with shining eyes and bounced on her toes with excitement. She was a cute little thing, probably five or six, wearing a pink cloth hat with "Florida" stitched in blue on the brim and a sparkly rhinestone palm tree decorating the crown. Her tee shirt had some kind of dragon on it. She laughed out loud when Hero came up and took the money out of her father's hand when he tried to hand it to me.

"Daddy, look!" she cried, pointing. "A yellow Bongo!"

I held the box open for Hero and he dropped the money in. "You have a good eye," I told her. "Hero is a Labrador, just like Bongo."

"Bongo knows lots of tricks," she boasted, then added doubtfully, "but I don't think he knows his fortune."

I said, "You know, the lady doesn't really tell Bongo's fortune. She just talks to him, and tells you what Bongo says back."

Her eyes went big. "Bongo can talk *too*?"

I nodded solemnly. "You can ask him anything, and Miss Sonny will tell you what he says."

She said, "Bongo doesn't talk to me. But he does lots of other cool things. He's the best dog in the world."

I smiled. "I can tell." I closed the cash box, and Hero and I escorted them the few steps into the tent. Sonny's table was draped with purple leftover Halloween fabric dotted with silver reflective stars and held a crystal ball—actually an upside-down fish bowl—filled with dog biscuits. "Sonny," I said, gesturing the man and child toward the lawn chairs set up before the table, "this is Bongo."

"Why hello, Bongo," she said warmly, smiling at him. "It's a pleasure to meet you."

His ears went up and he actually barked in reply. I have no idea how she gets them to do that, but it always makes me laugh. Even the weary-looking man smiled, and stroked the big dog's head affectionately as he sat down.

I went back to my table at the front of the tent in case anyone else showed up, but the demand for our services seemed to have slowed down—probably because everyone had had the same idea I had and was standing in line for barbecue. I angled my chair so I could watch the "reading."

Sonny said, "Bongo says he loves salmon snacks."

The little girl nodded vigorously. "They're his favorites. I give him apples sometimes, but he spits them out. He's not allowed to have Cheetos," she confided.

Her dad said sternly, "Neither are you."

She grinned up at him impudently. "I know."

He rested a hand briefly atop her head, smiling, and leaned back in his chair.

Sonny said, "Bongo says he has a room of his own at work. It's made out of wire and has a nice red bed in it."

The man sat up a little straighter, interested. Sonny didn't appear to notice. Bongo sat between the man and the little girl, panting happily, looking for all the world as though he was actually having a conversation with Sonny. I wished I had a camera.

"Bongo says he has a very important job," Sonny went on, "in the tech field. He says he's a very special dog. Everyone loves him."

Something had happened to the man. He had gone from being relaxed, if tired, to rigid. He sat forward in his chair, and his voice was hoarse. "What are you talking about?" he demanded.

The girl sang out, "I love Bongo!"

"He loves you too," Sonny said. "He wishes he could spend more time with you, but he has to work." She hesitated, looking thoughtful. "He loves his job. He says he can do things nobody else can. He finds things that are hidden. He—"

The man stood up so abruptly that his chair toppled over. "Celie, come on." He grabbed the child's hand, pulling Bongo around on the leash with the other. "We have to go."

"But I don't want—"

He swept her off the ground and onto his hip, ignoring her cries of protest. He strode out of the tent looking neither right nor left, his face white and strained. He held Bongo's leash so tightly that the big dog had to trot to keep up, and as I gaped after him, astonished, he picked up his pace until he was actually jogging down the street.

Sonny looked as dumbfounded as I was.

"What was *that* about?" I said.

"Weird," Sonny replied, shaking her head. "He kept darting his eyes around, like he was looking for something, and then…" She spread open her hands, palms up. "He left." She frowned thoughtfully and added, "But Raine, there was something about that dog…"

"Oh, crap."   I bent to scoop up the object I'd spotted beside the overturned chair in which the man had been sitting. "He dropped his wallet. I think I can catch him," I called over my shoulder as I ran out of the tent. "Keep your eye on the cash box!"

The roped off area between Valley Street and Courthouse Square was only three blocks long, and logic told me that anyone who'd left in that big a hurry probably wasn't going to lunch. He was most likely headed toward one of the two parking lots, either the one at the courthouse or the one at the north end of Valley Street. He'd turned south when he left the tent, so I took the shortcut across Kingston Alley and emerged across the street from the courthouse. I was in luck. As I paused at the corner to catch my breath, I caught a glimpse of a waving black Labrador tail, and next to it a man holding a little girl in a pink hat, making his way around the long line that had formed in front of the barbecue stand.

"Hey!" I called, waving the wallet.   "Hey, mister!"

The bluegrass music drowned out my voice, and he didn't even look around. I started running again.

I was right.   He headed across the street to the courthouse parking lot, and as he rounded the corner of Courthouse Square, the music became less blaringly loud.   We were only a few dozen yards apart now. "Mister! Hey!"

The displays on this side of the square were limited: the Chamber of Commerce had a booth with maps and brochures and homemade potholders, and the hiking club was selling trail maps and hickory walking sticks. There were a few people coming and going to their cars, tossing drink cups into the big trash cans, pausing to snap photos of the big "Welcome to Hansonville, Est. 1832" banner overhead with the brilliant vista of blue and green Smoky Mountains in the background. There really was no reason for the man not to hear me, so I tried a different tact.

"Hey!" I called, closing on him. "Bongo!"

Bongo swiveled his head around at the sound of his name and the little girl turned in her father's arms, pointing at me. But the man didn't look around. He jerked Bongo's leash and moved faster. "Hey!" I called again. "You dropped your wallet!"

Everyone else was staring at me now, but the man broke into a trot, running away from me. He might have out-distanced me, too, even with the burden of the child and the dog on leash, but he had to dodge the sudden opening of a car door. That's when I caught up with him, and grabbed his arm.

"Hey," I said, breathing hard. "You dropped your—"

He flung me off of him violently, his eyes wild. "Get away from me!" he shouted.

I staggered back, staring at him. Bongo started to bark, and the man jerked him close to his knee. The little girl cried tearfully, "Daddy, the fortune lady!" She buried her head in her father's shoulder. People were pointing their cell phones at us, hoping that in this day of viral social media, the altercation would escalate.

I managed, "I just wanted to return your wallet."
I held it up, but he didn't even look at it.

He took a step toward me, fury in his eyes, the
little girl weeping into his shoulder. "Do you think
I'm stupid enough to fall for that?" His voice had
deteriorated to something between a growl and a hiss.
"Who the hell are you? How did you find me? It
doesn't matter." He licked his parched, dry lips, eyes
darting back and forth. "Because you can tell
whoever hired you that it's over, they lost, there's no
way—"

"Everything okay here, Stockton?"

The low-key drawl was one I never thought I'd be
glad to hear. Jolene Smith, in full uniform, came into
my line of vision, resting her hands on her gun belt in
that very intimidating way law officers have of doing.
I think they teach that in police academy.

I said, "This man left his wallet at our booth. I
was just trying to return it."

She might not have noticed the wave of panic that
crossed his face, but I did. I held out the wallet to her
and she opened it. She looked at him. "Are you Jason
Broderick?"

There was a moment when nothing happened. He
just stood there, gripping the leash, his little girl
crying, panic churning in his eyes as he weighed his
options. Then he turned and started to bolt.

Bad decision. He was immediately stopped by
two deputies, one on either side. A word to the wise:
if you're going to have an angry altercation with
someone, don't do it in the parking lot outside the
sheriff's office.

Jolene said, "Sir, is your dog dangerous?"

The man said sharply, "Don't touch my dog." He pulled Bongo closer.

The little girl cried, "Don't hurt Bongo!"

I said quickly, "The dog's okay." I don't like to go out on a limb like that—after all, any dog with teeth can bite—but I could see the little girl was on the verge of a screaming, sobbing fit, and I didn't think any of us wanted *that* going viral.

Jolene repeated, "Is your name Jason Broderick?"

"Yes," he said. He was sweating now. "Yes, that's my wallet, okay? I dropped it like she said. I'm sorry for the confusion." He reached out the hand that held Bongo's leash. "Can we go now?"

Jolene looked at him for a moment, then removed his driver's license from the wallet and handed it to one of the deputies. "Check this out," she said.

Panic flashed across Broderick's eyes. "What are you doing that for? I'm not even in my car! You can't—"

Jolene said, "How much money did you have in here, sir?"

That sounded very much like she suspected me of taking some of that cash, and my outraged expression showed it.

He replied impatiently, "I don't know. About five hundred dollars, I guess."

"Five hundred eighty dollars in cash, three credit cards and a bank card," she specified. "Does that sound right?"

"Yes, that's right." He extended his hand for the wallet. "Can we go now?"

She returned the wallet politely. "It'll just be another moment, sir. Is this your daughter?"

I saw him swallow. "Yes."

"What's her name?"

"Celie. Celia."

"Where's her mother?"

"Her mother's dead," he replied briefly. "Look, you have no right to keep us here. All we're doing is driving through and we stopped for a bite to eat. I'm the one who lost my wallet. I'm the victim here. You can't..."

"Yes. sir," said Jolene. "You can be on your way in just a minute. Stockton." She jerked her head toward me, indicating I should join her as she walked a few steps away.

Keeping her back to the man and child, she lowered her voice and demanded curtly, "What's the story, Stockton?"

"I don't know." I tried not to glance over my shoulder. "There is no story. I'm working the Humane Society booth with Sonny Brightwell. She was talking to the guy—well, the guy's dog, Bongo..."

Jolene gave me a hard look, and I returned it levelly.

"You know how it works," I went on. "For a twenty-dollar donation, Sonny talks to your dog. That's what she was doing when suddenly the guy freaked, grabbed his kid and the dog, and ran out of there. He dropped his wallet in his hurry, and I ran after him. That's it."

It was her turn to frown. "What made him freak? Did he get a phone call or a text or something?"

I shrugged. "I don't think so. He just kind of went crazy and ran." I hesitated, uncertain, and then added, "There's something familiar about that name, though. Jason Broderick. Is he an actor or something?"

She replied impatiently, "Matthew. Matthew Broderick is the actor." Then she looked back at Broderick, her expression inscrutable. "Hang around for a minute, Stockton."

I protested, "I left Sonny alone at the booth. I need to get back." The truth is that nothing short of a gun could have persuaded me to leave before I learned the outcome of this little drama, and Jolene knew it. She ignored me, turning away as her cell phone buzzed.

I heard her say, "Yeah" and, "Right" and then, "Okay, that'll be an eight-three-three on the double. And get social services over here."

Our sheriff's office didn't generally use the 10-code system, except when the guys wanted to be cute on the radio, and even the private, internal 8-codes were rarely employed around here—except in case of extreme emergency. Buck had told me once what most of them meant, but all I could remember about the 8-3 sequence was that it had something to do with the way you approached a suspect who was considered dangerous. So far it did not sound good at all for Mr. Broderick. Or Bongo.

Jolene walked over to Broderick and said, "Mr. Broderick, please put the child down."

His arm only tightened, and horror slowly filled his eyes as he understood what was happening. Out of the corner of my eye, I saw three more deputies rounding the corner of the building, one of whom was my ex. They were coming toward us at a fast pace, but their weapons were not drawn, and they weren't running. The code was coming back to me now: three deputies, approach and surround but don't alarm. Right.

He said, "I will not! What is this? What's going on?"

Jolene said in her customary expressionless, no-nonsense tone, "Sir, there is an outstanding warrant for your arrest. We have to take you into custody. The little girl will be fine. Please put her down."

The little girl in question looked at us with big wet eyes, her arms wrapped around her father's neck in a death grip.

He just stood there, his chest rising and falling rapidly, his face sheened with sweat. "Listen," he said. "We can work this out. It's a mistake. I can explain everything."

"Yes, sir," Jolene said, "you'll have a chance to do just that once we get you inside. Do you have any weapons on you?"

"No. I don't... don't own a gun."

The little girl whimpered, "Daddy..."

He whispered, "It's okay, baby. It's okay."

Jolene held out her hand. "Give me the dog's leash."

Bongo sat alertly at his owner's side, bright eyes taking in everything that was going on. Jolene moved to take the leash, but Broderick took an abrupt step backwards, pulling Bongo with him. "No! Keep away from my dog."

The deputy who was guarding Broderick put his hand on his taser. Jolene put one palm out in a calming gesture, but I could see her shoulders stiffen.

"Take it easy, sir. You're frightening your little girl. Now, put her down and hand over the leash. You need to come with us."

I stepped forward quickly. "I'll take care of him. I'm a dog trainer." I glanced at Jolene and she didn't object, so I held out my hand for the leash. "People trust me with their dogs every day. I have a whole kennel full, and the golden you saw before, he's mine. Bongo will be fine."

He swallowed again, eyes darting, weighing his options. The other deputies were almost upon us. He was virtually surrounded and running out of options.

He unwound the little girl's arms from his neck and set her on the ground, comforting her protests with, "It's okay, sweetheart. Go with the nice police lady. Daddy's going inside to talk to these folks for a minute, okay? I need you to be a big girl."

She clung to his knee. "I don't want to be a big girl. I want to go with you."

Jolene bent down and held out her hand. "Come on, honey. We just need to talk to your daddy for a minute. How would you like to sit at my desk and color while we do that?"

She shook her head and buried her face in her father's knee. I can't say that I blame her. "Warm and nurturing" are not words I'd use to describe Jolene, even without her gun and badge.

"Well, how would you like to sit at my desk and eat ice cream?" said a familiar voice behind me. Buck knelt beside the child, smiling that smile that has won a thousand hearts. I could see the little girl relax when she looked at him. Being out of uniform, he was no doubt much less intimidating than the men with guns and radios who were surrounding her, although he did have a badge pinned to his belt loop. But it was more than that. Buck had always been the man they sent in to defuse a tense situation. He just had that way about him.

"Hey," he said, "I like your hat. I just got back from Florida, too. You know what my favorite part is? Mickey Mouse. What's yours?"

It always broke my heart a little, seeing how good Buck was with kids. He should have had children of his own.

She still looked reluctant, but there wasn't a female in the world who could resist Buck's charm. "Arial," she muttered, her face still half-buried.

"Sure, I know her. Didn't she make a movie? Cute chick, curly red hair?"

The little girl giggled, relaxing her grip on her father's leg a little.

Buck said, "So seriously? You got to meet her? I sure would like to hear about that. Maybe you could tell me all about your visit with her while we get that ice cream, okay?"

She looked uncertainly up at her father.

"It's okay, baby," he said, licking his dry lips. "Go with the man. He'll take care of you. But don't eat too much ice cream. You'll ruin your dinner."

She looked at Buck. "Can it be chocolate?" she said.

Buck held out his hand. "Honey, it can be any flavor you want."

She took his hand, and he led her back toward the building, making easy conversation with her the whole way.

Jolene turned back to Broderick. "We didn't want to cuff you in front of your daughter. Now, please give Miss Stockton the dog's leash and place your hands behind you."

There was a moment when I thought he would. He lifted the leash toward me and I reached to take it. But then, with a sudden flash of desperation he spun around, whirling Bongo with him, and bolted. "Bongo, run!" he cried.

Broderick was fast, and he had the advantage of surprise. He made it about thirty feet before two deputies tackled him. He broke away but lost hold on Bongo's leash. Bongo kept running for a few feet, and then turned around to see what had happened to the tension on his leash, as most dogs will. I dashed after him. I snatched up the handle on the lead at about the same time Broderick landed flat on his face in the grass beside the parking lot, a deputy's knee in his back.

You see such terrible things on television about police violence, but most of the time it's not like that at all—especially when there's a crowd of tourists standing around shooting video with their cell phones. There was a lot of shouting: "Don't move! Hands behind your head! *Behind your head*!" and one of the deputies drew his taser.

Jolene yelled at me, "Stockton! Out of the way!"

I quickly complied, dragging Bongo farther back onto the grass and then doing a quick about turn so that he could not see his owner. I walked briskly back toward the crowd of people to keep his attention and, sure enough, it worked. He trotted right along beside me with his ears up and his eyes watching my face. This dog had definitely seen an obedience school or two.

Jolene had her hand on her weapon, but I knew it would never leave the holster. Buck had taught me long ago that a good law officer never draws a weapon unless he intends to fire it, and there were children in the crowd, not to mention people getting in and out of their cars every minute. Besides, Broderick was subdued and compliant, and even as I hurried out of the way, the deputies were snapping cuffs on him, dragging him to his feet. No shots would be fired today.

I walked back to Jolene as two deputies, one holding each of his arms, turned Broderick toward the booking and holding area of the jail which was just a short walk across the parking lot. My heart was pounding and I could feel adrenaline like electricity in the air. Broderick twisted around, eyes searching until he found Bongo, and he cried, "What about my dog? What are you going to do with my dog?"

The deputies, out of good humor by now, pushed him forward and declined to answer.

I was in perfect sympathy, of course, and wished I could reassure him that Bongo couldn't be in better hands than mine. But even I had to wonder what kind of man would turn his daughter over to a perfect stranger, but would run from police when they tried to take his dog.

Jolene's voice, and her face, were tense as she said, "Can you get the dog to the shelter, Stockton? Or do you want me to get a deputy to drive him over?"

I said, "That's okay. I'll take him home with me."

She replied crisply, turning to follow her deputies to the jail, "Procedure, Stockton. The animal goes to the county shelter."

I ignored her. No way was I letting this beautiful dog spend the night in impound like a common street cur. After all, he hadn't committed any crime, no matter what his owner had done.

I kept up with Jolene, asking curiously, "So what was the warrant for? Some kind of custody thing?"

Jolene glanced at me, her expression impassive. "No," she said.

"What, then?"

She replied flatly, "Murder."

FOUR

Say what you will about Jolene—and I had said plenty—when it comes to grace under pressure, she could write the book. A lot of law officers, upon learning a suspect was wanted for murder, would have gone all Rambo on him, and not without justification. He could have pulled a weapon, or used his child as a shield, or commanded the dog to attack. A desperate man will do anything, and I can't think of anyone more desperate than someone who's already wanted for murder, whether or not he actually committed the crime. But Jolene hadn't blinked an eye, raised her voice or reached for her weapon, and she'd had the suspect completely under control until the moment he'd panicked over his dog. I guess Marshall had made the right choice for chief deputy after all.

"My goodness!" exclaimed Corny, breathless and big-eyed, when I finished my story. "What kind of murder? Who did he kill? Where?"

Corny is the head groomer and general manager at Dog Daze, the boarding and training facility I established in the remodeled horse barn fifty steps from my back door. Before Corny took over, grooming was more or less a sideline; now our grooming room is practically a spa, with classical music, a lavender diffuser, and, yes, a massage station. If dogs really could talk, they'd be begging their owners to come here.

Corny is also what you might call something of a character. With a halo of fuzzy orange hair, oversized glasses, and a propensity for dressing in primary colors—today it was crayon-green overalls and a red striped Henley shirt—he tends to leave an impression. And that's before we even get to his flair for drama.

In answer to his question—or questions, as the case may be—I could only frown and shrug uncomfortably. "I don't know," I admitted. Those were not words that came easily to me. In the old days, when my uncle or my husband—even when he was my ex-husband—was in charge, I would have known the answers to all those questions. It irritated me that all I could reply now was, "I guess he didn't kill anyone around here, or we would have heard about it. Anyway, I need you to take care of Bongo until I get back, okay? I left Sonny by herself at the booth—well, except for Cisco and Mystery, of course."

Corny looked thoughtful. "Jason Broderick," he said. "Why does that name sound familiar to me? Is he famous?"

"You're thinking of Matthew Broderick," I said, "the actor. *Ferris Bueller's Day Off?*" I had looked it up on my phone before I drove home.

"Oh," he said, although I wasn't entirely sure he recognized the movie. "Right."

Corny dropped to his knees and gave the glossy-coated Labrador a big hug. Bongo, who was panting a little with anxiety, licked his face once and then turned back to inspecting every inch of the office with his eyes.

"You can count on me, Miss Stockton," Corny assured me solemnly. "No matter what his human did, once he crosses this threshold he will be treated like any other guest—which is to say, like royalty."

I suppressed a grin. Despite his tendency to turn the simplest of jobs into a Grand Calling, or perhaps because of it, I would have trusted Corny with my own life, and even more so with my dogs. For all of Jason Broderick's panic, Bongo couldn't have been in better hands if the Secret Service had been assigned to protect him.

I said, "But put him in a quarantine kennel for the time being, okay? He seems healthy enough, but we don't have a shot record and we can't risk the other dogs."

"Absolutely." He picked up Bongo's leash and started to lead him back to the kennel area, then hesitated, looking troubled. "Miss Stockton, I was just wondering... don't you think it's a little strange that a man running from the law—I mean, someone who just killed somebody—would take his dog and his little girl with him?"

Don't think for one moment the same thought hadn't occurred to me. "On the other hand," I pointed out, "just because someone is accused of a crime doesn't necessarily mean he did it. Innocent until proven guilty, and all that."

Corny looked reassured. "Right," he said, looking down at Bongo. "It's probably just a huge mistake. That happens, right?"

I knew how he felt. It was hard to believe that anyone who could command the loyalty of such a beautiful dog could be guilty of murder. I managed a smile. "Sure. All the time."

Another thing Buck had taught me long ago was that ninety-nine percent of the time the person the cops think is guilty is in fact guilty. It's just the way it goes.

But in this particular case, I wasn't entirely convinced.

FIVE

Chaz Kramer spent the morning as any self-respecting CEO of a multi-billion-dollar global enterprise should have: playing golf on the award-winning course of his Bethesda, Maryland, country club. A member of the US Senate and a Saudi prince had joined him, but they had discussed neither politics nor foreign affairs. Saturday golf was sacred, an oasis from the concerns of business and the madness of the world. He had never made an exception to that rule.

Until today.

The foursome would have ordinarily included his son-in-law, David, who was not only an excellent golfer and a pleasant conversationalist, but Chaz's right-hand man. Every powerful executive needed such a person: someone whose loyalty was unquestioned and whose competence was absolute; someone who not only knew where the bodies were buried but who had done the burying. David was the person Chaz trusted, his detail man, his fixer. Today there was something that needed fixing.

David's spot on the course had been filled by a colleague of Chaz's, an interesting enough fellow who bred race horses, one of which was being groomed for the Derby this year. The prince had investments in several American stables and enjoyed talking to him. So did Chaz. The four of them finished their game with Bloody Marys and lunch at the club house dining room, whose floor-to-ceiling windows overlooked the fairway, and whose towering stacked-stone fireplace provided a cheerful blaze on the north wall. The ambience was casual but refined, with the clink of silver and the murmur of easy conversation in the background, waiters in white shirts and black ties anticipating every need while expensively groomed guests in their golf clothes enjoyed it all. The omelets were prepared to perfection, the company was congenial, and the view was spectacular. It was a perfect Saturday.

Almost.

When his phone vibrated in his pocket, Kramer excused himself to answer it. It was David.

"I just got word that the police picked up Broderick this morning," David said, "in some little town in North Carolina called Hansonville."

Kramer's shoulders relaxed fully for the first time in twenty-four hours. "And the dog?"

"The police report says it was taken to the county shelter."

Kramer frowned a little. "That doesn't sound good."

"I'm taking care of it."

"Excellent." Kramer paused, the frown lingering. "Hansonville. Why does that sound familiar?" But before he finished speaking he knew. "Right," he said softly. "Of course."

"The same thing occurred to me," David assured him. "I have someone on their way now, but I'm thinking this might be something I need to look into personally."

The frown deepened. "You may be right." Then, "We missed you on the course today."

"I missed being there," David replied. "Maybe you and Karen could come over for dinner tomorrow night. This Hansonville business shouldn't take long, and I know Angie would love it."

Kramer chuckled. "You don't know my daughter at all if you think she'd love having last-minute dinner guests. Suppose we take you both out instead? I'll have Karen iron out the details with Angie."

"Sounds great."

Kramer said, "You've got this under control?"

"Don't worry," replied David. "I know what has to be done."

"Then I'll see you tomorrow." He pocketed the phone and went back to the table, smiling. It was good to have someone he could depend on.

And it was even better not to know the details.

SIX

On a normal Saturday, it takes about fifteen minutes to get from my house to town. Even with the tourist traffic generated by Hansonville Day, the round trip took less than forty-five minutes, and I was back at the Humane Society booth by 1:30. I was also starving, since with all the excitement I had completely forgotten about picking up that barbecue plate.

Cisco greeted me with paws on the top of the ex-pen, which he could have easily knocked over with a single leap, and I corrected him with a quick, "Cisco, sit!" He sat, tail swishing and face grinning, and I rewarded him with a liver treat and a kiss on the nose.

"Cisco doesn't like being left behind," Sonny informed me, though it hardly took a pet psychic to figure that out. "He says you're a team. Deputy Smith was here to interview me about that fellow Broderick," she added, looking concerned. "Murder? Really?"

"That's what they say." I gave a noncommittal lift of my shoulders.

She said, with feeling, "That poor little girl."

I was about to agree, but just then my phone chimed. It was a text from Miles, who was taking advantage of two kid-free weeks to take a trip to Belgium, where he was building a resort hotel or buying a company or something of the sort. Our worlds intersected only on very specific levels, and his business was not one of them.

His message was: *Do you know what one of Belgium's main exports is?*

I was starting to feel like I was back in high school, with pop quizzes everywhere. *Chocolates?* I guessed.

Diamonds, he sent back.

Miles and I were at something of an impasse over the ring situation. It wasn't that I didn't trust his taste; he had given me some beautiful jewelry in the past—mostly, I suspected, with the help of Melanie. It was just that I wasn't really a diamond engagement ring kind of person. For one thing, a fancy diamond ring was completely impractical with the kind of work I did. For another... well, it reminded me a little of a brand, or a collar on a dog. I couldn't say that to Miles, of course.

So I typed back, *I'd rather have chocolates*.

He replied, *Chocolate diamonds?* This was accompanied by a photo of a really interesting looking emerald-cut jewel with a dark cast that didn't look much like a diamond at all. It was pretty. It was unique. But it wasn't me.

I like the kind with soft centers, I replied.

He sent back, *Not like you, then*.

I looked and looked but couldn't find that emoji Melanie was always sending me with the tongue stuck out, so I sent one with a halo and angel wings instead. He always got my sarcasm.

He replied, *I'll call you tonight. Love you.*
Me too.

I was about to tuck my phone in my pocket when it pinged again with another message. This one was from Corny and it said simply, *Is this him?* There was a link and I clicked on it.

The link was to an article from *Working Dog Today.* It was almost two years old, but I recognized it immediately. I read a lot of stuff about dogs, but this one stuck out because it was the first time I had ever heard of technology-detecting dogs. These dogs were trained to sniff out hard drives, thumb drives and even memory chips—all of which were of particular interest to law enforcement because they often contained evidence of criminal activity and were exceptionally easy to hide. Once hidden, these small pieces of technology were almost impossible to find, or at least they had been until the TDDs came along. At the time of the article, there had been only ten such dogs in the world, with demand far exceeding supply. One of the key researchers in the field was an animal behaviorist from Duke University by the name of Jason Broderick.

No wonder his name had sounded familiar to me, and to Corny. He was one of the leading pioneers in canine scent detection theory today.

Just to make sure, I thumbed down to the bottom of the screen, where there was a picture of Broderick in a lab coat, posing with a golden retriever and a yellow Labrador. It was without a doubt the same man I'd seen being led away in handcuffs an hour ago.

I dialed the kennel and Corny answered on the first ring. "Corny," I said, a little breathlessly, "check Bongo's ear for a tattoo."

Behind me, Sonny looked up with interest. The last rescue dog who had come to me with a tattoo had eventually been traced to a service dog organization. After they officially surrendered him to me, Hero had been adopted by Sonny. But during the search for Hero's owner I had learned that many service dogs and almost all dogs used in research facilities are tattooed, usually on the inner ear.

Corny understood immediately, and his voice reflected his excitement. "Was I right? Is that the same man? Miss Stockton, you don't think Bongo is one of *those* dogs, do you?"

As he spoke, I could hear him moving, opening the heavy fire door that led to the kennel area, being greeted by the excited barks of dogs he passed.

I said cautiously, "Could be." That would certainly explain why Broderick had been so concerned about the dog, although running from the police had been stupid. He could have gotten them both shot.

I heard the slide of a kennel bolt and Corny speaking softly to Bongo. In a moment he announced somberly, "Yes, ma'am. I have a tattoo on Bongo's right inside ear flap. Would you like me to read it to you?"

He sounded as full of import as an operator at Mission Control about to read the launch sequence, and I had to smile a little at his gravity. But my amusement was faint and short-lived. I had just found out I'd taken custody of a dog who was worth more than my house, my car and my business combined. There was absolutely nothing funny about that.

I said, "No, that's okay. Just take really, really good care of that dog. I'll be home as soon as I can."

"Yes, ma'am," he promised earnestly. "Don't you worry about a thing. I'll guard him with my life."

"I know you will, Corny."

I disconnected and turned back to Sonny, glancing thoughtfully at my watch. I knew Jason Broderick wouldn't be allowed any visitors until he'd been officially booked into custody, which might take another hour or two. And was I really that anxious to get into a discussion with Jolene—or Marshall, for that matter—about how I'd illegally taken a valuable dog home after being given a direct order to take him to the animal shelter?

But I really needed to talk to Broderick. What was he even doing with a dog like Bongo way down here in Hansonville? Maybe Bongo had been retired from the program. Maybe he was on his way to a new assignment. However he had found himself here in Hansonville—with a man accused of murder—Bongo was no ordinary dog and could not be treated like a household pet. He had special needs and the very least I could do for him was to try to find out what they were.

I looked at Sonny apologetically. "I know I haven't been much help to you today," I said, "but I really need to go over to the jail for a minute and see if I can talk to Bongo's owner. I'll get Casey to take the front, and I'll be back to help you pack up, I promise."

Before I even finished speaking, she was waving me off. "Go," she said. "Do what you have to. I'm fine here with Hero. And Raine..." She frowned a little. "I don't know if this helps, but one of the things Bongo told me is that he knows lots of secrets."

I sighed. "I wish he'd share some of them with me."

As it turned out, he didn't have to.

SEVEN

Buck dropped a folder on Marshall's desk and sank into the chair in front of it. "Jason Broderick, forty-two, professor at Duke University, specializes in animal behavior. Widower, one child. Broke into Hartwell Labs outside of Chapel Hill last night using a key card from when he had last consulted there two weeks ago. It should have been deactivated, but I guess it wasn't or he got into the computer and reactivated it. Anyway, the security cameras were out, but the time of entry was stamped 1:10 a.m. Between midnight and 2:00 a.m. a man by the name of Martin Anderson, an assistant of some kind at the lab, was shot dead by what looks to be a nine millimeter; forensics aren't back yet. Broderick's fingerprints were found at the scene—took them about two minutes to ID him since all they had to do was run his prints through the company computer for a match—and blood-stained clothes were found in his hamper at home, along with a nine-millimeter Glock, wrapped in the dirty clothes."

As he spoke, Marshall had been glancing through the file, but now looked up. "Talk about your lazy criminal," he remarked.

"Or panicked," Buck said, not disagreeing. "The theory is that this Anderson fellow surprised him in the act of a robbery."

"Oh yeah?" Marshall continued to flip through the pages. "What did he steal?" Then he stopped, having found the answer for himself, and looked up at Buck again. "The *dog*?"

Buck nodded. "Apparently the dog is property of Hartwell Labs. But it looks as though that's all he came for—nothing else was missing, and his fingerprints were on the kennel door."

Marshall gave a small shake of his head, muttering, "They do get stranger every day." He closed the file. "You called Raleigh?"

Buck nodded. "They said if we wouldn't mind holding him overnight they'd send a team down to take custody in the morning. Should be here before noon."

"Have you talked to the guy?" Marshall asked.

"I went back to give him a report on his little girl while he was being processed. All he wanted to know was what had happened to his dog. Then he started demanding to make a phone call. I told him he'd have to wait until we finished booking him."

"So did DFACS get here?"

"Yeah, Jenny came in to do the paperwork, and she's with the kid now. I think Mart is coming to pick her up; they usually turn the short-term emergency cases over to her and Ro."

Marshall nodded. "Couldn't find a safer place than with the former sheriff and his wife." Then he glanced up. "Ro's out in Vegas at that conference, isn't he?"

"Yeah. Mart'll be glad for the little girl's company, even if it is just overnight." Buck added, "I've got to tell you, this one has my curiosity up. What do you say I see what he has to say for himself once he gets settled in?"

"Ordinarily, I'd say why not," Marshall answered. "I'd like to have some answers too. But a professor accused of homicide? This one could get some attention, and we're better off going by the book. Unless, of course," he added meaningfully, "you can think of a legitimate reason the sheriff's department needs to talk to him. Say, clearing up his impound paperwork, finding a discrepancy in his vehicle registration, something like that. Then of course we'd have no choice but to get involved."

Buck smiled. "Right. I'll keep my eyes open."

Marshall closed the file. "Listen," he said, "I don't think I've had a chance to tell you, but I appreciate the way you handled everything. You made the transition a lot easier than it could have been."

Buck shrugged, mildly uncomfortable. "You wanted the job, I didn't. You're good at it, I wasn't. Just makes sense to me."

Marshall said, "For most of the boys who come in here it's an entry level job, they last a few years and move on. I want to change that, make this more of a career opportunity. We need experienced men and women on the force, and we need to find a way to keep them. I think we've seen over the last couple of years this isn't a sleepy little community anymore. The twenty-first century is here whether we like it or not. We need to be ready for it."

Buck said cautiously, "I won't argue with you there."

"I'm looking into state and federal funding for some of the improvements we need to make—better equipment, technological advances, things like that. We'll be adding more training hours and hopefully some salary and benefit package incentives, too."

Buck smiled a little. "Hey, this is starting to sound like a campaign speech. You already got the job, you know."

Marshall did not share his amusement. "The thing is, a lot of the guys are still loyal to you—to Ro, too, of course, but you were chief deputy for a lot of years, and then sheriff. They're used to having things done a certain way, and don't take easily to change. Some of them might be friends of yours, maybe even folks you hired, but I don't have time to coddle them along. They either get with the program, or get out. I just want you to know I appreciate your support."

Buck nodded. "The way I look at it, you're the man that gets paid to make the decisions I didn't want to. You're also my boss. The day I can't support you is the day I need to find another job."

Now Marshall smiled. "I'm going to do everything I can to see that day never comes. You did me a big favor taking this job."

Buck started to rise. "I'll let you know if I can come up with a reason to interview Broderick. You might want to sit in."

Marshall said, "There's one other thing."

Buck sat down again. Marshall looked a little uncomfortable.

"This is off the record," he said, "and normally I wouldn't ask. But I have some positions to fill, and like I said, I need experienced people. I know Wyn turned in her resignation last year, and I know she's still living in Asheville..." With this he looked a question at Buck, but the other man's expression was impassive. Marshall went on, "But she was a damn fine deputy, and the truth is I'd like to have her back. Like I said, this isn't the kind of thing I'd ordinarily bring up, but before I ask her to come back, I need to know what's going on with you two. Your W-4 says 'married.' Any plans to change that? And if so—or even if not—will it cause a problem if she comes back to work here?"

Buck said, without emotion, "Wyn makes her own decisions. And I'll let the front office know if I need to change my W-4." He stood to go, then hesitated. "Ask her if you want, but you'll be wasting your breath. She's done with law enforcement." He looked for a moment as though he might add something else, but then said only, "I need to get back."

"Yeah, Buck." Marshall made a dismissing gesture with his hand. "Thanks again."

Buck left without a reply, and Marshall watched him go, looking thoughtful.

EIGHT

I was surprised to see my Aunt Mart in the waiting area of the sheriff's office when Cisco and I arrived a few minutes later. She was chatting with Annabelle, who usually worked the desk weekdays but started taking on weekends in the spring to build up her vacation time. Annabelle greeted me, "Hey, Raine! What's up?" Then, "Hey, Cisco."

Cisco, ever the gentleman, returned the greeting by placing his paws atop the tall desk and waving his silky gold and white tail like a flag. This earned him a scratch on the chin and one of the dog biscuits Annabelle always kept in her drawer. He gulped it down, then turned to Aunt Mart, grinning and hoping for more. Aunt Mart and I hugged, Cisco slapped his golden tail all over her black slacks, and Aunt Mart gave him a perfunctory pat on the head. She was polite to all my dogs, but her heart belonged to Majesty the collie, who had found her forever home on a plush velvet dog bed in front of Aunt Mart's fireplace.

Cisco turned away, too interested in his new surroundings to show whatever disappointment he might be feeling over the scarcity of dog biscuits. Aunt Mart said a little breathlessly, "Raine, did you hear? Well, of course you did, it happened right here. I worked the women's club booth this morning and then went on home before lunch so I missed all the excitement, but what an awful thing! What kind of murderer takes his child with him on the run? The poor little thing!" She lowered her voice, cast a furtive gaze around, and added, "Is he a rough one? How did he look?"

Somewhere in the midst of all this I remembered that Aunt Mart and Uncle Ro were registered as an emergency foster home for children who only needed a night or two of care while relatives were located, and that she must have been called in to take temporary custody of Broderick's little girl—Carrie or Cassie; I couldn't remember which. I just knew she was one lucky little kid to get to have my Aunt Mart fussing over her for the next few days. I said, "Actually, he looked like a normal dad. He's a scientist. A researcher at Duke."

Aunt Mart looked surprised, and I reminded her, "Innocent until proven guilty, you know. It could all just be a mistake. Anyway, I have his dog back at the kennel."

"He had his dog with him too?"

I nodded and I could see her opinion of Broderick begin to transform into uncertainty as she took into account this new information. "Well," she said, "you might be right. It's probably some kind of mistake. But apparently it's going to take some time to straighten out, because little Celie is coming home with me tonight."

Celie. That was it.

"We're just waiting for the deputies to get her backpack out of the car," Aunt Mart went on. "I guess they have to search it first. Although what in the world they expect to find in a little girl's luggage besides PJs and a teddy bear, I don't know."

Despite the fact that she had been married to a law officer for close to forty years, my aunt could be incredibly naïve sometimes.

I was about to answer her when a small voice behind us cried, "Fortune-telling lady!"

I'm not one of those people who enjoys fawning all over kids—in fact, I don't enjoy kids at all, except for Melanie. But Cisco loves them, and when he heard Celie he whirled around to greet her. He sat beautifully and automatically as he had been trained to do in the presence of children, his tail sweeping the floor, his big grin beckoning. Celie pulled away from Jenny, the social worker who had brought her out, and ran up to us. "Where's Bongo?" she demanded. "Do you know where Bongo is?"

She wore a pink backpack shaped like a bunny with floppy ears, and she carried a fuzzy white teddy bear with a big polka-dot bow. All the county's first responders carried bears like that to give out to children at the scene of traumatic events, and I guess being turned over to strangers while your father went to jail in a strange town qualified as traumatic. She looked up at me with eyes that were both accusing and hopeful, and I was quick to answer her.

"I do know where Bongo is," I assured her. "He's at the doggie spa right now, having the time of his life."

She demanded suspiciously, "What's a spa?"

"It's like a vacation hotel," I told her. "There's a playground with teeter-totters and slides and tunnels to run through, and a wading pool to splash in, and lots of other dogs to play with. My friend Corny—he's the playground director—is tossing the ball for him, and after a while he'll shampoo his hair and do his nails. He'll even put on a DVD in the play room for him. Do you know what movies Bongo likes? Because I'm going to see him in a little while."

"Can I go?" she asked anxiously.

Jenny stepped up. "Probably not today, sweetie. Come say hello to Miss Mart. You're going to spend the night with her, won't that be fun?"

Celie ignored her. "Is this your dog?" she asked me, indicating Cisco.

"It is," I told her. "His name is Cisco. Want to see him do a trick?"

"Bongo knows lots of tricks," she informed me. "He gets his picture taken in an X-ray machine."

Jenny and Aunt Mart exchanged a look, but they didn't know what I knew: that Bongo was a research animal and had probably done stranger things than have his picture taken by an X-ray machine.

I said, "Cisco can do math."

She looked at me skeptically.

I stepped in front of Cisco and said, "Cisco, what is two plus two?"

Cisco barked four times. Jenny laughed and Aunt Mart clapped, and even Celie grinned a little. It's a pretty simple trick: Cisco starts to bark when I raise my pinkie finger and stops when I lower it, and since I'm standing in front of him no one sees me do it. We do quite a few appearances at schools and libraries every year to promote animal welfare, so Cisco has a repertoire of tricks to keep the children amused.

Celie said, "What else can he do?"

Cisco happily shook her hand, spun on his hind legs, and rolled over three times, and by the time he was finished a small crowd of deputies and civilian workers had gathered to watch. I said, "He can play basketball, too, but he misses the hoop a lot."

A shadow came over her face. "My daddy likes basketball."

Before she could ask the inevitable questions about where her daddy was and when she could see him, I said, "Hey, that's a cute bear. Cisco has one a lot like it. He loves it."

She hugged the bear a little tighter. "The nice man gave it to me."

I could imagine Buck had a drawer full of them.

Jenny stepped forward and tried to take Celie's hand. "Honey, come say hello to Miss Mart. She's so anxious to meet you."

Celie shrugged away and turned to pet Cisco. I said, "Boy, I'm jealous of you, getting to spend the night with Aunt Mart. Did I mention she's my aunt? And she has the most gorgeous collie dog in the world, named Majesty. You're going to love her."

Aunt Mart put in, "And there's nothing Majesty likes better than running around in the backyard with a little girl, unless it's walking around the neighborhood on her leash." She glanced at her watch. "Oh dear, it's almost time for her afternoon walk. She'll be waiting at the door for me to take her out. I don't suppose *you'd* be interested in walking her, would you, Celie?"

Celie hesitated, her hand falling away from Cisco's silky head. "Maybe."

Aunt Mart held out her hand. "And after that, maybe you can help me bake some cookies. What kind do you like?"

Celie took her hand. "Chocolate."

"What a coincidence! That's exactly what I was going to make!"

The two of them walked off, and Jenny turned to me, smiling. "Thanks for your help, Raine. You really calmed her down."

"I didn't do anything," I pointed out. "It was all Cisco."

Jenny bent to pet Cisco. "Well, sir, I think we may have to give you the unofficial title of Ambassador for Social Services. Good job."

Cisco beamed his pride and offered his paw for shaking. Jenny took it, laughing. But the next voice we heard was not so friendly.

"What are you doing here, Stockton?"

The small group of sheriff's office employees that had gathered to watch The Cisco Show dispersed hurriedly, no longer smiling. Even Jenny said, "See you later, Raine," and left. Jolene often has that effect on people.

I met her scowling gaze evenly. "I need to see the prisoner. Jason Broderick."

"Do you, now?" She walked to the reception desk, passed a folder to Annabelle, and said a few crisp words to her that I didn't quite catch. Even Annabelle's cheery disposition seemed to wilt a little beneath the force of Jolene's personality. She turned back to me. "I hate to break it to you, but this office doesn't run on what you need. And what is your dog doing here?"

I was prepared for this. Never mind that Cisco had been coming to this office since he was a pup-in-arms, apparently we now needed authorization. Fortunately, I had it. "Cisco is a therapy dog registered with the county to visit all public buildings including the jail," I informed her. "And right now we need to see the prisoner. Like I said."

She looked me up and down. "What for?"

I could have lied. I could have said something about therapy dog visits, or bringing a message from his daughter, with whom I'd just spoken, or made any number of other charitable excuses. But the truth is I didn't have time to make up a lie, and besides, experience has taught me that they hardly ever pay off in the end. So I faced her squarely and I said, "I need to ask him about his dog. The dog is in my kennel and I have some questions about his care."

Her eyes darkened. "Damn it, Stockton, I told you to take him to the shelter. I'll send a deputy out and—"

"And set yourself, and this county, up for a million-dollar lawsuit," I interrupted sharply. I had her attention now. "Jason Broderick is a world-renowned research scientist in animal behavior and Bongo—the dog—is one of his test subjects. That's why he was so anxious about keeping him safe. Who even knows how much that dog is worth? That's why I need to talk to Broderick and find out how to take care of him. And you're welcome, by the way. I wouldn't want you to get in trouble for turning over a valuable asset like that to the *pound*."

She glared at me for a moment. "How do you…?"

But a voice interrupted her from behind. "Well, that explains a lot," Buck said.

Of course, I knew he was there before he came through the swinging door that led to the office area. Cisco's ears pricked forward, his tail started doing the hundred-yard dash, and it was all he could do to keep his grin from splitting his sweet golden-retriever face. He strained at the end of his leash until Buck came over and ruffled his ears, and then Cisco flopped to his back, paws in the air, and wriggled on the floor with delight. Frankly, I thought he was going a little overboard, but I suppose seeing his hero twice in the space of a couple of hours was something that didn't happen every day.

Buck gave Cisco's silky white belly a good rub, then stood and told Jolene amiably, "I was on my way home, but I'll be glad to walk Raine over to the jail if you want. That'll give you time to check with the sheriff on how best to handle the dog situation. Come to think of it, he might be better off in the custody of a member of the sheriff's office, like yourself."

Jolene's jaw tightened. In the first place, it was common knowledge that the only canine she cared to take custody of was Deputy Nike, the Belgian Malinois who was the ranking member of the Hanover County Sheriff's Office's K9 Division. In the second place—and also common knowledge—she was distinctly uncomfortable around Buck. Four months ago he had been her boss, and their relationship had been rocky at best. Now they had to work together, not as employee and employer, or even as chief and subordinate, but as colleagues of equal rank whose areas of responsibility often overlapped. The fact that this didn't seem to bother Buck in the least would only rankle Jolene more.

She said stiffly, "Stockton doesn't have authorization to visit the prisoner. Are you taking responsibility?"

"Absolutely," Buck assured her, adding perhaps a touch too much solemnity to the word.

Jolene glanced at Cisco. "The dog stays here."

"I'll take him, Raine," Annabelle volunteered quickly and reached for the leash.

That was fine with me, and seemed more than fine with Cisco, who knew exactly where the dog biscuits were kept. Cisco is comfortable wherever he goes, but the only prison visits I ever made with him as a therapy dog team were with nonviolent offenders. I wasn't sure how I felt about taking my dog into a room with a stranger accused of murder, even if he *was* a famous scientist and someone whom, under other circumstances, I probably would have invited over for dinner and hours of intense conversation.

I handed over the leash to Annabelle, and Buck said to Jolene, "If you're going by Marshall's office, tell him I found something to talk to Broderick about, and he might want to turn on his monitor."

Buck pushed open the exit door and gestured me to precede him.

NINE

The jail is only a short walk across the courtyard from the sheriff's office, but it can seem like miles when you're trying to find something to say to your ex. I don't think I'd ever fully appreciated how valuable Cisco was in keeping a buffer of amicability between us.

Buck walked with his hands in the pockets of his jeans, the faint April breeze stirring his hair. Most guys on the force wore a buzz cut, but Buck never had. It made me sad to see the peppering of a few gray hairs here and there. The past year had not been easy for him.

He said, "She never knows what to say to me either."

I looked at him, confused. "Who?"

"Jolene," he explained. "It's not so much that she doesn't know what to say, but she doesn't know what to call me. Sir? Mister? I'm not really a deputy, and we don't have detectives with the county, just investigators. I told her to call me Buck, but she won't. Most of the time she ends up calling me

Major, which just pisses her off because it reminds her I outrank her."

I said, "You're a major now? I didn't know. Congratulations."

He shrugged. "It came with the job."

It was really none of my business, but to forestall an awkward silence, I said, "It's because she's afraid of you, you know."

He looked at me in surprise. "Who? Jolene?"

I nodded. "Or intimidated is more like it, I guess. I know she doesn't act like it, but I think she admires you. She really wanted to impress you when she worked for you, and you made her feel like she let you down. Now every time she sees you she's reminded of that. Who needs it? You should try being nicer to her."

I could feel Buck's thoughtful gaze on me, but all he responded was, "Huh." Then, as we reached the door of the jail, he said, "So what do you know about Broderick?"

"He's one of the people who helped develop the electronic device sniffing dog program," I explained. "You know, microchips, flash drives..."

"Yeah, I know about those dogs." Buck looked impressed as he pressed the button and waited for the jail door to buzz open. "No kidding, that's the guy? The SBI has applied for one of those dogs. I was just reading about it the other day."

The door buzzed and the lock clicked open, and Buck held the door open for me.

"It has to do with this chemical that all electronic devices have sprayed on them when they're manufactured," I said, recalling what I could of what

I'd read. "The pups are trained from birth to detect it, and their record is just about one hundred percent. This research group that Broderick is a part of has been working on the program for ten years—that's like forever in dog generations—and they just started placing dogs within the last two years. I don't think there are two dozen of them in the whole world."

"And you think that Lab of Broderick's is one of them?"

"I'm almost certain of it."

Buck was thoughtful as we approached the check-in desk. "The report on Broderick lists that dog as stolen."

"Well," I said, "I guess officially he does belong to the program. But Celie seemed to think of him as hers. Maybe Broderick did too."

I turned over my purse and walked through the metal detector, picking up my pass on the other side. Buck called for a deputy to bring Broderick to an interview room, and walked with me down the short corridor.

Our jail building was only ten years old, but already showed signs of wear—scuffed walls, stained linoleum, rusty spots on the ceiling tile. The building had room for only twenty-five inmates and was hardly ever full. Most people who checked in stayed less than twenty-four hours while waiting to bond out, but a few unlucky souls—vandals, deadbeat dads and the like—served their full sentences here. Serious offenders were transferred to Asheville as a matter of routine. All this is by way of saying that funding was limited and our detention facility was by no means state of the art. There was only one conference room, and it was used for suspect interviews, inmate visitations, and lawyer consultations. A deputy was waiting for us outside the door as we approached.

"Hey, Buck," he said, and gave me a noncommittal nod as he swung open the door.

Buck said, "How're you doing, Deke? Pulled jail duty this weekend, I see."

Deke was one of the senior deputies on staff, and for a brief, unmemorable time had been chief deputy during the last days of Buck's term as sheriff. He had the maturity of a thirteen-year-old and the brains of a goat—no offense to goats—but he took orders well, and he was loyal. This probably explained why he was cool to me every time we met: he still thought of me as the woman who'd done Buck wrong.

Deke said, "Yeah, well, it beats riding the road. I'll go get your prisoner."

"He giving you any trouble?"

"Nah. Of course, he ain't tasted the chow yet." Deke chuckled at his own joke and turned to go.

"Hey, Deke," Buck said, gesturing me to precede him into the room, "how about radioing across the street and tell the sheriff we're about ready to get started?"

Deke gave a lazy two-fingered salute in acknowledgement and ambled off.

The conference room was small and featureless, with overhead fluorescents, a scarred wooden library table and four matching chairs. There was a faded print of some sheep in a mountain meadow hanging on one of the industrial green walls, and a calendar for 2014 hanging on the other. I said, "Is Marshall coming over? Are y'all going to do some kind of formal interview? Because all I wanted was to ask him about the dog, and then I'll be out of your way."

Buck nodded toward the camera mounted in the corner. Underneath it, as well as on the other three walls at eye level, were signs that read, *CCTV Monitoring in Progress.* "Marshall can watch us through that camera, and so can anybody else who wants to save the walk over here."

This was new. I said uneasily, "Isn't that illegal?"

"Not unless an inmate is with his lawyer. Otherwise, you give up the expectation of privacy when you cross the threshold."

"I guess." It still seemed a lot like spying to me. "So when did this happen?"

"It was Marshall's idea." Buck shrugged one shoulder. "It was cheaper than putting in an interrogation room with security glass, and besides, Marshall's big on high-tech."

"I noticed," I muttered, and shot another uncomfortable glance at the camera.

He gave a small chuckle. "You don't sound like much of a fan."

"Of Marshall's?" I shrugged. "He's okay. I like his dog."

"I meant of technology. Modern crime fighting depends on it, you know."

I didn't like his condescending tone, particularly since he only echoed what Marshall had said to me earlier, and I knew he was right. Besides, I was *not* a troglodyte. "Well, give the devil his due, I guess," I admitted reluctantly. "There's a lot to be said for bomb-defusing robots and automatic license-plate checkers. I just don't think it's a good idea to rely too much on things we can't control."

Buck murmured, "Yeah, you never did much like things you couldn't control."

I could have nailed him with a look, but there was no way I was getting into an argument with him in the middle of a jailhouse conference room, particularly one that was being monitored on CCTV. So I took the high road by pretending not to hear.

I looked pointedly up at the camera. "Is he watching us now?"

Buck glanced at the camera and made a dry face, muttering, "Deke knows he's supposed to turn the camera on whenever we do an interview." He walked over to the corner and flipped a switch on the camera. "Now he is. You want a Coke from the machine or something?"

"No, I'm good."

I thought I should probably say hi to Marshall, but just then the door opened and Deke came in with Jason Broderick. The prisoner had already been issued the county's khaki jumpsuit, and his hands were cuffed in front of him, but otherwise he looked none the worse for wear. Deke escorted him none-too-gently to one of the wooden chairs and commanded, "Sit there."

Broderick did, and Deke retreated to the door to watch. Buck said, "Mr. Broderick, we met earlier. I'm Buck Lawson. I'm an investigator with the county, and this is Raine Stockton. She—"

"She stole my dog," Broderick interrupted lowly, glaring at me. "She stole my dog and I'm the one in jail! Where is he?" He lurched to his feet, his voice rising, and I took an involuntary step backwards. "What have you done with him? Where—"

Deke could move surprisingly fast when he wanted to, and he was upon Broderick in an instant, shoving him forcefully back into his chair. He drew his taser and demanded, breathing hard, "Do you want to try that again, mister? Do you?"

Buck lifted a staying hand toward Deke, but his eyes were not as friendly as they had been a moment ago, and his gaze never left Broderick. Deke backed off slowly and re-holstered his taser, but he kept his hand on his weapon. I thought that might have been a little showy, but I can't say I wasn't glad he was there. As frightened as he must have been by Deke's rough handling, the anger in Broderick's eyes had not completely gone away, and it was focused on me.

Buck said with very deliberate calm, "Let me start again. This is Raine Stockton, a member of our canine search and rescue team and an expert dog trainer, who generously volunteered to take care of your dog while you're our guest here at county detention. She also happens to be an old friend of mine, so I want you to think real carefully before you start yelling accusations at her again. As a matter of fact, what do you say we don't have any more yelling at all? You'd be doing Deke over there a big favor."

Broderick cut his eyes toward Deke, and I saw his Adam's apple bob as he swallowed. I ventured back toward the table, and Buck pulled out one of the chairs for me. "I did not steal your dog." I felt compelled to defend myself. "As a matter of fact, I kept him out of the animal shelter. That's what you wanted, isn't it?"

He still looked angry and unconvinced. "You knew who he was," he said. "That woman you were working with knew all about him. And then you tried to chase me down. I don't know how you found me or who sent you but—"

"That's all just a coincidence." I waved a dismissing hand and sat down. "I had no idea who you were or that Bongo was anything more than a family pet until an hour ago, when my kennel manager looked you up on the Internet." I worked hard to keep the excitement out of my voice as I added, "I read an article about you and your electronic device detection dogs. It was fascinating, the way you figured out how to isolate the scent and then train the dogs to detect it. And they have an almost one hundred percent accuracy rate! No other sniffer dog even comes close. I guess a lot of it has to do with genetics too, huh? I mean, training of course, but I read you've had your own breeding program in place since 2008."

Either he was unflattered by my enthusiasm or completely disinterested, because he didn't even blink an eye in response. So I tried again. "Bongo must be one of those dogs, right? From the training program?"

He looked from me to Buck, who had taken a seat in the chair next to me and was listening with mild interest. When Broderick looked back at me it was with a kind of bored bafflement, as though he was wondering why I had even been allowed in here.

I powered on. "Is he on food rewards? If so, what's the stimulus and the reinforcement ratio? I read that some of your dogs are trained not to eat at all unless it's in response to a stimulus. And I'll need to know his diet, of course. Whole food or raw? If you feed a specialty brand, I probably won't be able to get it until Monday. Is he allergic to anything? On any meds?"

He eyed me with cautious new respect, but when he spoke his tone was still grudging. "Bongo will eat any premium brand of kibble. He's a laboratory dog. We don't spoil them."

I have to admit, I was a little insulted. Here I was, going out of my way to accommodate his very special dog, and he was treating me like a sycophant. Which, in a way, I suppose I was. But still...

While I was still formulating a pithy response, Buck said, "So satisfy my curiosity. If he's just a lab dog—I'm guessing that you have a lot of them—why did you go to the trouble of stealing him?"

Anger flared again in Broderick's eyes. "I did not steal him! It's technically and legally impossible to steal your own dog, which you would know if anyone—*anyone*—in this two-bit outfit had bothered to check the papers in my luggage, the location of which I've given to at least three different deputies and processors. Bongo is part of a litter that I have raised from birth, registered to me personally, and given ownership to me personally by the tattoo in his ear. I and I alone own *all* the dogs in the research program. He was on loan to Hartwell, pending completion of the research and training, but *he belongs to me*. You cannot steal your own dog!"

This last was expressed with enough passion to violate Buck's "no yelling" request, and caused Deke's hand to tighten avariciously on his taser.

Broderick must have noticed, because he sank back in the chair and moderated his tone considerably.

"Look," he said, "I'm sorry." He turned to me and said, with as much sincerity as he appeared to be able to muster, "Thank you for taking care of Bongo. Really, I don't mean to be ungrateful. But you don't need to know about his training regime or his diet because I'm not going to be here that long." Now he turned back to Buck. "If your people would just check out what I told them, I'll be out of here before dark." Now he cast a quick and anxious look between Buck and me. "What about Celie? Is she okay? Is she very upset?"

I took the lead on that one. "She's with my aunt, who also happens to be the wife of the former sheriff. Celie's not happy, but my aunt is very good at turning that kind of unhappiness around."

"Small towns," he muttered, shaking his head. "I guess everyone knows everyone else."

I thought it was safe to offer, "If you had to get arrested, you couldn't have picked a better place. But Mr. Broderick…"

Buck interrupted me smoothly, "So you say the dog was on loan to this Hartwell Laboratory. What for? What kind of place is it? What do they do there?"

Broderick seemed to debate for a moment whether to answer, but apparently decided that cooperation would be better for his case than belligerence. He said, "It's actually the Hartwell Research Group—HRG. The lab is just a division. They're kind of a think tank, privately funded, with a number of projects under development at any one time. They funded the research into the sniffer dog program, provided kennel space, training equipment, staff, that kind of thing. That's why the dogs are considered 'on loan.'"

"And you worked for them?"

Broderick said stiffly, "I was a consultant. I work for Duke University."

"But you're not a consultant with Hartwell anymore," Buck said. "Your key card had been revoked."

Broderick's expression was determinedly neutral. "We had a disagreement about policy."

"So you decided to take your program elsewhere," Buck concluded with a nod. "I guess that kind of thing happens all the time."

Broderick said tersely, "It does."

I asked, "How many dogs were in the program?"

"Several dozen, in various stages of training. Not including the ones in the breeding program."

"So did they all live at the lab?" I couldn't think of a less fun life for a working dog... although I suppose a lot of people, at first glance, would think any kind of kennel life was no fun for a dog. Until, that is, they saw what kind of life the boarders at Dog Daze led. I should know better than to make snap judgments.

"Not all of them, no," Broderick replied, a touch impatiently. "Look, I don't see what—"

"So why did you only take the Lab?" Buck asked. I thought it was a very good question. "What's his name? Bongo? What's special about him?"

Broderick's lips compressed briefly and I thought he wouldn't answer. Then he said, "My little girl loves him. She thinks of him as her pet. That's what's special."

Buck nodded his understanding. "So I'm guessing this policy disagreement you had with the Hartwell group didn't end with you all on very friendly terms. Otherwise, you wouldn't have had to break into the facility in the middle of the night to get your dog back. I mean, couldn't you have negotiated with them over that? It sounds pretty harsh to me, holding a little girl's pet dog hostage like that."

I could see Broderick was growing uncomfortable, as well he should be. There was a reason Buck was the one who was always called in to ask the questions, and a reason Marshall had wanted him so badly for County Investigator. He had a way of getting to the truth of a matter before you were even aware that he was asking the questions.

Broderick stiffened and fastened his gaze on the blank wall opposite Buck's shoulder. "I don't know why any of this matters," he said. "What matters is that I did nothing wrong and you need to let me out of here so I can take care of my daughter and my dog."

Buck seemed to consider that for a moment, then he said patiently, "Mr. Broderick, you need to understand that's not going to happen. You don't have to talk to me, or to Miss Stockton, but I'm here to tell you that the two of us are probably the last people you'll meet here who are trying to help you. The Raleigh-Durham police are coming to take you back tomorrow morning, where you will be officially charged with breaking and entering, theft by taking, and murder. After that, everything is out of our hands."

I saw the color drain from Broderick's already pallid cheeks. He stared at Buck. "What?" His voice was hoarse. "Murder? What are you talking about?"

I looked at Buck, slowly starting to make sense of things. If Broderick thought he was being arrested for a simple theft charge, no wonder he hadn't displayed the kind of hysterical anxiety about his daughter that I'd expect from a doting parent. All this time, he must have thought he was going to bond out in a couple of hours and be reunited with his little girl, who would be none the worse for wear. What he was worried about was that the stolen property—Bongo—would be taken into custody, and *that* was why he ran.

On the other hand, as I'm sure Buck would have been quick to point out, running from the law was also fairly common behavior for murderers.

Buck said, "Do you know a Martin Anderson?"

Broderick swallowed hard and blinked, flicking his gaze briefly away and back again. "He's an assistant at the lab. At Hartwell. He takes care of the kennels, helps set up tests, documents the research, that kind of thing."

"Was," corrected Buck, watching him. "He *was* an assistant at the lab. Now he's dead."

Broderick's jaw went slack with shock, and for a long moment he just stared. Then he said hoarsely, "Martin? Dead? But I just..." He broke off with a breath and his shoulders went slack. "My God."

Buck's careful, observant gaze took in everything about the other man as he added, "And it looks like it was your gun that killed him."

Broderick sank back in his chair, although I couldn't tell whether the expression on his face was astonishment or relief. "Impossible," he said. "I don't own a gun."

Buck nodded. "Well, I guess that's something you're going to have to work out with the police when you get back home. Because according to the report, they found a gun that fires the same kind of bullets that killed Martin Anderson in your clothes hamper, wrapped in a shirt that was spattered with the victim's blood."

"That's insane." Broderick's voice was hoarse, his eyes horrified. "Martin was alive when I saw him. We talked. He was on his way home. I figured that was how…that's who told the police I was there. But if he's dead…"

Broderick grew still and seemed to withdraw into himself, his eyes flickering back and forth as he reviewed options in his head. "I need to make a phone call," he said at last, tensely. "I have a right to make a phone call."

Buck took a cell phone from his pocket and placed it on the table. "You can use this one," he said. "It's unlocked. Sheriff's Office issue, so there'll be a record of the call." He glanced at me. "Come on, Raine, let's give him some privacy."

Of course I knew he wouldn't *really* be making his phone call in private, since Deke wasn't about to leave him alone and Marshall was presumably still watching from the closed-circuit camera. But I took this to mean civilian visiting time was over, so I stood.

"I guess the lab will be sending someone for Bongo," I said. "But don't worry, I'll take good care of him until they get here."

Broderick started to reach for the phone with his cuffed hands, and then stopped, staring at it.

Buck gave him a sympathetic smile that wasn't entirely sincere. "Sorry," he said. "We can't uncuff you. But I'll dial the number if you want."

Broderick said dully, "I don't know it."

"Do you want me to look it up on your cell phone? I'll need your password."

He shook his head. "It's a local number. There's a business card in my luggage..." He glared at Buck. "The same luggage that has the papers that prove I didn't steal Bongo."

Buck said, "I can get you a phone book. But if you're trying to get a lawyer out here, I've got to tell you, it's a waste of time. You're going back to Raleigh tomorrow, and there's not a thing anybody can do for you until then."

Again, Broderick shook his head. "No. It's not a lawyer, and I don't think he'd be in the phone book." He looked at Buck hopefully. "But he lives here in Hanover County. Maybe somebody can Google his contact info. His name is Miles Young."

TEN

After that, things got a little strange. I typed in Miles's phone number and handed the phone to Broderick. Buck and I, who no longer had any intention of going anywhere, listened without shame as Broderick identified himself as "Jason Broderick. That's right." He darted a glance at Buck and lowered his voice a fraction as he added, "The Coyote Project. You said I should contact you if…"

I could feel Buck's surprised and curious gaze on me, but I was stone. At least on the outside I was stone. On the inside I was churning with so many emotions it was impossible to isolate, much less define, even one of them.

Broderick went on to say he was being held in the Hanover County jail and that the charge—which was absolutely, unequivocally erroneous—was murder. Yes, he had Bongo with him, but "some woman" had taken him to her kennel. That was when Jason Broderick's surprised gaze swiveled to me. That was right, he admitted. Her name was Stockton.

There was nothing of interest after that: "Yes, I will.... Okay, yes. I appreciate it... No, I won't...I'm sure. I will. Thank you, Mr. Young."

When he finished his phone call he was taken back to his cell, disinclined to talk to either Buck or me further. No doubt one of the things Miles had told him was not to say another word to the police. Miles wasn't a lawyer, but he was incredibly smart, and you didn't have to be either one to know the best thing you can do when facing a murder charge was exercise your right to remain silent. I was starting to see the wisdom in that myself.

For my own part, I remained stone. Shoulders squared, jaw clenched, I walked back to the front with Buck. He knew better than to waste time questioning me about the obvious. It was clear that I didn't know any more than he did, and it was also clear that I was humiliated by that fact.

I retrieved my phone and checked it immediately. The text from Miles had been sent three minutes earlier and it said: *On my way home. Whatever you do, don't let that dog out of your sight.*

Buck read the text over my shoulder. I didn't try to stop him.

He said, "Any ideas?"

I replied tersely, "No."

"So I take it Mr. Young is out of town?"

I pushed on the door to the courtyard, but it was of course locked. A moment later it buzzed and the lock turned. We walked out into the sunshine.

Buck went on, "So where is he?"

A direct question from a law officer. I answered, "Belgium."

"When was he due back?"

"Next week."

"And he's flying back early because of this Broderick person." He glanced at me. "Or maybe the dog."

I said nothing.

"Did he ever mention Broderick to you? Or the dog?"

I replied, "No." And that of course was the most confusing, and infuriating, part. Why wouldn't he have? Of course he rarely talked to me about his business, and I didn't expect him to. But if he had connections with a world-famous researcher into canine behavior who also happened to be the head of an exclusive working dog program, *of course* I'd want to hear about it. Just knowing such a person would have made him a hero in my eyes, and Melanie's too. So why keep it a secret?

"You've got to wonder," Buck said, "whether the reason Broderick turned up here in town was to meet with Young. Seems like too much of a coincidence otherwise."

"I have no idea." I pushed open the door to the sheriff's office before Buck could, and Cisco came bouncing out from behind Annabelle's desk. I grabbed Cisco's leash before he could run to Buck, thanked Annabelle for dog-sitting, and told her I had to hurry back to my booth—which of course I did. But first I had to do something else.

I walked to my car so fast that Cisco had to trot to keep up, and I could feel Buck's thoughtful gaze on us from the glass-fronted door of the sheriff's office every step of the way.

I got Cisco settled in the backseat and dialed Miles's number from behind the wheel of the car. He answered without preamble.

"Baby, listen to me." He knew I hated to be called "baby"—who didn't?—and the fact that he wasn't doing it to annoy me only demonstrated how distracted he must be. "This is serious. I'm not going to explain anything over the phone, so—"

I burst in incredulously, "*Serious*? Don't tell me about serious! I just spent twenty minutes in the county jail talking to a man accused of murder, and who does he make his one phone call to? His lawyer, his mother, his boss, his best friend? No! None of the above! He used his one and only phone call on *my boyfriend*!"

"Fiancé," he corrected automatically.

"While I'm sitting next to an investigator looking like the perfect fool because I had no idea he even knew you!" I stormed on. "Who is he to you, Miles? Why did he drive all the way down here from Raleigh with a stolen dog and his little girl and a murder warrant hanging over his head just to see you? And why didn't you ever mention him to me?" This was the part that was most hurtful, and most inexplicable. "You knew I'd want to know! Why keep it such a secret?"

He said, virtually ignoring me, "Is Bongo with you?"

I blinked, the rhythm of my tirade disrupted. "He's with Corny, at Dog Daze. Aunt Mart is taking care of the little girl."

"Good." He sounded busy, distracted. He had a habit of doing two or three things at once when he was on the phone, and usually he was pretty good at hiding it. This was not one of those times. "I'm going to send somebody from my security team—"

"If even one of your security goons sets foot on my property," I told him tightly, "I swear to God I'll shoot him." Miles's so-called security force and I had a history. Enough said.

Miles went on, "It looks like I'm not going to be able to clear a private jet from here, so I'm trying to get a direct flight to Atlanta. That'll put me in Hansonville around eight in the morning if I can charter a chopper from the airport. I'll explain everything, every single thing, then. Don't shoot my security guards. I love you."

Again I was taken aback. Chartering a helicopter was not a stretch for him by any means, but to do so just to save the drive from Atlanta was not his style. I started to think that the entire situation had probably been accurately summed up by his first words to me: *This is serious.*

I repeated, very deliberately, "I. Will. Shoot. Them. Swear to God. Love you back."

I disconnected and sat there for a long moment staring at the phone as though expecting it to somehow give up the answers I was looking for. It did not, and I started the engine and put the car in gear, still looking.

ELEVEN

Amos T. Gerrard arrived in Hansonville at 4:45 in the afternoon. The downtown area was blocked off due to some kind of festival, but that turned out to his advantage, because one of the first things he saw was a big banner waving over the Humane Society booth. He took advantage of the free parking, walked a block to the booth, and casually picked up a brochure. The address of the county animal shelter was conveniently listed on the back. He dropped a dollar into the dog-shaped collection jar and got a "Thank you!" from the girl at the table and a cheerful bark from the golden retriever by her side. Gerrard rubbed the dog's head and grinned. He actually liked dogs, which made him perfect for the task at hand.

The brochure said the shelter was open until 6:00 on Saturdays, and GPS took him right to it. There were a couple of other cars in the gravel parking lot in front of the low concrete block building, and the sound of barking greeted him when he got out. The inside of the building was tiled in linoleum and smelled of disinfectant. A plump middle-aged woman greeted him from behind the desk, and he introduced himself.

"I was driving through town and stopped for the festival," he extemporized, "and my dog got away from me. I was hoping somebody might have turned him in. Big black Lab, really friendly, he would've gotten into the car with anybody."

"Oh, dear." The woman looked sympathetic. "I'm sorry, but no one has turned in a dog like that this weekend. Or anytime, really. Mostly what we get are hounds," she confided, "pits, feists, a lot of mixed breed puppies. But you should fill out a lost dog form, in case he turns up later."

She rummaged through her file drawer and came up with the form, which she passed across the desk to him.

"Thanks, I will." He took the paper and kept the anxious look on his face. "But would it be okay if I had a look for myself? It's just that I've had him since he was a pup and I don't think I could sleep tonight unless I looked at every dog in here, just to make sure."

"Well..." She looked uncertain. "If he came in today, he'd still be in quarantine, but I guess I could get someone to take you back. Hold on a minute."

He had to wait fifteen minutes, but eventually a teenage boy showed up to take him on a tour of the facility. There was nothing in the quarantine room except one wild-eyed shepherd mix and a mangy hound. The kid took him down the rows of the general population and around to the outside runs. Before he left, Gerrard made certain he'd seen not only every dog in the place, but every place a dog could possibly be kept. He filled out the lost dog form with a phony name and phony number and left it at the desk, remembering to look dejected as he walked away.

He called from the car.

"No dog," he reported. "Maybe the cops haven't brought it in yet."

"It's been six hours since the arrest," replied the man on the other end, "and it's a Saturday. If they were going to take him to the shelter they would have. They must've found out what the dog is worth."

"Do you think they're keeping him at the jail? Or maybe one of the cops took him home?"

"That's what you're there to find out," returned the other man shortly. "I don't care what it takes, you are not to leave that place without the dog. Is that understood?"

"Yes, sir," replied Gerrard. "I understand. Whatever it takes."

Gerrard disconnected the phone, smiling to himself and feeling quite optimistic about the future. There was nothing he liked better than a job on which he was authorized to do whatever it took. The possibilities were endless.

TWELVE

It's hard to stay mad at a man who stocks your freezer with homemade gourmet meals every time he leaves town and who over-nights a ten-inch chocolate torte because he'd had a slice for dinner at some fancy restaurant his first night in Belgium and thought you might like it. There was still half a torte left, and a sliced pork roast with cherry sauce and new potatoes in the freezer, so after I closed up the Humane Society booth and turned in the receipts, I called Corny and invited him—and Bongo, of course—to the house for dinner.

Part of Corny's salary package—if it could be called that—is the bunk room in the back of the kennel building, where he lives rent free. It's not such a bad accommodation for a single guy—it has a TV, a shower, and access to the kitchen in the break room for meals. But I still think I got the better part of the deal, since someone is on the premises virtually twenty-four/seven, and being able to brag about that is a huge coup for the kennel business. Nonetheless, I try to give him his privacy, and usually the only time we have dinner together is when it's a family thing with Miles and Melanie. Tonight, though, I wanted someone to talk to about all this who, even though he might not be entirely neutral, at least didn't look at me as though he was trying to find a way to put my boyfriend in jail.

And I also didn't want to spend the entire evening checking my phone and getting more and more frustrated when Miles didn't call.

Cisco and I were greeted by a barrage of scrambling paws and wagging tails when we came in the door. Mischief and Magic, my twin Australian Shepherds, raced down the corridor from the kitchen, with Pepper, Melanie's golden retriever, only inches behind. Pepper stayed with me whenever Miles and Melanie went somewhere they couldn't take her, which was perfectly fine with me. The first rule of southern hospitality and purebred rescue is that there's always room for one more.

I dropped to my knees, laughing and scrunching up my face against dog kisses as Pepper, who was the youngest and generally the least disciplined, barreled into me paws-first. Mischief and Magic jumped over her back like two dolphins and wiggled their way underneath my arms. Cisco, not to be outdone, spun and play-bowed and launched himself into the melee. I generally prefer more civilized greetings, but I felt a little bad about leaving the three of them behind while Cisco and I had gone to the festival. So I rubbed ears and hugged necks and kissed noses for about thirty seconds before I declared firmly, "Okay, that's enough." I got to my feet and held out my palms, and all four dogs sat, watching me attentively for the treat they knew was coming. They weren't disappointed. I dug into my jeans pocket and came up with four liver treats, which they gobbled down without tasting.

"Okay, go play," I told them, and the four of them raced back to the kitchen like a herd of wild mustangs. There is nothing more joyous than a house full of dogs.

There was still enough daylight left for them to play in the exercise yard, so I let them outside while I prepared their dinner. My house runs on almost as strict a schedule as Dog Daze does, and we're fairly synchronized. My four had no sooner finished wolfing down their meals than I saw Corny lock the front door of Dog Daze and start across the yard toward the house. He had Bongo with him, as I'd requested, so I let my pack out into the backyard play area again and went to the front door to let Corny and Bongo in.

"Hi, Miss Stockton," Corny greeted me and led Bongo across the threshold. The big black Lab went to the end of his leash, checking out the room with his nose and his quick, interested gaze just like any other dog would do. Corny followed him, adding, "He's been fed and exercised. No trouble at all."

Bongo walked the perimeter of the room, sniffing where the other dogs had been, paying particular attention to the place where someone had dropped a few crumbs of a liver treat, then he looked up at me, clearly deducing where the treat had come from. I told him to sit, and found another treat in my pocket for him when he obeyed.

"That's odd," I said. "He didn't even notice the television or the laptop. I thought that's what he was trained to alert to."

"I noticed the same thing," admitted Corny, "when he was around the computer and the cell phone in the office. He probably needs a release word, like Cisco does before he tracks."

"Right," I agreed. "That's probably it." But I have to say I was troubled by how much I didn't know, and disappointed that, even though I had possession of one of the most advanced dogs in the world of sniffer training, I wouldn't even get to see him perform. I should have asked Broderick for the release word.

Everyone has her own method of introducing a new dog into the existing pack. I've generally found it works best to crate the resident dogs while allowing the new dog to explore the house, becoming familiar with the sound and scent of the others dogs while he, in turn, feels safe in letting the others get used to him. None of my dogs is particularly dominant or overly territorial, so I've always had good luck with this. Since Bongo was a temporary guest, however, it seemed better to crate him and let the other dogs get used to him at their own pace. A lot of dogs come in and out of my house, and I think over the years my pack has learned that a dog in a crate is only a visitor and none of them have to worry about being usurped.

So while Corny set the table and I microwaved pork roast, Bongo made himself at home in the wire crate beside the kitchen door. I had already outfitted it with clean bedding and a barely used Nylabone. He did not seem particularly interested in either one, but settled down with a grunting sigh and rested his head on his paws, watching us prepare dinner. I suppose he had logged a lot of hours in a crate watching people, but still, I felt a little sorry for him. I hoped I got to keep him long enough to take him for a nice run.

I put together a quick salad and told Corny about the interview at the jail, ending with Broderick's phone call to Miles. I was almost as surprised by Corny's reaction as I had been by the phone call itself.

"Well, that makes sense," he said with a nod. He had just finished filling two glasses with iced tea and placed one in front of each plate on the table. "He was probably expecting Mr. Young could get him out of jail in a matter of minutes. I guess he didn't realize Mr. Young was out of town when he started out for here. Or if he was, you know, on the run with Bongo, he didn't have time to check. "

I blinked at him. "What?"

"I did some research on the computer after I got Bongo settled," he explained, then glanced at me with quick apology in his eyes behind the overly magnified glasses. "The kennel is pretty slow and I had some time…"

I waved him on. "It's fine."

"Anyway," he said, "I was reading about the Hartwell Group that Dr. Broderick works for—he has like three doctorates, by the way—and learned that Mr. Young is one of the founders and primary investors. What do you call it? Majority shareholder? Maybe that's just for corporations."

There was a scratch and a demanding bark at the door, and Corny went to open it. "According to the article, there was Mr. Young, and some fellow who owns an airline, and this other person who has like a dozen companies all over the world—rich people, in other words, venture capitalists—who got together with Jonathan Hartwell, a professor at Duke. He was a genius, had all kinds of inventions, but he must've been pretty old because he died about three years ago."

He opened the back door and a flurry of golden tails and black-and-white faces burst through, making a beeline for Bongo's cage. Bongo stood up, tail up and eyes alert.

"Ladies! Gentleman!" Corny reprimanded. "Manners, please!"

All four dogs skidded to a stop in front of Bongo's cage, cast a quick eye toward Corny, and sat, one by one. I swear I sometimes think Corny is Dr. Doolittle in disguise, although I don't think even the great doctor himself could exercise the influence over my dogs that Corny does.

"Much better," Corny said, even as Cisco craned his neck toward the crate for a better sniff. "Mr. Bongo is our guest. Show some respect."

The dogs got up with low wagging tails and friendly ears to check out the crate, and Corny turned back to me. I kept a wary eye on the dogs, because Bongo would have been perfectly justified in feeling defensive while he was being surrounded by three strange dogs, and I didn't want any incidents.

"Anyway, it worked out well for the investors," Corny went on, "since they hold the patent on whatever comes out of the think tank for ten years, and they get twenty percent of whatever an invention sells for. Like, say, I don't know, somebody invents a solar water filter and the Navy wants to buy it for all their ships. That could be twenty percent of like billions, right?"

I said uncertainly, "Is that the kind of thing they do there? Water filters? And microchip-sniffing dogs?"

He waved a hand airily, "Oh, a lot more interesting things than that. Drug research, nano-science, bio-tech, all kinds of cool stuff. And, well, obviously, they're very successful or Mr. Young wouldn't be involved, right?"

If Corny has one fault, it's his blind loyalty. He had decided early on that Miles could do no wrong, and nothing would ever sway that opinion.

I smiled weakly and set the salad bowl on the table. "Right."

The microwave beeped, and Corny used potholders to remove the ceramic dish of pork and cherry sauce. I poured the buttered new potatoes into a separate dish and sprinkled them with dried parsley, as instructed by the label on the vacuum-sealed container, because Miles knew there was no chance I would have fresh parsley.

"I have a theory," Corny confided, "about why Dr. Broderick broke into the lab to steal Bongo."

"He claims he didn't steal him," I pointed out. "He says he has papers that prove he owns Bongo."

"That makes even more sense," Corny said with a decisive nod. He sat down across the table from me and cast a guilty look over his shoulder at Bongo. "I probably shouldn't say this in front of him," he said, lowering his voice. "But I read this article online about a drug dog that had made so many busts the cartel actually put out a contract on him."

"I saw that on the news," I said, surprised. Usually I greeted anything that began with "I read online" with a healthy amount of skepticism. "This dog was costing the drug cartel so much money that they thought it was worth it to put up $50,000 to the hit man who could take him out. The DEA took the threat seriously enough to bump up the dog's security."

Corny nodded enthusiastically. "So Bongo is one of the top tech-detecting dogs in the country, right? What if someone—or a lot of someones—think they'd be better off if he were... you know..." Again he cast an apologetic look over his shoulder toward a completely unconcerned Bongo. Corny lowered his voice to a near-whisper. "Not in the picture."

Mischief and Magic, whose attention spans were notoriously short, had already wandered off in search of something more interesting than a black Lab in a cage. Pepper stretched out in front of Bongo's crate, watching his Nylabone with tail swishing, and Cisco brought a rubber ball over to the crate and dropped it deliberately on the floor. Bongo watched it bounce.

I said thoughtfully, "Huh." I helped myself to pork and potatoes and passed the dish to Corny. "You mean like some mob kingpin who keeps evidence of his crimes on flash drives that he's afraid Bongo will uncover?"

Corny nodded enthusiastically, scooping potatoes onto his plate. The kitchen light glinted off his glasses with the bobbing of his head. "Exactly. And Dr. Broderick was just trying to keep Bongo safe."

"So why did he murder the lab assistant?" I inquired, willing to play along.

"Maybe," opined Corny, "the lab assistant was the hit man."

I wrinkled up my nose skeptically. "I don't know, Corny. This is starting to sound a little bit like a game of *Clue*." I didn't want to hurt his feelings, so I added, "Anyway, Bongo's not the only tech-sniffing dog in the world, so doing away with him wouldn't help any mob boss who wanted to keep his secrets safe." *And*, I thought but didn't say, *it didn't explain how Miles was involved.* "That was a good theory though," I said. "I just think it's something … I don't know. Simpler. Or at least I hope so."

"So," Corny asked me plainly, pausing with his fork midway to his mouth. "Do you think Dr. Broderick did it? Do you think he's a killer?"

People killed for a lot of reasons, I knew: passion, impulse, rage, revenge, to name a few. Deliberation—the kind of crime that was plotted out, thought through, and executed—really accounted for only a small percent of homicides. Of course, it was entirely possible that even a prominent scientist like Dr. Broderick had been cornered, desperate, and thought he had no choice, or that a gun had accidentally gone off in the heat of the moment. But he had defended himself so clearly, so convincingly. All he wanted was his dog. How could you convict a man for that?

And Miles was on his side. Despite the fact that he wouldn't tell me why, Miles believed in him.

I gazed cross the room at Bongo, who was on his feet now, watching the ball roll across the room with that cute puppy expression Labs get when their ears go forward and their foreheads wrinkle. I said, "No.

I don't think he's a killer. I think the police have got the wrong man."

Not, of course, that it mattered what I thought.

After Corny left, I took a page from his book and did a little Internet research myself on the Coyote Project. The results were less than satisfactory. I learned about a plan to tag and monitor the coyote population in the southern Appalachians, a conspiracy theory that the government was importing coyotes from Alaska to keep down the deer population in our national parks, an outbreak of some kind of coyote flu, and, bizarrely, an inner-city program to teach art to gang members. And then there was this:

Coyote: Native American symbol of the evil deity; devil dog

Terrific.

THIRTEEN

Buck tapped on Marshall's half-open door before he realized the sheriff wasn't alone. It was 8:00 a.m. on a Sunday morning and the truth was Buck was surprised to find him there at all. As a general rule, the sheriff, whose job was mostly administrative, worked 9:00 to 5:00, Monday through Friday. Buck had found that rule hardly ever applied when he'd been sheriff; it looked as though Marshall had already begun to discover the same thing.

Jolene, who was on duty all weekend, was standing in front of Marshall's desk, and she turned when Buck knocked. Marshall was dressed for church, as Buck would have been under different circumstances, and he stood on the other side of the desk, half-bent over the computer screen as he scrolled through pages. He gestured Buck inside.

"I didn't know you were busy," Buck said, indicating a thin manila file folder in his hand. "It can wait."

"Jo was just bringing me up to speed on the Broderick situation," Marshall said. "It looks like we're very close to stepping into the middle of a mess here."

"I can't say I'd argue with that," Buck said, coming into the office. He nodded at Jolene. "Morning, Chief Smith."

She nodded back, and he could see her shoulders tense. "Morning."

Marshall started to straighten up from the computer screen, then scowled and held up a finger for patience. "Hold on a minute." He picked up the phone and dialed a couple of numbers. "Jackie, this is Sheriff Becker. Is Deke on duty today?" A pause. "Well, tell him he left the camera on in the interview room last night. Somebody needs to get down there and turn it off. Deke knows damn well it's his responsibility to make sure the camera is off in that room every time somebody leaves it. We've got two lawyer meetings set up there today."

He hung up the phone, still scowling, and gave a short shake of his head. He muttered, "If you ever wonder how a man can be at a job for twelve years and not get a single promotion, that's why."

Then he blew out a big breath, returning his attention to them, and rubbed at his mustache. "So," he said. "I had a call from Miles Young last night, asking if there was any way we could hold on to Broderick for another twenty-four hours or so, until he got back from Europe."

Buck tried to keep his expression neutral, but his jaw tightened briefly. It was no secret that Miles Young and Marshall Becker were personal friends;

Young had almost single-handedly underwritten Marshall's campaign for sheriff. And that was only one of the reasons such a request was completely inappropriate.

Buck regretted the words even before he spoke them, but he said them anyway. "So we're taking orders from Miles Young now?"

Marshall regarded him levelly, his tone unaltered. "We are not, which is exactly what I told him. As far as I'm concerned, the sooner this particular prisoner is out of our custody the happier I'll be. Unfortunately, it would appear the matter has been taken out of my hands."

He glanced at Jolene, who supplied, "There was a transfer of custody order for Broderick on my desk when I got in this morning. From the FBI."

Buck frowned. "The Feds? How do they fit in to this?"

"My question exactly," Marshall replied. "So I put in a call to Jake Benson at the Charlottesville field office. He wasn't in on a Sunday morning, of course, so I dropped every name I knew, even tried to call in a few favors, and finally got a call back from the special agent in charge basically telling me to mind my own business. All I was able to find out is that Broderick was at the center of an investigation for corporate espionage even before the murder charge; that's how he lost his job at Hartwell."

Buck said, "Corporate espionage? Must be a pretty big deal for the FBI to get involved."

"It's always a big deal when a military contract is at stake," Marshall replied. "Apparently Broderick was a member of a team working on a special project for the military when classified materials started making their way into the private sector. Broderick wasn't officially charged, but it's starting to look like he got himself tangled up in a pretty big squirrel's nest."

"This project for the military he was working on," Buck said, "did it happen to have a name?"

This time it was Jolene who spoke. "It did." She looked at Marshall and explained, "I was curious about the FBI warrant and had time to do a little research myself before you got in. It was pretty easy to find out what kind of things Broderick was involved with at Hartwell, and the most recent was a government contract for something called the Coyote Project."

Buck grunted thoughtfully, unsurprised.

Marshall said, "What?"

"It's just that I was in the room yesterday when Broderick was talking on the phone to Miles Young," Buck said. "The only thing he mentioned by name was the Coyote Project."

Jolene said, "That's interesting. When I tried to look it up, all I could find out was that it's classified."

"That *would* be interesting," Marshall corrected mildly, "if this were our case. I appreciate your curiosity, but we've got our hands full dealing with what we're responsible for around here. Two agents will be down sometime tomorrow to take over. Meantime, we're to consider Broderick a high-security prisoner."

"That should be no problem," Buck said. "I don't think anyone has broken out of this jail since it was built."

"Why should anyone want to break out?" Jolene said. "Most of the people we arrest have a better life in jail than they did before they were convicted."

Jolene had been with the Sheriff's Office less than a year and rarely offered an opinion about anything not directly related to a case, particularly not in jest. But she had a point. Most of the crime in Hanover County was poverty or drug related, and for those perpetrators, incarceration was a definite step up. The food was good, the showers were clean, and most of the time the people who wanted to kill the inmates were on the outside. For the average defendant, there was no safer place to be than the Hanover County jail.

Buck said thoughtfully, "So it looks like Young got what he wanted after all. Broderick will be our guest for another night."

Marshall said, "Do you have a problem with that?"

"None at all." Buck tapped the file folder in his hand against his thigh, hesitating for a moment. Then he said, "I don't mean to complicate things with the FBI, but I thought you'd want to see this. I ran it past the prosecutor last night and he said it's up to you, how far you want to continue the investigation. I know he'll be out of our custody in twenty-four hours," he added, "but it looks like we have cause to bring charges against Broderick ourselves."

Both Jolene and Marshall looked at him with surprise, and Marshall scowled as he reached for the folder in Buck's hand. "What kind of charges?"

Buck handed over the folder. "Child abuse."

"Oh, Raine, honey, it was just awful," Aunt Mart said. Her tone was hushed and tight with stress over the phone, and I could picture her glancing over her shoulder as she spoke, trying not to wake the subject of our conversation. "I wish Ro was here."

It was not quite 8:00 in the morning, and I guess Aunt Mart had forgotten that, with Corny on site, I didn't always get up at 6:00 a.m. to open the kennel as I used to do. In fact, I'd had a restless night with dreams of men in lab coats chasing Labrador retrievers with hunting knives, and when I tried to call 911 for help, all I got was Miles's voice mail. I'd slept late, and somewhere in the back of my mind I'd half-expected to be awakened by the smell of coffee and something scrumptious baking in the oven. This was Miles's typical way of letting me know he had returned from a trip, and it was particularly effective when he knew I was upset with him. Miles had not called last night. I was still upset with him, and instead of the aroma of baking muffins, I'd been awakened by the jangling of my land line and Aunt Mart's distraught voice on the other end of the phone.

The Labrador retriever who'd inspired the nightmares now regarded me with baleful eyes from behind the door of his wire crate, while I ran a hand through my short, sleep-tangled curls and dangled my feet over the side of the bed, searching for my slippers with my toes.

"Of course I had to call Jenny," Aunt Mart went on fretfully. "The protocol is very clear about that. And she came over and took pictures, and then she thought we'd better call Buck. Normally she said she'd file a report with the sheriff's department on Monday, but with the poor little thing's daddy being in jail and all..."

I found one of my slippers and thrust my foot inside. The other one was clenched in the jaws of a grinning, tail-wagging, golden-haired slipper thief who danced across the room with it and play-bowed, inviting me to chase him. I said, "I don't understand. You said she was covered with bruises when you went to get her ready for her bath. How did she get hurt?"

"She wouldn't say," Aunt Mart replied.

Cisco pranced close to me and I made a grab for the slipper, almost falling out of bed in the process.

Aunt Mart went on, "Jenny said a mixture of old and new bruises like that usually indicates long-term abuse. When Buck asked if her daddy ever hurt her, she just started crying." Her voice went misty. "Oh Raine, it just breaks my heart to think of that sweet little girl going through something like that. Why do there have to be such monsters in the world?"

A knot had formed in my stomach before she finished speaking. Of course, I knew everyone had secrets and people were hardly ever who they appeared to be, but this was Dr. Jason Broderick she was talking about, a genius in his field, a man I admired... a man who had been arrested for murder, and whom my boyfriend had dropped everything to rush home and help. Something was very wrong here.

I slid out of bed, wincing as my bare foot struck the cold floor. Typical of a mountain spring, it had started to rain overnight and the temperature had dropped precipitously. My bedroom was freezing. "I'm so sorry, Aunt Mart," I said. "But… is there any chance there's been some kind of mistake?" I limped over to Cisco, wrestled his prize from his mouth, and thrust my foot into the soggy slipper. I shivered and pulled on a robe. "I mean, Celie didn't seem like an abused child to me."

On the other hand, Broderick had not exactly shown an abundance of concern for his daughter, either. And I had seen far too many abused dogs come slinking back to their owners with ears back and tails wagging low, begging for affection and more than ready to give it in return, to believe in the law of natural consequences.

She sighed. "I know. And until all this happened, she really seemed to be settling in, playing in the backyard with Majesty, swinging on the tire, dressing up her Teddy bear…but in the end, she cried herself to sleep. I feel just awful. But what else could I do?"

"Nothing," I assured her firmly. "You did exactly the right thing."

"I won't keep you on the phone, honey," she said. "I know you've got a lot to do this morning. I was just wondering if maybe you could bring Celie's dog over to play after church today? I think it would really cheer her up."

I glanced at Bongo, who stood up in his crate and returned my gaze, almost as if sensing we were talking about him. "I think that's a great idea," I said. "What time?"

We agreed on 1:00, and as soon as I hung up I grabbed my cell phone and checked for messages.

There was a text from Miles that had come in at 3:00 a.m.

Didn't want to wake you. Delayed in London. I'll call when I get to the States. He included a link to The Weather Channel, which described a freak spring snowstorm that had shut down Heathrow. I dialed his number and it went straight to voice mail. "Damn it," I muttered, and hung up without leaving a message.

Bongo pawed the gate of his crate and Cisco wagged his way over to me, his stuffed duck having replaced my slipper as the prize of the morning. As much as I would have liked to have stood there for another minute or two feeling angry and worried about Miles, I didn't have time. The day had begun.

FOURTEEN

Marshall took his time studying the file, examining the pictures, the social worker's report, Mart's statement, Buck's report on his interview with the child. He closed the folder grimly and returned it to Buck. "We're not turning over a suspect with an incomplete jacket. See what you can get out of Broderick. Find out what you can from the kid's doctor, the emergency rooms in her hometown. Get a report ready to hand over to the FBI when they get here."

Buck said, "You got it."

Marshall glanced at his watch and frowned. "I've got to get going. I'm supposed to give the devotional to the Sunday School class this morning, but I'll be back after lunch. Jo, text me if anything else develops. Buck..." He hesitated for a moment, his expression tight and frustrated. "No more complications, okay?"

Buck touched the corner of file folder to his forehead in a light salute and replied, "I'll do my best."

Broderick was being kept in a holding cell, temporary housing away from the general population and about as secure as it got for a county jail. It was an 8x10 concrete box with floor to ceiling bars on the corridor side, a cot bolted to the wall, and a steel toilet. Most people who stayed there moved through fairly quickly, so amenities weren't a priority.

Broderick was lying on the cot, one arm over his eyes, but he got to his feet when he heard Buck approach. Buck stood outside the cell and waited until Broderick came to the bars. He took a paper from the file in his hand and held it up. It was a picture of Celia Broderick in short pajamas, the bruises on her arms and legs clearly visible.

Buck's amiable manner from the day before was completely gone. He said, "Tell me how your daughter got these bruises."

Broderick's jaw tightened. He seemed to be considering whether or not to answer.

"We can subpoena her medical records," Buck said, "but this is the second day off I've wasted on you, and I'm starting to lose my sense of humor. Answer the question."

Knowing the FBI would be taking over, Buck had half-expected Marshall to shut down the investigation, since it was pretty clear it wouldn't be going anywhere. But he had reckoned without Marshall's propensity for doing things by the book. Buck had taken the report, and the sheriff wanted follow-through. So, as a matter of fact, did Buck.

Broderick drew a breath, and there was a slight hitch toward the end when he released it. "She's okay? Celie's okay?"

Buck held his gaze and nodded once.

Broderick rubbed a hand over his stubbly face. "Celie has a blood disorder," he said. "It's like hemophilia, only trickier. She can get a bruise from her mattress, or a button on her dress. When she was a toddler she had to wear a football helmet every minute she was awake because one fall could've caused a brain bleed that would have killed her. The past year she's been taking treatments that have helped, but there's no cure."

Buck said, "You didn't think any of this was worth mentioning to the social worker?"

Broderick burst out, "I was trying to protect—" And he broke off in mid-sentence, snapping his mouth shut with an almost audible click of his teeth.

"Protect who?" Buck demanded. "Who is more important to protect than your daughter who could die from a fall off a tricycle?"

Broderick drew in a sharp breath through his nostrils, his eyes blazing briefly. Then he said, with a visible effort to keep his tone even, "I told the social worker Celie couldn't have aspirin. I saw her circle that in red under allergies on the medical form. There's nothing more I could do! I'm not even supposed to be here! We should be in Florida by now. She..." He drew another sharp breath, fingers closing into fists at his side. "She just had a treatment," he said. "I knew she'd be fine for another couple of weeks. But don't you see that's why I've got to get out of here?" Now desperation crept into his voice and he wrapped his hands around the bars. "Everything I did was for her! But it's all going to be for nothing if you don't let me out of here!"

Buck stepped away from the bars and tucked the picture back into the file folder. He said, "I need the name of your daughter's doctor."

Broderick released the bars, his shoulders sagging with defeat. "Jackson Lyon," he said tiredly, "with a 'Y.' Family Medical Center in Raleigh. He's a pediatric oncologist. He'll confirm everything I've told you."

Buck walked away without replying.

FIFTEEN

I'm careful about introducing new dogs into the pack. Cisco is generally the most amiable dog you'll ever meet, but he does have a jealous streak, particularly when it comes to male dogs he considers rivals for attention. That was one reason I'd let Bongo sleep crated in my room last night, so that Cisco could get accustomed to his scent and realize he was no threat. The other reason was that, even without Miles's instructions on the matter, I wasn't about to let Bongo out of my sight.

Of course, there isn't room for *everyone* in my room, so I knew there'd be a flurry of sniffing and reacquainting to be done that morning, so I let Mischief, Magic and Pepper out into the backyard first, then went back upstairs for Bongo and Cisco. The morning was still cold and misty, so I pulled a coat over my sweat suit before going out onto the back porch to watch the dogs go through their greeting rituals. Fortunately, the girls were happy to see Bongo again, and Cisco seemed pleased to be reintroduced. Bongo was far more interested in relieving himself than in any of the dogs, and I felt a little guilty. He was probably accustomed to being released from his crate much earlier in the morning.

I let them run around for a few minutes, splashing in puddles and sniffing blades of grass, then grabbed a towel from the hook by the back door and called them to me, one by one. As soon as I dried each set of muddy paws, I let them back into the house. Mischief and Magic are lightning on the recall, and Cisco is pretty good. Pepper is going through that gawky teenage phase in which her brain is almost as clumsy as her body, and seemed much more interested in a bug she'd found floating in a puddle than in the sound of my voice. Eventually, however, she looked up, remembered I was the one who was responsible for her breakfast, and raced up the steps to me. Bongo sniffed the perimeter of the fence while I dried Pepper's paws and ushered her inside.

When I opened the door to let Pepper in, I heard the distant ringing of my cell phone, and swore to myself as I remembered I'd left it upstairs in its charger. I slammed the door shut and raced up the stairs, trying not to trip over the dogs who thought this was a great new game. By the time I reach the phone, it had stopped ringing, and I saw, just as I suspected, I had missed a call from Miles. Frustrated, I dialed my voice mail.

He said, "Hey, babe. I'm just getting on a flight out. ETA is probably another six to eight hours. I'm turning off my phone for takeoff but I'll call when I land. I know you've got everything under control. Just hang tight until I get there. Love you."

"Thanks for the vote of confidence," I muttered, "but I'd rather have some answers." I dialed his number as quickly as I could, but he hadn't lied. His phone was off.

I went back downstairs, trailed by a pack of hungry canines. I pushed them aside and went back outside for Bongo. But the backyard was empty.

My heart jumped to my throat with such force that I actually choked on my indrawn breath. "Bongo!" I called. I plunged down the steps, grabbing the rail to keep from slipping. "Bongo!"

My fenced exercise yard is not that big, and designed in a perfect square around the back side of my house. There's only one small area that can't be seen from the back porch or the kitchen window, and that's on the side where the gate is. "Bongo!" I cried again, and ran in that direction.

The minute I rounded the corner I could see that the gate was standing open, and Bongo was nowhere in sight. I did not slow down. I screamed again, "Bongo!"

The next thing I knew I was flat on my back on the soggy ground, staring up into the face of a big-chested stranger in a black coat.

SIXTEEN

A lot of things happened at once. Four dogs came scrambling down the steps from the kitchen, whose door I'd apparently neglected to close tightly, barking and kicking up sprays of muddy water. I heard Corny cry, "Miss Stockton!" The fierce-faced stranger grabbed me by my arms, and I kicked and twisted, fighting off muddy paws and happy dog kisses as much as I did the grip of the stranger. And, out of the corner of my eye, I saw Bongo.

The escape of the pack turned out to be in my favor. As soon as they got over the novelty of finding me on the ground, the dogs turned their attention to the stranger, circling and barking and jumping on him in excitement, startling him enough that I was able to wrench away and lurch to my feet. No sooner had I done so than Corny, in a bright yellow rain slicker, came trotting up with Bongo on a leash. "Miss Stockton! Are you all right?"

"I'm okay!" I gasped. I grabbed Pepper's collar and pulled her with me as I backed away, commanding, "Cisco! Mischief, Magic! Here!" One lost dog—or almost lost dog—was quite enough for one morning.

Corny snapped the gate closed and I herded my dogs back toward the house. Fortunately, dogs are a living example of the law of inertia: once in motion, they tend to stay in motion, and in only a matter of seconds they were back in the house and secured behind the closed door. I spun back to the stranger, breathing hard. "Who are you?" I demanded. "What are you doing in my backyard?"

Corny said accusingly, "I saw him lurking around the house, and then noticed that Bongo was out in the backyard by himself. So I came into the yard to check on Bongo—you said we weren't supposed to let him out of our sight—and when I turned around this man was standing there with the gate open." The outrage in his voice suggested that the worst of all possible offenses the stranger could have committed was to open the gate—which I suppose was true. "Good thing I already had Bongo on a leash."

The man said politely, "I didn't mean to cause all this confusion. I went to the front door, but then I saw this gentleman"—he nodded to Corny—"and followed him around back. That was quite a fall you took."

I glared at him. My backside was cold and soaking wet—not to mention bruised—my hands were mud-caked, and it had started to drizzle rain again. Water slithered off my hair and inside my collar, inching a slow cold path down my back. "Who are you?" I demanded again.

"My name is Darrel Grayson." He extended a hand, which I ignored. "I take it you're Raine Stockton, and this..." He turned to Corny, but looked at Bongo. "Must be Bongo. I'm here from Hartwell to take him off your hands."

My eyes met Corny's. Corny's hand tightened on the leash and Bongo, sensing it, sat down on the wet grass. I could tell that Corny and I were thinking exactly the same thing: Something was very off here. No way was this guy taking Bongo.

I said, "Not without a court order, you're not. This dog was taken into custody by the Hanover County Sheriff's Office, and they're the only ones I'll release him to."

Grayson seemed more amused than surprised. "I'm sure you meant to include his rightful owner in that."

I replied, "I said exactly what I meant. I need you to leave now."

He looked around, quick eyes searching the house, the fence perimeter, the kennel building. He nodded toward the kennel. "Is that where you keep him?"

I said nothing, my heart pounding. Corny inched his hands down lower on the leash, taking up the slack.

Grayson's eyes landed on the gate. "You might think about a lock for that."

I said, "I can have a police car here in ten minutes."

He smiled. "I won't bother you again."

He turned and walked through the gate, closing it carefully after himself. I could hear his footsteps crunching on the gravel drive as he walked away.

Corny inched closer to me with Bongo, his eyes frightened behind the rain-streaked glasses. "Miss

Stockton," he said, keeping his voice low, "I don't like that man."

I wiped my muddy hands uneasily on my sweatpants. "Me, either."

"The way he was walking around your house," Corny said, "checking the windows and doors... it was like he was looking for a way to break in. And where is his car?"

I looked quickly at Corny, then went to the gate, peering around the side of the house. There was no car in my driveway. The man who'd called himself Darrell Grayson was moving casually down my drive toward the road, on foot.

I said, "The sound of a car would have alerted the dogs." And there aren't too many good reasons for wanting to approach a stranger's house in silence.

"He gave up pretty easily," Corny observed.

"He'll be back." I was sure of it.

"Do you think he really was from Hartwell Labs?"

"Maybe," I said, turning away from the gate. "But if he is, we've got bigger problems than we thought. When I was fighting with him on the ground his coat fell open, and I saw a shoulder holster." I looked at Corny, not wanting to frighten him further but understanding that knowledge was the best defense. "He had a gun."

SEVENTEEN

The man who waited for Jason Broderick in the interview room was wearing an expensive-looking knee-length overcoat with pearls of misty rain still clinging to it, dark leather gloves, and a well-fitting gray suit with a Harvard tie. There was a calf skin briefcase and two paper coffee cups with lids on the table, and he stood with his hands in the pockets of his coat, examining the print of the sheep meadow on the wall. He turned when Broderick came in.

"Dr. Broderick." He came forward with his hand extended. "I'm David Sutherlin, from the law firm of Sutherlin, Feinstein and Rich. Miles Young asked me to stop by."

Broderick looked at the attorney's extended hand, then lifted his own cuffed hands in a wry apologetic gesture. Sutherlin looked sharply at the deputy who had escorted him in. "Uncuff my client's hands," he demanded. "There's absolutely no directive that requires a suspect to be restrained while meeting with his attorney."

Deke hesitated, clearly uneasy with words like "directive" and "restrained." He had already gotten in trouble with the sheriff once today. He said, "We're not supposed to…"

"Cuff him to the table, then," replied Sutherlin impatiently. "That's what the restraint ring is there for, isn't it?"

This time Deke's hesitance was slightly less. He had seen Buck do that, so it must be okay. Besides, the lawyer was right. That was what it was there for.

He ordered Broderick to be seated, then unfastened one of the wrist restraints with the key from his belt, and immediately snapped it around the iron ring bolted to the table, leaving Broderick's right hand free. "I'll be outside when you're done," he told the lawyer and left.

Broderick flexed his free wrist, and the attorney smiled, again extending his hand. "As I said, I'm David Sutherlin."

Broderick shook his hand. "Jason Broderick."

Sutherlin made an apologetic face as he withdrew his hand. "Sorry about the gloves," he said, plucking them off by the fingers. "It's bitter outside." He nodded toward the cups on the table. "I brought you some coffee. It wasn't easy, finding a decent cup of coffee in this berg, but it's got to be better than the jailhouse variety."

Broderick pulled one of the cups toward him with his free hand. "Thanks." He looked at the other man anxiously. "Is Celie okay? The investigator who talked to me this morning… is this about that? Because—"

Sutherlin interrupted calmly, "Your daughter is fine. This is about making sure you're fine, too, and seeing that the two of you are reunited as soon as possible."

Broderick's shoulders relaxed visibly. "Right. Good." He took a sip of the coffee, and then looked at the other man. "I didn't ask for a lawyer."

"Mr. Young is covering the cost," Sutherlin assured him.

Broderick shook his head. "That's not what I meant. I can pay. It's just that..." He leaned forward urgently, his hands wrapped around the coffee cup. "I'm innocent. This is crazy. Like I told the investigator, Martin was alive when I left him. My little girl needs me. You've got to get these charges dropped so I can get back to her, and I mean as soon as possible."

Sutherlin opened his briefcase. "That's exactly why I'm here." He took out a legal pad and a pen, folded his hands atop them, and leaned forward earnestly. "Tell me what happened."

Buck hesitated a moment, then made the turn that took him to Jolene's office. "Office" was something of an exaggeration; it was really little more than a cubicle at the back of a room filled with communal deputy desks, and it had been his cubicle for almost eight years. She had made some changes. Nike's wire crate took up the wall space between two filing cabinets, but it was empty now, since the rain had stopped and Jolene usually let Nike enjoy the outdoor chain-link run during good weather. There were framed photographs on the desk and a child's artwork on the wall. There was even a fern sitting on the filing cabinet. It looked like silk, but still. A fern.

He rapped lightly on the particle board wall, poked his head around the corner and said, "Hey."

Jolene looked up from her computer.

Buck jerked a thumb over his shoulder. "I'm headed out. I finished the report on Celia Broderick and left it on Marshall's desk. Make sure he sees it, okay?"

She said, "What did you find out?"

That surprised him a little. Jolene was very much a stay-in-your-lane kind of person, and he had never known her interest to stray over the line into cases that didn't concern her.

He stepped inside the cubicle. "I'm having a pretty good day. I didn't think I'd be able to get through to Celia Broderick's doctor on a Sunday, but I guess it's not every Sunday he gets a call from an out-of-town sheriff's office, either. So after a little back and forth about release forms, he confirmed she was being treated for a form of Von Willebran's Disease. It's a clotting disorder that causes bruising, which matches Broderick's story." He shrugged one shoulder. "It doesn't prove anything, of course, but I remember hearing about a case in Texas where DFACS actually took a baby away from the parents because the kid kept coming in to the pediatrician with unexplained bruises, and it turned out to be the same kind of thing. So I guess it happens." He hesitated, and added, "The doctor did say something odd, though. He seemed surprised that I was asking about Celia Broderick because, he said, she wasn't 'officially' his patient any more. Apparently her dad had put her in some kind of clinical study and he'd just transferred all her records to a doctor in central Florida. That's why he remembered so much about her case when I asked."

"Who was the Florida doctor?"

"Somebody Liebowitz. It's in the report. Do you want me to e-mail you a copy?"

She hesitated, and then shook her head. "No. The FBI's got this."

"My thoughts exactly."

He turned to go, then Jolene said, "She was wearing a Florida hat."

Buck said, "I tried asking her about it when I was talking to her before, just to make conversation, but you know how kids are. She said she didn't remember where she got it, or when." Again he shrugged. "Anyway, not our case. The prosecutor wouldn't be able to make charges even if he wanted to, so my job is done."

He started to leave, then hesitated, glancing at a photo on Jolene's desk of a gap-toothed, chocolate-skinned little boy with a riotous headful of curly dark hair. He couldn't help smiling. "Is that your little guy? He's going to be a real heartbreaker when he grows up, with that grin and all that hair."

Her hand touched the photo in an almost unconscious gesture of affection, and her lips turned down ruefully. "He's got the devil in him already, that's for sure."

"When's he coming down here?"

"Another month. I'm still looking for a place for Mama to stay, and she thought it was better to let him finish out kindergarten in Raleigh."

That was the longest conversation they'd had about anything personal since he'd hired her last spring. Buck remembered what Raine had said about Jolene being afraid of him, and he didn't like the possibility. The way it looked right now, neither one of them was going anywhere. They may as well try to get along. Besides, she was good at her job. And these days he could use all the help he could get.

Buck said, "Gerald Winters has a little place over on Spring Street that he rents out. I don't know how much he gets for it, but I heard it was empty, and it's not that far from you. It might be worth giving him a call."

She tried to hide her surprise, but wasn't quite quick enough. "Yeah, okay. Thanks. I will."

She turned back to her computer and he had taken a step into the corridor before she said, "It's just that…"

He came back inside the cubicle and waited for her to go on.

"There's something screwy about this case."

Buck agreed without a trace of humor, "A lot of things."

She frowned determinedly at her monitor, which was locked on the HCSO logo, her fingers resting lightly on the keyboard. "I was getting ready to file the custody transfer request we got on Broderick from the FBI when I noticed that the crime scene report had been updated since yesterday. It seemed a little soon for forensics, so I went to have a closer look and saw that the list of evidence now includes security camera footage." She clicked her mouse and typed in a few characters. "I put in a request for a copy for our records and, what do you know?—they actually e-mailed me a copy within the hour. I guess whoever works the records desk in Charlottesville on Sundays doesn't know about red tape. Here it is."

Buck rested his hand on the back of her chair as he leaned in to watch the video.

The footage was grainy and low-light. The view was of a white tiled corridor. In the background a dog barked. A short, bespectacled man in a white lab coat came around the corner, moving quickly. Less than two seconds later, according to the video time stamp, another man came into view from the opposite corner. He was wearing a baseball cap and a dark windbreaker, and although the camera angle only partially captured his face, there was little doubt the second man was Jason Broderick. He stopped short with a muffled expletive, his surprise evident. "Martin?" The voice was definitely Broderick's. "Martin, what are you doing here?"

The man in the lab coat seemed startled, uncertain, frozen in place. He looked as though he was about to reply when Broderick stepped backwards, partially out of frame. Two soft gunshots whooshed from a silencer in rapid succession. The first one caused Martin to jerk to his right, a bright spray of blood bursting from his head. The second caught him in the chest and he fell backward, still and bleeding. Jolene stopped the playback.

Buck straightened up, his expression thoughtful. "Not looking good for our friend Broderick. I wonder why this wasn't included on the original evidence list?"

"There's something else," Jolene said. "The report we got yesterday said the security cameras were off at the time Broderick entered the building."

"So they were," agreed Buck. "But apparently not on this floor."

"These systems usually work in tandem, on a single circuit," Jolene said. "But okay, maybe not this one. What I don't understand is why Broderick took that step back just before he shot him. It's not like the victim was rushing him. He was in point-blank range. Who steps back from three feet away to get a better shot?"

That wasn't the only thing that was bothering Buck. He stared at the frozen footage, frowning. "Sounds like a question Broderick's lawyer should be asking a jury, for sure," he agreed absently.

Jolene closed out the window on the footage. "Or maybe he should ask Broderick. He's with him now."

Buck glanced at her. "That was quick. I didn't think he'd called a lawyer."

"I guess Mr. Young sent him. The jail called over to see if we wanted to make an exception, since we usually don't allow lawyer visits until 2:00 on Sundays. I figured somebody would be crying foul if he didn't get to see his lawyer before he left here, so I okayed it."

Buck said thoughtfully, "I did a little research myself yesterday after Broderick made his phone call. Turns out Miles Young is one of the owners of this think tank, the Hartwell Group, where Broderick worked. The same place Broderick's accused of stealing intellectual property from, not to mention the dog. The owners make money by licensing or selling whatever the think tank develops to private companies. So when ideas go missing, it's money out of their pockets. So why do you suppose Broderick would use his one phone call from jail to call the man he's accused of stealing from? And why would that same man send him a lawyer?"

"Maybe," suggested Jolene, "he thought he could make a deal with Young if he returned the stolen property. And maybe that's what the lawyer is trying to work out with him now."

"Maybe," agreed Buck absently. "Or maybe they both thought they could make a deal with somebody else."

Jolene said, "Either way, I don't see how it ended up murder. Or what any of it's got to do with the Coyote Project."

"Yeah." Buck gazed at the computer monitor thoughtfully. He wanted to see that footage again. He pointed to the window she had just closed and started to speak, but was distracted by another icon blinking at the bottom of her screen. "What's that?" he said, even though he knew the answer.

She said under her breath, "Crap!"

She clicked the mouse and the screen was filled with an image of the interview room at the jail. Two men sat across the table from each other. One was Jason Broderick. The other, who had not bothered to remove his raincoat, had a briefcase open before him. He could only be Broderick's lawyer.

"Son of a—"

Jolene's expletive was cut off by Buck's. "Damn it, Deke, you idiot! You're going to get this whole case thrown out!"   He grabbed the mouse from Jolene's hand and closed the screen. "Call over to the jail and get somebody in there to turn off the camera."

Jolene was already dialing the phone.

Buck pushed away from her chair and bolted out of the cubicle. "I'll get over there and try to do some damage control."

But by the time he got there, it was already too late.

EIGHTEEN

It seemed a little melodramatic to call 911 about a crime that hadn't happened, particularly when the perpetrator was long gone. I thought about reporting the incident to Jolene, but, honestly, I was afraid she would order me to surrender the dog. I was pretty sure she was still annoyed with me for not taking him to the animal shelter in the first place, and this incident would only prove her right—despite the fact that the animal shelter was possibly the least secure place in the world on a weekend. In the end I decided the best thing to do was to call the sheriff himself, who I was pretty sure would not be in on Sunday morning. That way no one could say I hadn't at least tried.

"You didn't miss him by much," Annabelle said. "He came in for about an hour this morning—you know how it is when you have a high-profile prisoner—then went on to church. He said he'd be back after lunch. You want to leave a message for him?"

"Yeah, just tell him to call me back when he gets a chance," I said. "You know I'm taking care of the dog that belongs to the prisoner they brought in yesterday, and I just wanted to check in."

"Sure thing." I could tell she was already scribbling a reminder to herself.

I added as casually as possible, "I don't suppose you know anything about anyone from Raleigh coming by to get the dog, do you?"

"No, I haven't heard anything. I can ask Chief Smith if you want to hold on."

I said, "No, that's okay. I'm sure she'll let me know if she hears anything."

I was calling from the kennel office, where I'd spent the morning helping Corny clean the indoor runs and wash bedding, which always took a beating on rainy days. We only had three boarders left of the ten we'd cared for over the weekend, so it was pretty easy duty. Also, all things considered, the kennel seemed safer than the house at present.

My soul might be in jeopardy for skipping Sunday services, but after the unexpected visit from Mr. Grayson—or whoever he was—there was no way I was leaving Bongo alone, even long enough to go to church. His leash was clipped to my belt; he went where I went. Cisco and the girls were in the playroom, and I felt a little sorry for Bongo, whose ears would prick up every now and then at the sounds of merriment coming from that direction. But I would be even sorrier if I lost him.

When I hung up the phone, Corny tapped lightly on my doorframe. "Do you want me to take Bongo to play with the others?" he volunteered. "I'll stay with him, of course."

I glanced at my watch and shook my head. "No, I just have time to get the towels out of the drier, and then we'll have to leave."

"All taken care of," he said, which was hardly a surprise. Corny was the most efficient person I'd ever known.

"Thanks," I said.

He stood there at the threshold of my office, hands shoved into the pockets of his bright red overalls, faint lines of puzzlement furrowing his brow. "So I went to the Hartwell website," he said, "to try to find that man who was here this morning, that Darrell Grayson. He wasn't on any personnel list. No one by that name works there."

I nodded. "I'm not surprised."

"Sooo…" His brows drew together in deepening perplexity as he went on. "If he doesn't work for Hartwell, and if the police didn't give him permission to take Bongo, how did he know where to find him? I mean, the only people who know you even have Bongo are the police and us. And Mr. Young, of course."

My expression was uneasy as I glanced at my phone. How long did it take to fly from London to the United States, anyway? "Right."

"And another thing I don't understand," Corny went on, "is why he left without Bongo. I mean, you said he had a gun. Unless he wasn't authorized to shoot us. Sometimes they're not, you know."

I was confused. "Who?"

"Operatives," he explained patiently. "You know, NSA, Black Ops, things like that. They have to follow a very strict set of parameters or risk blowing the whole mission."

Corny's tastes in video entertainment were almost as extreme as Melanie's, which explained where they both came up with their somewhat outrageous theories. I said doubtfully, "I don't know that retrieving Bongo would necessarily justify a Black Ops mission."

Bongo thumped his tail on the floor, though I wasn't sure whether that signified agreement or disagreement. I scratched his ear again.

"Maybe not," Corny admitted, not in the least offended. "But PIs aren't allowed to shoot people either. Maybe somebody hired him to steal Bongo. Maybe it was even somebody at the Hartwell Group. And that would explain why he wasn't listed as an employee."

"Yeah," I agreed thoughtfully, looking down at Bongo. "It would." There were far too many unanswered questions rolling around in my head, and the one person who could answer all of them was right now somewhere over the Atlantic, refusing to take my calls.

I said, "Maybe I'll try to call Miles again."

I reached for my phone, but as I did it rang. I lifted an eyebrow. "Speak of the devil," I said, and even allowed myself a small leap of hope.

But it wasn't him. It was instead the devil's daughter—who would have been amused and delighted to hear herself described that way—and I swallowed back disappointment as I answered the call.

"Hey there, kiddo," I said, forcing cheerfulness into my voice. "How're those dinos treating you?"

Buck strode into the interview room and switched off the monitor himself. "Damn it, Deke," he said, "you're going to get us both fired. What's the matter with you, for crap's sake?"

"I'm telling you, I turned it off!" Deke objected. "The minute Jackie told me the sheriff called over this morning saying it was on, I came right in and turned it off. I guess I left it on yesterday after you interviewed Broderick, and that's on me, but I turned it off this morning."

"*Jackie* turned it off this morning, you idiot," Buck said in exasperation. "You must've turned it back on again."

Jackie was the receiving deputy with whom Marshall had spoken that morning. She had been on her way to the interview room to turn off the camera yet again when Buck arrived, but he had already figured out what had happened. The only good news was that Broderick's lawyer had just left, sparing Buck the embarrassment of explaining what happened. Someone—hopefully not him—would have to write up an incident report, of course, but as long as no one from the Hanover County Sheriff's Department was ever called to give evidence in the Broderick case, the damage should be minimal.

"Anyhow," Deke said, not entirely echoing Buck's thoughts, "I don't see how it can be that big a deal. They couldn't have been in there more than five minutes. Ten at the most. Just long enough for the lawyer to say who he was." He picked up the two coffee cups that had been left on the table and dropped them in the trash can, apparently in an effort to demonstrate his thoroughness to Buck. Unfortunately, both cups were partially full and coffee splashed all over the plastic trashcan liner, so his point was lost. "Next thing I know, he's knocking on the door, saying Broderick wants to go back to his cell. So that's exactly where I took him."

Buck ignored the mess in the trash can and pointed to the monitor. "Look," he said, "the green light is off. That means the camera is off. Check it next time, will you?"

"Yes sir, Buck, I'll surely do that."

Buck strode to the door and then hesitated, glancing back. "So what happened? Didn't Broderick like his lawyer? Did anybody say anything when they left?"

Deke shrugged. "Just that Broderick didn't feel good. Tell the truth, he didn't look all that good either. All sweaty and shaky-like, and he didn't say a word all the way back to his cell. Every other time he can't stop talking, you know what I'm saying?"

Buck frowned. "Was he sick when you brought him up here?"

"Not so's you'd notice."

Buck frowned. "Has anybody checked on him?"

"Hell, Buck, it wasn't more than a minute ago that I left him, sound asleep on his cot."

Buck felt a prickle on the back of his neck. He looked at the two coffee cups in the trashcan. He looked at Deke. He left the room, walking fast. But before he reached Jason Broderick's cell, he was running.

Melanie hadn't talked to her father since last night, which, as she pointed out to me, was really this morning since London was five hours ahead of us. She knew he was coming back early but didn't know why and wasn't very interested as long as it didn't mean she had to cut her trip short. Melanie was at an age where nothing was very interesting that didn't directly affect her—an age which, as I knew from personal experience, was destined to last well into her twenties. She was full of chatter about all things prehistoric, including, according to her, the food at the campsite and one of the team leaders. I told her I wished I was there, and meant it. She replied generously that she wished I was there too.

I was in a slightly better mood when I put Bongo in his crate in the back of the SUV and started out for Aunt Mart's. For one thing, Melanie almost always made me laugh. For another, the sun was actually starting to peek through, showing patches of blue sky between gray-edged clouds. The air was still wet and cool, and tendrils of wispy cloud-smoke drifted from the tops of the distant blue-green mountains, but the promise of sunshine made it feel like spring.

Aunt Mart and Uncle Ro live in a neat brick ranch just outside of town, with a couple of acres of fruit trees and a flowing green lawn that Uncle Ro enjoys keeping in shape with his riding lawnmower. The pea-gravel drive is lined with bright pink and deep red azaleas, and today they were in full bloom.

I could hear Majesty barking as I went up the front steps with Bongo on his leash, but the barking sounded muted, as though it was coming from the back of the house. I took that to mean that Aunt Mart had locked Majesty in a bedroom so that I could bring Bongo in without any drama, which I appreciated. I knocked lightly and opened the front door, calling, "Hey, Aunt Mart, it's me!"

There was no response except that muted barking, which meant Aunt Mart was probably in the kitchen and hadn't heard me drive up. I remember thinking, as I guided Bongo from the small foyer toward the main living area, that I hoped she was baking cookies.

"Hey!" I called again. "Where's Celie? I've got—"

And that was when my breath left my body. I dropped the leash and stood frozen in place, the scene throbbing in front of me.

The television was overturned. Glass from a broken lamp was scattered across the hardwood floor. A stack of magazines had been dislodged from the coffee table, strewn like birds with broken wings from the fireplace to the sofa. Water dripped from an overturned vase of daffodils. And in the middle of it all my Aunt Mart sat strapped to a kitchen chair with duct tape, small desperate mewling sounds coming from her duct-taped mouth as she struggled against her bonds, her face streaked with mascara and tears.

I stumbled across the room and fell to my knees beside her chair, gasping for breath. I tried to gently pry the tape away from her mouth with shaking fingers but she jerked her head so violently to one side that the tape came off in a single rip.

"Celie!" she cried, sobbing. "She's gone! He took her! He took that little girl!"

In the background, Majesty barked and barked.

NINETEEN

Two patrol cars were in the front drive before five minutes had passed, but the first thing I did was scream at them, "Where have you been? What took you so long?"

Bongo was locked in Uncle Ro's office, and Majesty was still in the bedroom. Both dogs started barking at the sound of the cars in the drive, and for perhaps the first time in my life my head didn't automatically swivel toward the sound of the barking.

I knew both the deputies, and both of them knew me. They also knew they were responding to a crime at the former sheriff's house, and could see the former sheriff's wife huddled on the sofa, trying to repair her face with shaking hands, and I knew they were intimidated by the fact. But they remained professional. Jamie, who had been hired by Uncle Ro five years ago, said, "Can you tell me what happened?"

Aunt Mart, only slightly more composed now than she had been moments earlier, repeated what she'd told me. "Celie—the little girl I'm fostering— and I had just finished lunch. I was expecting Raine to come over with Celie's dog, so when I heard a car drive up I thought it was her. I went to put my collie in the bedroom so that Raine could bring the dog in, and when I came back the front door was open, and when I went to close it somebody grabbed me from behind. I screamed and fought and"—there was a hitch in her voice—"things got broken. Celie... Celie came down the hallway and I yelled at her to run, but she ran the wrong way, back to her room. The man...he was dressed in black and had a ski mask over his face. Just the sight of him must have terrified her. He pushed me down on the floor and..."

She was weeping openly now. I sank down on the sofa beside my aunt and grasped her hand. She clutched my hand back with such force that it hurt. Jamie glanced at the other deputy, Leon, who quickly went outside to secure the perimeter. By the book.

Aunt Mart sucked in a breath and went on, "He taped my hands behind my back and put tape over my mouth. I thought he was going to... to..." Her nails dug into my hand. "But he just dragged me over to the chair and taped me to it."

She nodded to the kitchen chair that sat at the edge of the room, remnants of the tape I'd cut away still dangling from it. I could feel a tremor run through her, and I patted her hand. "And then he left, and when he came back he had Celie, carrying her like a rag doll, and the poor little thing was too scared to even cry. She just buried her face in her teddy bear and looked at me with those great big scared eyes as he carried her out the door..."

Her voice went high and tight, and I whispered, "You're doing great, Aunt Mart. Everything's okay now."

It wasn't, of course. Everything was very, very far from okay. The evidence of that was not so much in the trashed room, the missing child, the deputy sheriff taking notes about an assault and kidnapping in my uncle's house—*my uncle*—but in the fact that my aunt, whom I had once seen fight off a would-be thief in a church lobby with an umbrella and shoot the head off a rattlesnake at a Kiwanis picnic before calmly going back to serving potato salad—that this woman, gentle, kind-hearted, soft-spoken and as solid as an oak—was now shrunken and broken and weeping in my arms—that was not okay. That was as wrong as anything ever got.

Even Jamie's eyes were softened with compassion as he said, "I'm so sorry, Miss Mart. But you just take it easy now. We're going to take care of this. How long ago did it happen?"

Aunt Mart covered her face briefly with both hands, then drew in a wet breath and squared her shoulders, glancing uncertainly at the clock shaped like a ship's wheel on the wall. "About half an hour. It was over really quickly. He never said anything. He just took Celie and ran. I heard the car start up, but I didn't see it."

I felt a stab of agonizing remorse. If I had been here earlier...why hadn't I been here earlier?

Another patrol car pulled up and two more deputies got out. They left their blue lights swirling as they went around the side of the house, presumably to get the report from Leon. Aunt Mart pulled her hand from mine, swiped at each eye with her fingers, and pressed her hands to her thighs in preparation for rising. There were still red stripes around her wrists from the tape. "Well," she said, with only a little shakiness in her voice. "I'd better get a pot of coffee going. These boys'll be needing it."

I started to object, but quickly saw that she needed to keep busy, so I let her go. "Where's Buck?" I demanded of Jamie as soon as she was out of earshot. "Where's Marshall? Why aren't they here?"

"They're probably on their way," Jamie said. "Do you mind if I look around?"

"Don't let the dogs out."

I started to dial my uncle's cell phone number, surprised to see my fingers were shaking. Aunt Mart, with that peculiar intuition all mothers seem to have, turned back from the kitchen as I was dialing and caught me in the act.

"You're not calling Ro, are you?" she said. "Don't you bother him with this! He's been looking forward to this trip all year! Why would you call him? He can't do anything from there!"

She tried to take the phone from me, and I blocked her with my shoulder. "Because he'd kill me if I didn't," I replied. "And he'd never forgive you." And also because I had to do something, anything, that felt like the right thing after so much else had gone wrong.

I spoke to Uncle Ro briefly, then turned over the phone to my aunt, who took it into the kitchen. After a while I could hear her crying softly. I've never felt so helpless in my life.

"The docs think it was fentanyl," Buck told Marshall when he arrived. His expression was grim. "He's still unconscious."

They were in the corridor outside the ICU waiting room. Except for a few people in pastel scrubs, and the deputy stationed in front of the glass cubicle where Broderick was kept, tethered to life by tubes and monitors, the place was deserted. Occasionally a phone rang at the nurses' station, or the elevator pinged with a delivery of supplies or test results; otherwise, it was silent.

Marshall's face was tight with anger, his voice terse. "How in the *hell* did one of my inmates get hold of a controlled substance?"

"It had to be in the coffee the lawyer brought," Buck said. "Nobody else has had access to him except the jail staff. He's in holding, with no other inmates. His clothes were taken at booking, so he couldn't have concealed anything on his person. His breakfast meal was sealed until delivery, the deputy on duty will swear to that. Scrambled egg sandwich, hash browns, fruit cup, OJ. We've eliminated everything but the coffee the lawyer brought in. We got the cups and some of the coffee from the trash can. The hospital lab is testing it now."

Marshall asked the obvious question. "This lawyer—is he legit?"

Buck said, "According to the bar association, he is. His name is David Sutherlin and he's licensed to practice in North Carolina, Delaware, Maryland and

DC. He works for some big pharmaceutical company called Entretex that makes, among other things, fentanyl." He watched Marshall for a reaction as he added, "Miles Young sent him."

Marshall said only, "A corporate lawyer for a criminal case? That doesn't make a lot of sense."

"No," agreed Buck, though reluctantly, "it doesn't. Miles Young knows every criminal lawyer in three states, and he could have his pick of them down here in the time it takes to fuel up a private plane. We've both seen him do it."

Marshall's expression was unreadable. Buck went on, "But the fact remains, Jason Broderick used his one phone call to contact Miles Young. Young made a personal request of the sheriff to have Jason Broderick held over in Hanover County until he got here. Twelve hours later, a man shows up to meet with Broderick, claiming to be a lawyer sent by Miles Young. And less than an hour after that Broderick is in the hospital with a fentanyl overdose. One way or another, it's starting to look to me as though Miles Young always gets what he wants."

Marshall just nodded. "So why would a lawyer want to poison his own client?"

"That I don't know," Buck admitted. "But we picked Sutherlin up before he even left town. Jolene is interviewing him now, although I'm guessing her questions will carry a little bit more weight once the tests come back on the coffee."

Marshall jerked his head toward the elevator. "There's no point standing around here. We're not going to be able to talk to him today. They'll text you with the lab results, right?"

"Right."

They walked to the elevator, and Buck pushed the button. Marshall was thoughtful as they waited for it to arrive.

"So this lawyer uses his real ID to gain access to the jail, poisons his own client in front of a deputy watching through the observation window, then gets in his car and drives away," Marshall said. "Doesn't even try to evade detection. Make any sense to you?"

"Not a bit," admitted Buck.

Marshall glanced over Buck's shoulder at the deputy guarding Broderick's room. "Could he have been trying to get Broderick out of jail and into the hospital? Part of an escape plan?"

"If he was, it was overkill, pardon the pun. The man's on life support, and we've got him under twenty-four-hour guard. There's no way he's leaving the hospital except in handcuffs."

"Or a casket," said Marshall, frowning.

"Yeah."

The elevator doors opened and they stepped in. The two men stood side by side, watching the LED display count down the floors. Marshall said, "I'm going to have to fire Deke."

Now it was Buck's turn to remain silent.

"He's a screw-up, always has been. Something like this can ruin a department's credibility. It might've lost the whole case."

The doors pinged open in the lobby. Buck said, "I'm going back to the office and see what I can put together on this Sutherlin character. I'll let you know what we hear from the lab."

Marshall said absently, "Sorry about your Sunday."

Buck smiled faintly. "Same to you."

They walked toward the glass double doors and the parking lot beyond. The lobby was pleasantly quiet on this Sunday afternoon, frequented by visiting families in their Sunday best carrying flowers or balloons, and women in pink-striped aprons arranging flowers and magazines on a rolling cart.

Marshall said thoughtfully, "You know, I've seen a few murders and attempted murders in my career. But you've got to wonder why anybody would try to kill a man who's already behind bars for homicide."

The same thing had been bothering Buck. "The list of motives is pretty short," he admitted.

The sliding doors opened, and they stepped out into the muted sunshine. Marshall said, "You're checking all other possible ways he could have gotten the fentanyl?"

But before Buck could answer, his phone buzzed. Less than a second later Marshall's phone chimed as well. Buck felt his gut tighten as he dug his phone out of his pocket, and he went cold as he read the text.

"Damn it," he whispered.

Marshall looked up from his own phone, his face grim. "Go," he said shortly. "I'll get a command center set up at the office and be out there as soon as I can. Go."

Buck was already gone.

TWENTY

Things do not happen quickly in a crisis. In the movies, swarms of cops arrive within minutes, interviews are conducted, evidence is collected; the FBI sets up wire taps, command stations and task forces are organized, road blocks are put in place, and the manhunt is on. In real life, events unfold with maddening slowness. There's a lot of standing around and talking, a lot of crackling radios, a lot of uniforms moving in and out. The same questions are asked and answered over and over again. Someone said the FBI had been called. Someone else said it would take the State Bureau of Investigation two to three hours to get agents on the scene, and their crime scene van might not arrive until the next day.

Do you know how people say life is funny? As in, a few hours ago, my biggest concern was that someone would try to steal the dog that was in my care, and now a child had been kidnapped. That should put everything into perspective. Well, let me tell you something. It's not funny at all, and perspective depends entirely on who's doing the looking.

It was thirty-five minutes before Buck got there. That can seem like a lifetime when someone you love is terrified and in pain.

I let the dogs out of their confinement because the barking was getting on everyone's nerves and because Aunt Mart kept casting distressed looks toward the door that restrained Majesty. Majesty was far too aloof, and much too well-behaved, to get underfoot, and I knew that just having her near would comfort Aunt Mart. So after checking with Jamie— who was as close to being in charge as anyone was at that point—I opened the door and let Majesty out. Just as I predicted, she trotted straight into the living room, ignoring all the invaders in her home, and hopped up on the sofa beside Aunt Mart. Aunt Mart wrapped her arms around her and buried her face in Majesty's fur.

I had no intention of giving Bongo free run in a strange house, but he had been such a quiet, well-behaved dog since I'd had him that I didn't expect any trouble out of him either. I had hung his leash on the coat rack just inside the door, next to Uncle Ro's battered John Deere hunting cap and a lightweight cotton camo jacket. But the minute I opened the door, before I could even reach for the leash, Bongo charged past me down the hall. I cried, "Hey!" but he didn't look back.

I thought he'd go toward the front of the house, where all the people were, following Majesty's scent. But he dashed the other way, toward the back bedroom. When I reached the threshold, I saw immediately it must have been the room in which Celie had stayed: her backpack was open on the bed, her pink Florida hat was on the nightstand, and a pair of child-sized pink slippers was on the floor. Bongo raced from corner to corner, sniffing frantically. Before I could stop him, he jumped on the bed and pawed at the covers, bumping the backpack with his nose.

"Bongo, off!" I shouted and rushed in to grab his collar. He outmaneuvered me and sprang off the bed.

"Oh!" Aunt Mart touched my shoulder and I abandoned the chase, glancing at her. She brought a hand to her throat, and tears trembled on her thin wet lashes. "He's looking for her!"

Bongo snatched the hat from the nightstand, gave it a shake and dropped it on the floor, then resumed his excited, sniffing circuit of the room.

"He's looking for something," I agreed, frowning thoughtfully. That was the most animated I'd seen Bongo since I'd had him. It was as though someone flipped a switch. "I've never seen him act like that before."

When he swung toward our side of the room, I stepped in front of him, grabbed his collar, and snapped on the leash. "Bongo, let's go." I tugged the leash lightly, but he swiveled his head away from me, planting his feet. I snapped the leash and repeated more sternly, "Bongo! Let's go!" But in the end I had to practically drag him from the room.

"That was weird," I murmured. I studied Bongo, whose neck was still craned toward the guest room, his eyes focused and intent. "I wonder if…"

I was distracted by the opening of the front door and a familiar voice, first speaking shortly to the deputies in the front room and then calling, "Mart?"

Aunt Mart's face sagged with relief as she turned, holding open her arms to Buck. He was there in two strides, drawing her into a hug. Every muscle in my body seemed to relax all at once, just at the sight of him, and there was a moment when something in me instinctively leaned toward him for comfort and reassurance, just as I had done all my life. Just as Aunt Mart was doing now. It caught me off guard and threw me off balance, and before I could stop myself, I heard my voice demanding sharply, "Where have you been? What took you so long?"

Buck glanced at me, but didn't answer. He held Aunt Mart's shoulders and looked down at her gently. "How're you holding up?"

Aunt Mart compressed her lips and gave a brave nod, obviously not trusting her voice as she stepped away from him, fumbling in her skirt pocket for a tissue. I supplied, "Uncle Ro is flying into Asheville tomorrow. He'll be here by noon."

Buck gave Aunt Mart a reassuring smile. "I talked to him on the way over, promised him you'd have a deputy by your side every minute 'til he gets back."

Aunt Mart sniffed into the tissue. "The fool wanted to take a flight out this afternoon, but it wouldn't get here until midnight, and he knows how I hate him driving over the mountains after dark."

"I'll send a unit to pick him up at the airport tomorrow," Buck assured her. "We'll have him back here in no time."

"You will not!" Aunt Mart was horrified. "You need every man on the force out there looking for that little girl!" Her expression quickened into despair as she added, "Buck, you've got to find her. It's my fault she's gone and... and she's just so little, and so scared! You've got to find her!"

"We'll find her," Buck told her firmly. "The sheriff's already setting up road blocks on every road leading in and out of these mountains, three counties and four police departments are joining in the search, state troopers checking every vehicle, and the FBI is on the way. We'll find her."

Dogs can always tell when you're not paying attention to them, and Bongo was no exception. The leash must have slackened in my hand while I was listening to Buck, and Bongo took advantage of it. He lunged back toward the guest room with such determination that if I hadn't let the lead slide out of my fingers he would have broken them. I snatched up the trailing leash when Bongo was only a few feet inside the room, and Buck was right behind me.

"Is this where the little girl was staying?" he asked, sweeping the room with his gaze.

Aunt Mart stood next to him, pulling at her fingers, biting her lip briefly. "She ran back here when—when he broke in. But he found her and carried her out."

"Bongo acts like he's on the trail of something," I put in quickly. "He ran around the whole room, sniffing for something—"

"You let him in the room?" Buck turned on me, his eyes flashing. "Damn it, Raine, this is a crime scene! What's the matter with you?"

He turned back toward the front room and called down the hall. "Atkinson! Jefferies! Get back here and tape off this room!"

I said, "Buck, I'm telling you, this dog was tracking! He's supposed to be trained to alert to electronic devices, but there's not even a television in this room. So it has to be something else, something either Celie or the kidnapper had, or maybe even dropped. It could be evidence!"

Buck gave me a hard stare. "If there *was* evidence, you and that dog just made it harder to find. What's he even doing here, anyway?"

"I asked her to bring him," Aunt Mart put in quickly. "I thought it would cheer up poor little Celie. She's been through so much. But by the time Raine got here…" She broke off, biting her lip.

Buck glanced at her and softened his tone, though not his expression. "Did the dog find anything?" he asked me.

"No, but…"

He cut me off as one of the deputies arrived with a role of yellow crime scene tape. "Nobody goes in this room until the FBI gets here," he said to the deputies. "And close the door so the dogs don't go in."

"Yes, sir, Buck."

Buck turned to Aunt Mart. "I know you're tired of telling it," he said, "and you're going to get more tired before the day is done." He gave her an encouraging smile that hardly seemed forced at all. "But I need to hear what happened from the beginning, so maybe you could pour us a couple of cups of coffee and we can sit down and try to figure this out, okay?"

There was tenderness behind her weary smile. "Buck, have you had lunch yet?"

"No, ma'am," he admitted. "Not yet."

She patted his arm again. "You come on in the kitchen and I'll fix you a sandwich."

He said, "That sounds real nice. I'll be there in a minute."

He turned back to the two deputies who were taping off the doorway as she left. "When you get done here, go outside and tag footprints and tire tracks for the photographer. I know there's been some traffic in and out, but with all this rain, the perp had to have left tracks. He for damn sure didn't fly in."

"You got it, Buck."

"And get a couple of guys to route everybody else to the back door," Buck added. "No point in contaminating the scene any more than it already is."

"Yes, sir."

They finished the taping and left, and I said, "Does Marshall know?"

He glanced at me. "Know what?"

"That the men still take their orders from you."

He returned an impatient frown. "Did you give your statement already?"

"Some of it," I said.

The frown sharpened. "What do you mean, 'some of it'?" Then, gesturing to the front door, he said, "Let's get away from all this noise. Come on outside."

I followed him to the front of the house, the tightly wound leash in my hand tugging Bongo into position beside me. The farther we moved away from Celie's room the more cooperative he became, seeming first to grow resigned to losing whatever treasure he had been seeking, and then to forget about it. Could Aunt Mart have been right? Could he only have been looking for the little girl he adored?

We went out onto the wraparound porch, then around to the side porch, out of the way of the deputies who were taping off the steps and placing small cones at the edges of anything that might have been a footprint on Aunt Mart's immaculately painted porch floor. Some of those footprints were actually paw prints, and I felt bad for possibly destroying evidence. But how could I have known?

The sun was shining now with an almost obscene serenity on the expanse of baby green grass, dancing off azalea blossoms and glinting on puddles. In the shadows of the porch it was still chilly, though, and I shivered a little, thinking about how carefree I had been when I had gotten out of my car less than an hour ago, and how very quickly everything had gone wrong. And how much worse it could get.

"I told Jamie what time I got here and what I saw and what I did," I said without preamble. "But there's more. I thought I should wait for you. Also," I admitted, "I didn't want to scare Aunt Mart any more than she is already."

He waited for me to go on.

"Somebody tried to break into my house this morning," I said. "Or at least my backyard. He said he was from Hartwell Labs and he had come to take Bongo, but I wouldn't turn him over. He had a gun. And he was wearing a black windbreaker, just like the one Aunt Mart said the kidnapper was wearing. I think it might've been the same man."

Buck said, "What time?"

"A little after eight."

I described what had happened the best I could, and Buck jotted a few notes down in the little book he kept in his pocket. When I was finished, he asked, "Can you give a description?"

"Yes, and so can Corny. A little over six feet, big shoulders, maybe 220 pounds. Thinning brown hair, about forty. And he gave a name—Darrel Grayson. I don't know if it's real or not. I didn't see any ID."

"Why didn't you report it?"

My jaw tightened. Bongo, perhaps sensing my tension, stretched out at my feet and looked up at me with big brown eyes as though trying to encourage me to chill. I said, "I did try to report it. I called the office, but the sheriff wasn't in."

"And 911 was out of service?"

I drew a sharp breath but controlled a snarky retort. "I didn't call 911 because there was no emergency," I explained simply.

Buck said impatiently, "Listen, Raine, if you haven't figured it out by now, this office doesn't work like it used to when Ro was sheriff, or even me. You don't have any special privileges. You've got to go through channels like everybody else. When you have an incident to report, you call 911 and you report it to the officer on duty just like any other citizen, do you understand?"

But even before he finished speaking, I knew what he was getting at. I'd screwed up. It had already occurred to me, with a slowly creeping uneasiness, that if the man who'd tried to take Bongo was in fact the same one who'd kidnapped Celie, and if I *had* reported the incident when it happened, maybe, just maybe, things would have turned out differently at Aunt Mart's house today. I no longer felt quite as angry, or as cocky, as I'd been before. In fact, I felt a little sick. Was this my fault? Could I have stopped it?

Buck must have seen the dismay on my face, because his own anger faded. "Okay," he said, "I'll get a man on this. It's a good lead."

He glanced back toward the house. "I need to get back in there." But he made no move to go. Instead he blew out a breath, his eyes bleak. "That poor little kid. She must be scared to death. Nobody should have to go through what she has."

I asked, "Do you think... Aunt Mart told me about the bruises. You don't really think her father did that to her, do you?"

He pushed a hand through his hair, squinting in the sun as he gazed out over the lawn. "Ah hell, I don't know. Probably not. Her doctor says she has some kind of bleeding disorder that causes bruising. So now we've got a kidnapped child out there with a medical condition and no way to even know how bad it is."

I was confused. "What do you mean? Why don't you just ask her dad?"

Buck looked back at me. "Jason Broderick is in the hospital, in ICU," he said. "It looks like somebody got to him in jail, tried to poison him with an overdose of fentanyl."

"Oh, my God." I just stared at him. "But...but I don't understand! Who could have gotten to him *here*? Who even knew he was here? The only person he called was…" I broke off, the words dead in my throat.

Not a flicker crossed Buck's face to reveal what he was thinking. He said, "The only person to see Broderick before he collapsed was a lawyer by the name of David Sutherlin. He brought coffee, probably tainted with the drug. He said Miles Young sent him."

There was a hollow feeling in the pit of my stomach that slowly spread upward to my chest. I stared at him.

Buck stared back, his gaze steady and strong. He said, "What have you heard from Young?"

I swallowed. "There was a snowstorm in London. His flight was delayed."

Buck said, "Tell him I want to talk to him when he gets in."

I refused to let my gaze, or my voice, waver. "Buck," I said quietly, "what is going on?"

He shook his head again. "You know why I took this job?"

It was a question I think everyone had been asking. Why had he come back here, why had he dropped out of an election he was almost certain to win, why had he taken a job with the sheriff's department serving under the man who had taken his job as sheriff? Why wasn't he with his wife in Asheville? Those were only a few of the things I wanted to know. But I said nothing.

"Because I was done," he said. He took a step back and leaned his shoulders against the wall, focusing on the lawn, looking tired. "Done with pulling bodies out of wrecked cars, done with facing down crazy drunks, done with wondering whether the next traffic stop I make is going to be the one where the driver pulls a gun. Just done. A small-time county investigator looks at credit card fraud, burglaries, identity theft, shoplifting. Oh yeah, now and then you can expect a case that'll turn your stomach—child molestation, a bad drug deal. But mostly it's routine. And I was done."

He gave one slow shake of his head, as though trying, with that motion, to reconcile the events of the past twenty-four hours. "We picked the guy up on somebody else's warrant. He was supposed to be out of here by morning. It wasn't even our case. Now he's in ICU with an overdose that will probably turn out to be a homicide attempt, his child has been kidnapped, and it all happened on my watch. Not in the plan."

My heart ached for him. I wished I knew what to say to comfort him, but I didn't. Besides, that wasn't my place. Not anymore.

So what I said was, "Buck, Jason Broderick is a respected professor, a researcher, an animal behaviorist. Yesterday, when he ran from the police, he was trying to save his dog. Do you really think he killed that guy?"

He replied, without meeting my eyes, "It doesn't matter what I think."

"And now somebody tried to kill him and kidnapped his daughter," I plowed on stubbornly, "not to mention tried to steal his dog. Did it ever occur to you that whoever did those things might be the real killer?"

He said impatiently, "Look, Raine, I know you've got personal reasons for wanting to believe this guy is innocent."

Personal, I thought. *By personal he means Miles.* But he was wrong. Miles had nothing to do with this.

Or at least not much.

"And I wish I could say you're right," Buck went on, "but we've got security footage of the shooting at the lab. It was Broderick on the video. As for everything else... like I say, the FBI is on the way. As soon as they get here, it's their mess. Until then, I'm just the evidence-gatherer."

I said, puzzled, "But Dr. Broderick said the security cameras were off that night, remember?"

"I guess not all of them."

He pushed away from the wall and looked at me, his expression businesslike again. "This whole thing is going sideways fast, and I don't like the idea of civilians being in the middle. So I need you to take the dog down to the sheriff's office and turn him over to Chief Smith."

I gaped at him. "Jolene? But she doesn't want him. Besides, why isn't she out with Nike looking for Celie? Isn't she working this case?"

"We're all working this case," Buck replied brusquely. "The K-9 team is on standby until needed. And," he added pointedly, "like I said, as soon as they get here, the FBI will be in charge."

"But she's not set up for another dog. You know Bongo is better off with me than he would be anywhere else."

"That may be," Buck said, "but both of you are going to be safer with the dog in police custody."

I am not an idiot. I knew he was right. If that man had taken out his gun this morning, there would have been nothing Corny nor I could have done to stop him from shooting all of us—Corny, Bongo, and me. I couldn't protect Bongo. My aunt hadn't been able to protect Celie. He was right. Nonetheless, I felt compelled to argue.

"But I promised his owner," I objected. Before he could say something stupid about promises made to homicide suspects being invalid, I added with more than a touch of self-righteousness, "I promised Celie I'd take care of him!"

Buck turned to go inside. "A deputy will follow you back to the office. Now that this creep, whoever he is, knows you have the dog, I'm not taking any chances."

Under ordinary circumstances, I would have instinctively objected to having a babysitter—or a police escort, for that matter. But my head was reeling with questions and my instincts were off. The only thing I could think to say was, "I'm staying with Aunt Mart tonight, and I need to go by the house to pick up a change of clothes. I'll drop Bongo off afterward."

Buck replied briefly, "Drop him off first. Let me know when you're ready to leave."

I watched him go back into the house, but I didn't follow. I sank down into one of Aunt Mart's green wicker chairs, dropping my hand over the side to stroke Bongo's head. Jason Broderick, poisoned. His child kidnapped from my aunt's house. Bongo threatened. And all of those things tied together by a single thread. How *did* the bad guys find out I had

Bongo, anyway? How did they know where Celie was? How had Jason Broderick's enemies traced him to the Hansonville jail?

Despite my defiant front to Buck, I was scared. There was one person who knew all those things. And I had been the one who told him.

TWENTY-ONE

Word gets around quickly in a small town like this, especially when a prominent citizen is involved. Not long after Buck left to start interviewing neighbors, those same neighbors started showing up with casseroles and pound cakes, just as they would have after a funeral. I knew they meant well—or more likely, were just curious—but it was a little creepy. No one was dead yet.

One of the kind and the curious was Sonny, who, even though she lives on what is possibly the most remote mountaintop in the county, likes to have lunch at Miss Meg's diner in town on Sundays when she's able. While there, she had heard rumors of the kidnapping and had called me to confirm. She placed one of Miss Meg's lattice-topped peach pies on the dining room table, which was already overflowing with plates and platters, and told my aunt, "I know it's like bringing coals to Newcastle, but I figured your house is likely to be filled with hungry lawmen for a while." She squeezed Aunt Mart's hands and told her seriously, "You let me know if all this gets too much for you. You know I'm a lawyer, which means I'm authorized to kick ass on your behalf."

That was designed to make Aunt Mart smile, and it did, however wearily. "Oh, Sonny," she said. Her voice quavered just the slightest bit. "I just want them to find that little girl."

"Buck says Celie has a medical condition," I told Sonny when Aunt Mart turned away to greet more newcomers. "And they can't even find out how bad it is because her father was rushed to the hospital this morning."

"Good lord," said Sonny, her brows drawing together sharply.

I could tell she was about to ask questions I probably wasn't authorized to answer, so I went on, "And somebody tried to break into my yard to steal Bongo this morning." At the sound of his name, Bongo looked up, and I dropped a reassuring hand on his head. "It might have been the same man. Now Buck wants me to turn him over to police custody." I gave a resigned sigh and added, "I heard somebody say that the FBI would want to talk to anyone who'd had contact with Celie while she was here, so it's good you stopped by."

"Yes," Sonny murmured and dropped her thoughtful gaze to Bongo. "Buck interviewed me on the phone last night about what happened at the festival."

She bent down and caressed Bongo's head. "How're you doing, big fellow?"

I was about to answer for Bongo, as I usually did, when she straightened up with a small frown. "He says he's worried about bears," she said.

Okay. For the second time that day I didn't know what to say.

Fortunately, I was spared the effort by the arrival of the long-awaited FBI—or at least two special agents representing the same. Accompanying them was Sheriff Marshall Becker. I listened while Marshall told us all what we already knew: Everything possible was being done to locate the child, all leads were welcome, and no one was to leave without giving his or her name to one of the deputies. While the agents brought in their technical equipment and explained to Aunt Mart what they intended to do with it, I called Corny and brought him up to date. He was horrified, of course, and anxious to do something to help, but I assured him I'd be home in a couple of hours and the best thing he could do was to keep everything running smoothly at the kennel.

After I hung up, I checked my messages. Still nothing from Miles.

We heard a helicopter go over, and Aunt Mart looked hopefully toward the sky. Both the forest service and the SBI had helicopters that they made available to the county for emergencies, including manhunts. I assured my aunt this meant they were searching for Celie. I didn't say anything about the chances of finding her.

The dining room table was commandeered as an electronics center, and some of the women from the church were busy trying to find a place in the kitchen for all the food people had brought. A half-dozen laptops were set up on the eight-foot-long dining table, each one of them showing an overhead view of various roads in different sections of the county. A larger screen displayed a satellite view of the entire county with a map overlay with different-colored dots representing various police agencies in each section.

A nice young fellow from the Charlotte field office of the FBI—Dale somebody—explained to Aunt Mart that law enforcement was checking motels, campgrounds, rental cabins and the like within a fifty-mile radius, but that such efforts would take time. He didn't add, but I could tell Aunt Mart knew, that the thirty-minute head start the perpetrator had would not make the job any easier.

By this time, Jenny, the social worker who had placed Celie in Aunt Mart's care, had arrived. She held my aunt's hand and listened intently to every word that was said. She, like Aunt Mart, took her responsibility very seriously.

"We're also using helicopters and drones," Dale added, gesturing to the feed from the computer monitors, "from the local sheriff's department and other agencies, to scan the woods from overhead. The footage is recorded and time stamped, and we have agents watching in real time from various locations. If we spot a vehicle parked where it shouldn't be or movement in a place that should be deserted, we can zero in on that."

I felt compelled to point out, "The trees are starting to leaf out. You're not going to be able to see much from the air."

He glanced at me. "Yes, ma'am, that's going to be true in some places. But it's still a lot faster than a foot search." He turned back to the two women and added somberly, "Most of the time in a case like this, all we can do is wait for a ransom demand."

While he spoke, his partner set up monitoring equipment on the telephone and explained that they would be staying until the ransom call came in, which was usually within twenty-four hours. I stood in front of the satellite map, studying it. Bongo's leash was clipped to my belt, and despite all the activity around him, he remained calm, seeming almost bored. Majesty wasn't above an interested sniff or two when someone new arrived with food, but for the most part she remained pressed to my aunt's knee, within easy reach whenever Aunt Mart needed the comfort of a silky collie head.

I asked Dale, just to make sure I'd heard him correctly the first time, "These little dots are where you have checkpoints and men on the ground patrolling, right?"

He glanced up from unrolling a coil of cable that he was trying to weave behind the table and in between the chairs. "Yes, that's right."

I pointed. "It looks like you've got everyone concentrated here, within a mile or two of town, and along the major highways."

"We're checking every car that comes in and out of town, as well as all the public areas—gas stations, campgrounds, motels, convenience stores and the like. That's why you see so much police concentration in one area."

"But sixty percent of the roads in this area aren't even paved," I pointed out, "not to mention the logging roads and hiking trails..."

He gave me a tolerant look. "Yes, ma'am. That's why we have drones surveying the outlying areas."

"But this whole *county* is an outlying area," I objected. "So is the entire ridge between here and Asheville. You can't possibly cover this whole area with aerial surveillance."

He straightened up from laying the cable and looked at me with a raised eyebrow that might have been meant to intimidate, or it might have reflected genuine puzzlement. "I'm sorry," he said politely. "Who are you again?"

Marshall Becker spoke up behind me. "This is Raine Stockton," he said and touched my shoulder lightly. "She's one of our most valuable search and rescue volunteers, and, I'm told, an expert on the back country around here. When it comes to wilderness searches, she's the one you want on your team."

I appreciated his support; I really did. But I had a feeling that, implicit in that compliment was a caution: this was not a wilderness search and I would be well advised to mind my own business.

He glanced down at Bongo and said, "Is this Broderick's dog?"

Bongo was sitting nicely at my side, panting a little from stress, which was only natural. I put my hand on the leash, feeling a little protective. "Buck told me to turn him over to Jolene. I'm on my way there. But Marshall..." I turned back to the screen, drawing a circle with my finger a few inches above it. "There's a lot of territory you're not covering here.

Maps of the county just like this are available at every rest stop on the expressway, not to mention the welcome center and pretty much every booth at the festival yesterday. If I were a kidnapper, I'd go for the quickest cover closest to town." I pointed. "What about the old shirt mill factory?"

He gave me an indulgent look. "We've already searched that."

"Okay." I turned back to the map. "What about the train depot? It's only half a mile from town and it's been deserted for years."

He replied patiently, "Cleared."

Somewhere in the background I heard Sonny explaining to a deputy that no, she didn't consider herself a real psychic, and that yesterday's performance was only to raise money for the animal shelter, but, yes, sometimes she guessed right, who could say why, and that somehow she'd guessed close enough about Jason Broderick to spook him…

I remembered what she'd said about Bongo being worried about bears. I knew it was stupid, but my eyes went to the line on the map that represented Bear Gap Road. It was only six miles from here and accessible by two cross streets out of town. There were, I recalled, a collection of vacation rental cabins at the end of the road, and none of them was open yet.

"There!" I declared, punching a finger at the screen.

The scene enlarged so abruptly that it startled me and I stepped back. The screen was filled with an abstract swirl of green and brown, which it took me a moment to realize was actually a magnified shot of the tops of trees and the road below. Marshall reached around me and used two fingers to pinch the screen down into a more recognizable view. I could see the path of a dirt road and the half moon of a blue lake in the distance. Now that I realized how sensitive the screen was to touch, I was more careful, and gently used my fingers to move the view until I saw the glint of a metal roof. "The rental company doesn't open these cabins until May, and they're far enough off the beaten path that no one would notice somebody breaking in. This guy can't know the area that well. He'd look for someplace close but isolated."

Leaning around me again, Marshall zoomed in on the cabin and the small cleared space around it. "Good theory," he said, "but as you can see, there's no sign of activity."

"You can't see everything from that shot," I protested. "You need people on the ground, searching."

"We can see enough." He zoomed in again until I was staring at a high-definition close-up of the dirt road and turn-around in front of the house. "No tire tracks," he pointed out. He straightened up. "We'll check it out, but no one has been down that road since the rain."

"And we're not limiting this to a local investigation," Dale pointed out. "There's absolutely no reason to think the kidnapper would stay in the area. So while we appreciate you wanting to help, Miss, er…"

"Stockton," I said.

"It's probably best if we let you know if we need you," he concluded. Then, with a polite smile he added, "Excuse me. I just need to get there, where you're standing."

I clucked my tongue to Bongo, and we moved out of the way.

The house was filling up with people—neighbors, people from church, law enforcement, even a reporter from the local radio station. It was maddening, standing around and watching nothing happen. Usually when a child goes missing, I'm among the first on the scene, along with Cisco and my fellow SAR volunteers, plotting a search grid, talking to the parents, coordinating our strategy and taking to the woods. But this wasn't a missing child, this was a *taken* child, and even if it hadn't been a police matter, I lacked the skills to join the search. I couldn't even talk to the father who, last I heard, was still unconscious in the ICU with a ventilator doing his breathing for him.

Since I'd been all but summarily dismissed by the FBI and since Aunt Mart certainly wasn't lacking for people to give her moral support, I decided this was a good time to make my escape. I kissed Aunt Mart on the cheek and told her I'd be back in an hour.

She looked up at me with eyes that were tired of being anxious. "Oh, honey, you don't have to—"

"I'll be back," I told her firmly.

Bongo and I had almost made it to my car before Jamie intercepted us.

"I'm supposed to give you and the dog a ride back to the sheriff's office," he said. He was a little out of breath from jogging down the steps to catch us. "And then take you back to your house to pack." I rolled my eyes a little but followed him to his patrol car.

"Don't you think your time would be better spent out there looking for the kidnapper?"

"Yes, ma'am, I do," he replied, opening the door for me. "But the FBI is in charge now, and I do what I'm told."

You'd think that with a major crime in progress, the sheriff's office would be buzzing with activity, but in fact the opposite was true. During a manhunt, every deputy on the force is either in the field or getting ready to relieve someone who's already been there twelve hours, and except for the team that was gathered inside Marshall's office, poring over maps and barking out orders on their telephones, the inside of the building was practically deserted. The office phones, however, were ringing off the hook, and a harried Annabelle barely looked up when Jamie entered with Bongo and me. He pushed open the swinging doors to the bullpen where, during normal times, the deputies would sit at the desks and fill out reports or take complaints, and pointed me toward Jolene's office. Of course I already knew where it was.

"I'm going to get a cup of coffee and call my wife," he said. "We were supposed to go to her mama's for supper tonight, but that's off, I reckon. Give me a holler in the break room when you're ready to go."

Bongo did his usual alert eye-sweep of the room as we made our way through the maze of desks to Jolene's office, but his behavior was nothing resembling that which he'd displayed in Celie's room. In fact, now that he was away from the place the little girl had been, he seemed bored.

Jolene was not at her desk, and Nike's crate was empty. I was annoyed. Surely Buck did not intend for me to simply leave Bongo in the crate and walk away, did he? If so, he was very much mistaken. Either he had forgotten to tell Jolene that she was supposed to take custody of the dog or—more likely, I had to admit, under the circumstances—something more urgent had demanded her attention. Come to think of it, it would have been unusual to find the chief deputy at her desk with a kidnapping in progress, not to mention the attempted murder of an inmate. Whatever the reason, I had just wasted time I could have spent being with my aunt in her time of crisis, and I was not inclined to wait around for Jolene to finish whatever she was doing and return to her office. I hadn't wanted to leave Bongo with her in the first place. If she wanted him, she could come and get him.

I sat down at her desk to leave a note to that effect. Bongo stretched out at my feet with a sigh.

The surface of her desk was neat and organized, which was not surprising. Jolene was ex-military and very precise; some might even say rigid. There was a framed photograph of her little boy in one corner, but no other ornamentation. Pens were placed in their organizer, next to a box of extra staples and a stack of business cards. *Jolene Smith, Chief Deputy, Hanover County Sheriff's Office.* Beside that was a pad of Post-Its. I took a pen from the holder, but as I reached for the Post-It pad my elbow jostled the mouse of her computer. Immediately the sheriff's office logo on her monitor was replaced by another image. It was Jason Broderick, frozen mid-stride against the backdrop of a large dimly lit room. A black bar at the bottom of the screen showed a "play" arrow. I hesitated for just a moment, and even glanced over my shoulder, but no one was around. I clicked on it.

The sound of barking came from the computer speakers. Bongo's ears pricked and he turned his head toward the sound. Almost all dogs will show interest in the sound of another dog's barking, even if it is artificially reproduced. But this must have been particularly confusing for Bongo, because the sound of the barking was his own. I could have sworn to it. Hadn't I just spent half an hour listening to that same bark from behind the closed door of my uncle's home office? And if you're thinking one dog's bark sounds just like another, talk to me after you've spent ten years running a boarding kennel. There's a difference. That was Bongo barking in the background, and Jason Broderick striding forward in the foreground. This video must have been taken at Hartwell Labs.

I saw the man in the lab coat. I heard Jason say, "Martin? What are you doing here?"

I saw Jason step backward, out of frame, and I flinched as the other man jerked to the side, as blood bloomed, as he fell, as he died in real life right before my eyes.

But something was off.

My mouth was dry and my chest was tight, and I really, really did not want to watch that video again. But I clicked the rewind arrow and watched it play out. The walking, the barking, the man in the lab coat, the barking, the backward step, the shots…

"Damn it, Stockton! What are you doing?"

Jolene burst into the cubicle, shoved me aside, and grabbed the mouse from my hand. With a single click the image disappeared.

She slammed a legal pad down on the desk and turned on me, fuming. "I could put you behind bars right now! That's police evidence! What the hell are you doing here, anyway?"

I scrambled to my feet and so did Bongo, who looked at us both with alarm. I tried to transmit calm through my grip on the leash, but my own composure was not so easy to fake. My heart was pounding. "The dog stopped barking," I said.

She stared at me. "What?'

"In the video," I explained, "you can hear Bongo barking the whole time. If this was taken the night Dr. Broderick stole Bongo, that was him barking in the background through every frame—except when the shots were fired. Dogs don't just stop barking like that for no reason, especially when something happens to upset them, like the sound of gunfire. So what made Bongo stop barking?"

I saw her face tighten as she glanced involuntarily at the blank screen, then quickly back to me. She said, "What are you talking about?" But there was more curiosity than accusation in her tone now.

"Jason Broderick said Martin Anderson was alive when he saw him," I explained, "and that he, Jason, left through the kennel area door after he got Bongo. He wouldn't even have come back past the corridor where Martin was shot. So maybe..." I hesitated, trying to think it through. "Maybe the reason Bongo wasn't barking when Martin was shot was because he wasn't there."

Jolene scowled at me, but in an absent way. I could tell she was thinking about something else. "Damn it," she said softly. "I knew there was something wrong with that video."

She sat down at her desk and said briskly, "Get out of here, Stockton." Her hand reached for the mouse.

I said, "I'm supposed to turn Bongo over to you."

"Put him in the crate." Her tone was short, distracted as she brought up the video again.

"He eats at 5:00," I said. "I give him premium kibble mixed with—"

"I know how to take care of a dog, Stockton." Her attention was on the screen. The video began to play. The dog barking in the background. Broderick saying, "Martin, what are you doing here?" The *pop, pop* of a silenced gun.

Jolene whispered, "Damn it." She started the video again.

I put Bongo in the crate and latched the door. He stood there, looking at me and panting anxiously while I clipped his leash to the crate. "Sorry, bud," I said softly, and I scratched his chin through the wire.

Jolene did not look up from the monitor as I left. The sound of a barking dog followed me all the way outside the building.

Although it seemed like days since I'd left the house, in fact I'd only been gone a couple of hours. The kennel was quiet, as it should be this time of day since playtime was over and feeding time wouldn't begin for another hour. There were no cars in front of the building, which meant no drop-offs or pick-ups, and all was quiet inside the house. Instead of going around back, where visitors usually park, Jamie pulled the cruiser up to the front steps. I opened the door.

"It won't take me long," I said. "I'm just going to throw some things in a bag and take the dogs down to the kennel to spend the night with Corny. Do you want to come in? I think I've got some sweet tea in the fridge."

"Nah, that's okay." He took out his phone and started checking his texts. "I need to stay by the radio. Take your time."

I put one foot on the ground and then froze. A man had just rounded the corner of my house, coming from my backyard, and was headed down the path to the kennel. My throat clenched involuntarily. Black windbreaker, broad shoulders, thinning hair. It was the man from this morning. Darrel Grayson.

"Jamie!" I gasped.

He looked up.

"That man!" I pointed, half whispering, half screeching. "That's the one who broke into my backyard this morning! The one who tried to take Bongo! He may be the kidnapper!"

Jamie said, "You're sure?" But his door was already open, his hand on his gun belt.

"He has a gun!"

Jamie drew his weapon and got out of the car, using the open door to shield most of his body as he shouted, "Police! Stop where you are!"

The man was only about twenty yards away, but the house had shielded our arrival from his view. He stopped when he heard Jamie's command, and started to turn. It was him. It was definitely Grayson.

Jamie shouted, "Hands behind your head! Stay where you are!"

Grayson clasped his hands behind his head and didn't move.

Jamie eased his way out from behind the door, leading with his gun. "Get down on your knees," he commanded, loudly. "Keep your hands behind your head. Do it now!"

My heart was pounding and my throat was dry as I watched the scenario unfold. And suddenly there was a sound that didn't belong. My head swiveled toward the porch as my screen door squeaked open and Cisco, Pepper, Mischief and Magic barreled out, racing down the steps toward me.

Miles came out onto the porch behind them, taking in the scene with one sweeping glance and an expression that registered absolutely no alarm.

"Easy, Deputy," he said. "He works for me."

TWENTY-TWO

Buck got the text just as he was getting into his car after talking to the last of the four neighbors who shared the dead-end street on which Mart and Ro lived. No one had noticed any strange vehicles, or heard or seen anything unusual that day. This was not surprising, since it was too early in the season for open windows or sitting on the porch, and most folks had been sitting down to Sunday dinner when the kidnapping took place. Someone did say he thought he might have heard a car go by a little after 1:00, but was not able to provide any more details. Buck was considering swinging back by the hospital to check on Broderick's condition when he got the text from the office of the director of the hospital laboratory.

He stared at it in disbelief. "Son of a bitch," he whispered. He dialed Jolene's number as he slammed the car door.

"Do you still have Sutherlin on hold?" he demanded.

"I do," she replied, "but I don't know how much longer I can keep him. The man's a lawyer. He came in of his own free will and he knows perfectly well he can leave that way too. I'm about to run out of soda and cookies to bring him from the vending machine, and he's about to run out of patience. Tell me you've got something."

"I've got something all right." He started the engine. His tone was bitter. "The coffee came back clean. We're going to have to cut him loose."

Jolene's stunned silence reflected exactly the way he felt. "I don't understand."

"Yeah, well, there's a lot about this situation that I don't understand." He put the car into gear and backed out into the driveway, slinging gravel. "Is the sheriff in?"

"He's in the field." She hesitated. "But there's something you should see if you're coming back to the office."

He brought the car to a rolling stop at the end of the driveway and turned right. "Talk to me."

"That video of the shooting at Hartwell Labs we were looking at earlier," she said. "I figured out what was off about it. A couple of things, in fact. Actually," she admitted reluctantly, "it was Stockton who spotted the first one. Long story, don't ask." She took a breath and plunged on. "That section right before the shots, where Broderick steps out of frame, is different from the rest of the tape. The dog isn't barking. And when the gun is fired, the victim jerks to the right."

Buck's foot left the accelerator as he suddenly understood. "But Broderick was standing in front of him."

"Yes, si—" He heard her cut off the "sir" and try to cover it quickly with, "That's right. The shots were fired from the corridor to the left, and it's entirely possible Broderick wasn't even there at the time. It'll take a forensic team to prove it, but this video has been doctored. It's starting to look like our prime suspect has been framed."

Buck was thoughtful for the time it took him to wait for cross traffic at the main intersection leading into town—two cars—and to make the turn onto Main Street. He said, "Who do you suppose would want to do a thing like that?"

"My guess is the real killer," she replied.

"Yeah, mine too," Buck said. "And I'd further guess that the same person who tried to frame Broderick for murder might also want to keep him from talking, especially if he knew something that could prove his innocence and point to the real killer."

He made the turn onto Courthouse Square. "Do me a favor. Keep Mr. Sutherlin entertained for another five minutes, will you? I'm on my way in."

"I can do that." She paused. "Anything on the little girl?"

Buck's mouth tightened grimly as he pulled into one of the spaces reserved for courthouse employees. He had his pick; they were almost all empty. "Nothing yet. But I'll tell you this." He slammed the car door and started up the courthouse steps, two at a time. "When we find the person that put Jason Broderick in the hospital, we are going to find her kidnapper."

There was a small visitor's room in the sheriff's office which was sometimes used to counsel victims or interview witnesses. It was furnished in a slightly more inviting fashion than the interview room at the jail, with a round Formica-topped table and a couple of folding chairs, a sagging plaid sofa, and a wall-mounted television currently tuned to ESPN, volume muted. David Sutherlin looked as out of place as a show dog at a rodeo in his three-thousand-dollar suit and five-hundred-dollar tie. His haircut alone cost more than the average Hanover County deputy made in a week. He sat on the sofa, immersed in his phone, and barely looked up when Buck walked in.

"I'm sorry to keep you waiting, Mr. Sutherlin," Buck said. "It's a mess around here today." He extended his hand. "I'm Buck Lawson, an investigator for the county."

Sutherlin took his time finishing the text he was sending, tucked his phone in the inside pocket of his jacket, and stood to shake Buck's hand. "They told me my client was taken to the hospital," he said with a fair imitation of concern. "How is he?"

"Not good, I'm afraid." Buck dropped a legal pad onto the table and sat down in one of the plastic chairs, gesturing for Sutherlin to take the other one. "Mr. Broderick is suffering from a fentanyl overdose and is still unconscious in ICU."

"So the deputy informed me," replied Sutherlin severely. "It sounds to me as though you have a serious security problem with your jail."

"I agree," Buck said, "and that's why I'm investigating." Again he gestured. "Please sit down. This won't take long."

Sutherlin glanced at his watch. "I hope not. I have a flight to catch out of Asheville this evening."

Buck pretended surprise. "You're not staying over?"

"I'm afraid not, no."

"It just seems like a lot of trouble for you to fly down all the way from..." He flipped a page on the notepad Jolene had given him. "Maryland to spend less than five minutes with a client."

"There is very little I can do for Mr. Broderick while he's unconscious," replied Sutherlin. "And I do have to get back."

"Right." Again Buck pretended to consult the notepad. "To Entretex Pharmaceutical." He looked back to Sutherlin. "They make a good many products containing fentanyl there, don't they?"

Sutherlin smiled without humor. "I couldn't begin to list the products for which Entretex is responsible. They number in the thousands."

Buck nodded thoughtfully. He knew Sutherlin expected him to follow up on that, so he didn't. He said, "There's more bad news for your client, I'm afraid. His daughter was forcibly abducted from her foster home this morning by a man in a ski mask."

Buck waited for a reaction, but he got nothing. Not the flicker of an eyelash, not a ghost of surprise. Not even a pretense of concern. The slow boil of anger in Buck's gut tasted like sour ashes, but he managed to keep his expression neutral and his voice even.

"What I can't figure out is why anyone would do that," Buck said. "The child's father is in a coma, he couldn't pay the ransom if he wanted to. Of course, the Hartwell Group has deep pockets, but why would the kidnapper think they would be inclined to ransom the child of a man who's accused of murdering one of their employees?"

The other man's expression was implacable. "I'm afraid I can't help you there, Mr. Lawson."

Buck nodded. "I suppose not. Criminal law isn't your specialty, is it?"

He did not answer.

Buck said, "You told our check-in officer that you'd been sent by Miles Young. Is that the truth, or did you just say that because you figured that was a way to get Broderick to trust you?"

Sutherlin regarded him with a trace of amused condescension. "Mr. Lawson, I've already given my statement to the deputy. I barely had a chance to explain Dr. Broderick's legal options to him before he started to complain of a headache and difficulty concentrating. I asked if he wanted medical attention and he said he just wanted to lie down. The deputy came to remove him from the interview room and I left. Now, unless you have a follow-up question on that statement, I think we're done here."

Buck gave a small, self-deprecating grunt of laughter and leaned back in his chair, running a hand over his face. "You know, you're right. I'm just a country lawman trying to act like one of those fancy detectives on TV, and I'll tell you something—I'm just no damn good at it. So I'll just ask you straight." The amusement faded from his face. "Did you come down here to keep Jason Broderick from identifying the person who really killed Martin Anderson? And did you do that by slipping him an overdose of fentanyl during your client-attorney conference?"

David Sutherlin's pleasant expression did not change as he stood. "As I said, Mr. Lawson, we're done here."

Buck looked at him for another long moment, then picked up the legal pad. "I'll take that as a no," he said, standing. "Thank you for your time, Mr. Sutherlin. Like I said, we're a little shorthanded around here today, so if you don't mind hanging out for a few more minutes, we'll get your statement typed up for your signature. It shouldn't take long."

For the first time, there was the faintest hint of a fissure in Sutherlin's cool façade. "I do mind! I mind very much. I've already been here an hour and a half, and I've done more than enough to demonstrate cooperation with your investigation. This is a tremendous inconvenience and you have no cause to keep me here any longer." He turned for the door.

"True enough," agreed Buck. "No hurry to get this done today. We can always subpoena you to come back down here, but it seems to me that would be a *real* inconvenience."

Sutherlin turned back to him, his jaw set.

Buck smiled. "Like I said, it won't take long." He picked up the remote control from the table and turned the sound back on the television. "Hey, look. The game's on. Are you a Hornets fan?"

TWENTY-THREE

Miles came down the steps toward me and I closed the distance between us in a turmoil of emotions, pushing through the dogs who tangled around my feet. I was angry, I was relieved, I was scared, I was so damn glad to see him and so furious at what he'd put me through the past couple of days that I didn't know whether I wanted to fling myself into his arms or punch him in the chest. I'm sorry to say that when we met at the bottom of the steps I went with my lesser instincts. I drew back my arm to strike, but he caught my wrist before I could finish the motion.

"There's my girl," he said, with just a trace of amusement in his tone. "Hit first and ask questions later."

I wrenched my arm away. "You *jerk!*"

I was already sorry, and determined not to let him know it. He was here. He was here, and he looked so damn good in faded jeans and one of those silky long-sleeve tees he got in Hong Kong that clung to every muscle of his torso that I could have eaten him with a spoon. The stem of a pair of amber tinted sunglasses was tucked into the neck of his shirt, and he wore moccasins with no socks on his feet. I drank in every detail. He was here and he was going to explain everything. He was here and his calm gray eyes told me he wasn't going to let anything else bad happen and somehow, just because he was here, I wanted to believe that. But my nerves were still drenched in adrenaline and I was still breathing hard and, ten feet away, a deputy sheriff was still holding a gun on a man who'd tried to break into my house only this morning. The one thing I was *not* going to do was tell Miles how glad I was to see him.

At least that was what I told myself right up until the moment I flung myself into his arms and hugged him as fiercely as I have ever hugged anyone in my life. "Thank God you're here," I whispered. "I missed you so much!"

He held me tightly, dropping his head to kiss my hair. When I stepped away, he smiled down at me and said, "Love to hear more on that subject, sweetheart, but…" His eyes floated over my shoulder to Jamie, and to the intruder who still had his hands clasped behind his head. "I need to talk to the deputy before someone gets shot." He grabbed my fist, which was still balled up from tension, kissed my fingers, and walked quickly away.

Pepper jumped up on me, clawing at my legs for attention, and I automatically swiveled away from her with a sharp, "Ank!" Cisco nipped playfully at her tail. Mischief and Magic made straight for a mud puddle in the middle of the drive. I called them back and managed to corral all four dogs on the porch, which I blocked off with a portable gate I kept for that purpose. It didn't take long, and when I trotted across the yard to the place where Jamie, Miles and that man Grayson were standing, Grayson was offering an ID wallet to Jamie. Jamie had already confiscated his gun.

Jamie examined the ID, then looked back at Grayson. "Private security?"

"That's right," Grayson said. "I was hired by Mr. Young to keep an eye on Ms. Stockton's property while she had possession of a valuable canine."

Jamie looked in some confusion toward the four valuable canines on the porch. I glared at Miles, and without taking my death stare off of him, explained to Jamie, "He means Bongo. Jason Broderick's dog."

Grayson looked at me. "I'm sorry I frightened you this morning, Miss Stockton. I pretended to be from Hartwell so that I could assess how secure the animal was in your care. I had strict orders not to tell you who I was really working for."

Because, as I might have mentioned, I have a history with Miles's security force. Damn it.

Jamie looked from me to Miles. There was no point in pretending he didn't know who Miles was; everyone knew Miles. But he obviously felt obligated to conduct some line of questioning, so he said, "What are you doing here, sir?"

"I just got back from a trip abroad," Miles explained. "I came to let Raine know I was home, and when I couldn't find her I asked Grayson to check with Corny in the kennel as to whether he knew when she was expected back. That's when you drove up."

Jamie said, "How did you get in the house?"

"I let myself in with my key."

I was barely paying attention to the interchange so I had no chance to object before Jamie asked, sounding slightly puzzled, "How'd you get a key?"

That was when I started paying attention. I saw the amusement in Miles's eye and I knew what he was going to say. Nonetheless, I tried to drill holes in his brain with my eyes while thinking, *Don't say it, don't say it, don't...*

Miles said, "My fiancée gave it to me."

Jamie repeated, "Your fian—" But then he looked at me and understood. He tried to cover his shock by looking quickly back at the ID in his hand. "I have to check this out," he said. "Please wait here."

He re-holstered his weapon and went back to his patrol car. Grayson lowered his hands.

I turned on Miles, a thousand things bubbling to my lips. But what I said was, "I thought we weren't telling people."

He lifted an eyebrow. "No," he corrected. "*You* weren't telling people." He looked at Grayson. "I don't think the deputy would mind if you went and sat on the porch while he runs your credentials."

"The dogs are on the porch," I objected.

"That's okay." Grayson smiled. "I like dogs."

I watched him amble away, and then turned back to Miles. "Somebody tried to poison Jason Broderick in jail," I blurted. "He's in the hospital. Right after that, somebody broke into my aunt's house and kidnapped his little girl."

"I know." Miles looked at me, his expression grave. "Another part of Grayson's job was to keep me up to date. How's your aunt?"

I replied briefly, "Upset."

"And the dog? Is he still in police custody?"

"I left him in a crate in Jolene's office."

He nodded. "Probably safer for everyone that way."

I hated that he knew so much, and was grateful for it. I said, "Buck wants to talk to you. He thinks…" I searched his face. "He thinks you're involved somehow."

Miles nodded grimly. "He's right about that."

"That lawyer you sent," I pressed on. "They think he's the one who poisoned Dr. Broderick."

He frowned in puzzlement. "What lawyer? I didn't send anyone."

I allowed myself the tiniest frisson of relief. But there were still too many questions, and he was the only one who could answer them.

"I need to know what's going on, Miles," I said tightly. "Tell me what's going on!"

He dropped a hand onto my shoulder, his fingers lightly kneading the muscles there. His expression was troubled. "At this point," he said, "I'm not entirely sure I know. But I'll do the best I can." He nodded toward the house, where Grayson was kneeling on the porch, wrestling with Cisco and Pepper. He didn't look nearly as menacing now as he had earlier in the day. "Let me get this squared away and then we'll talk. You're probably in a hurry to get back to your aunt, and I need to check on Dr. Broderick."

There was nothing, at this moment, more important than hearing what Miles had to say, and I was about to tell him so when I heard the sound of the door to the Dog Daze office opening. I turned and saw Corny step outside, look around for a moment, and then start to jog toward us. I was sure he'd been alarmed by the sight of the patrol car in the driveway, not to mention Grayson playing with the dogs on the porch. I was about to call out to him that everything was okay, when I caught sight of his face. He looked terrified.

"Miss Stockton," he gasped. He barely glanced at Miles, but grasped my arm, tugging me back toward the kennel. "Something happened. I didn't know what to do. You need to come. I think—I think it's something bad!"

TWENTY-FOUR

Bongo stood up in the crate expectantly when Buck returned to Jolene's cubicle, thumping his tail against the metal wires with a clanging sound. Jolene looked up from her computer. "Anything?"

"That son of a bitch did it," he said, slapping the legal pad down on Jolene's desk. "I just don't know how. He didn't even blink when I told him the kid had been taken."

Jolene said, "Any way he might've substituted the coffee cup we found in the interview room for the one Broderick actually drank from? Smuggled the drugged one out somehow?"

Buck frowned. "Maybe. I don't see how though. The clerk logged two cups of coffee going in and there were two cups of coffee on the table."

"Briefcase?"

"Searched."

Bongo plopped back down in the crate with a sigh, rattling the metal. Buck nodded toward the image on Jolene's screen. "What's that?"

She glanced back at it. "Real-time feed from our drone. The sheriff's got it set up so that any of our computers can access it. I guess he figures the more eyes the better."

"Anything?"

She shook her head. "They spotted a little girl matching her description—same sweater, same tennis shoes and everything—coming out of the restroom at Holiday Park. But when they sent a team in all they managed to do was scare the hell out of the kid *and* her folks, who were up here camping with their two other children and the family dog. If you ask me, it's a waste of time."

"Time is the name of the game in a case like this," he replied absently, watching a dirt road lined with wild dogwoods drift by on her screen. His eyes wandered down to the icons at the bottom of her screen.

He looked at her abruptly. "Did you delete that camera footage from the interview room this morning?"

She looked insulted. "Of course not. I would never do anything like that without a direct order from the sheriff or the county attorney."

"And the sheriff doesn't know about it yet?"

"Not from me, he doesn't."

Buck was thoughtful for a moment, gazing at the screen. Then he said, "Why don't you go get a cup of coffee?"

She did not move. "I don't like coffee."

"Then get me one." He glanced at her. "Please."

"No." But she stood up slowly. "What are you going to do?"

The minute she relinquished her place in front of the computer he leaned forward and commandeered the mouse, closing out the drone feed. "Something that could cost me my job. It would be better if I didn't have a witness."

"You can't look at the video," she said. "It's a confidential exchange between a lawyer and his client. Policy is very clear—"

Buck said, "I doubt that policy was meant to protect a lawyer who tries to kill his client. And this is the only chance we have at proving he did it." He clicked on the icon at the bottom of the screen.

"It's poison fruit," she objected. "Even if you do find proof you can't use it."

"Yeah, yeah, yeah," he said impatiently, "Nardone v. United States, 1939, evidence obtained in an illegal search is considered fruit of the poisonous tree and therefore not admissible in court. I studied criminal justice, too, Smith."

"I really can't allow—"

"Look," he told her, "my computer isn't connected to the jail system, and if I e-mail the file to myself from your computer there'll be a record. So I'm going to suggest you find something important to do away from your desk." Buck slid into her chair. "This footage is going to come up in about two seconds."

Jolene hesitated. "You mean the footage of the interview the sheriff authorized you to conduct at the jail yesterday with Jason Broderick? That's what you're looking for, right?"

He looked up at her.

Her expression remained stoic. "Because I would never let you use my computer for any other reason. I just hope you don't accidentally stumble onto an illegally obtained recording of a lawyer with his client in that same interview room. Because," she repeated very clearly, "that would be poison fruit."

Buck turned back to the screen to hide his surprise, but he wasn't entirely able to hide the flicker of a wry smile that twitched at his lips. He clicked the mouse.

He fast forwarded through the first two hours of an empty interview room, then slowed to normal speed when Deke opened the door for a man in a dark raincoat, one of those expensive designer models that fell just above the knee and was splotched with water from the morning rain. Sutherlin carried a briefcase and two paper cups of coffee from a fast food place on the highway north of town. He set the coffee on the table beside the briefcase and Deke could be heard telling him it would take about five minutes to bring the prisoner up. It actually took ten, but Buck and Jolene watched every one of them. Sutherlin did not sit down. He didn't open his briefcase. He stood with his hands in the pockets of his raincoat, gazing out the window at the parking lot, walking the length of the room, standing in front of the pastoral print on the wall.

Broderick came in, hands cuffed in front of him, Deke holding his elbow. David Sutherlin turned, extended his hand.

"Dr. Broderick. I'm David Sutherlin, from the law firm of Sutherlin, Feinstein and Rich. Miles Young asked me to stop by."

Broderick couldn't shake hands, and Sutherlin made a fuss about his client being in cuffs. Deke freed Broderick's right hand and cuffed the other one to the table. The two men shook hands, and Sutherlin sat down. Sutherlin apologized about the coffee, took the lids off both cups, passed one to Broderick. Sutherlin drank from his cup, opened his briefcase, and took out a legal pad.

"Tell me what happened," he said.

Broderick sipped from his cup.

"It had to be the coffee," Buck muttered. "It had to be."

Broderick said, "I talked to Mr. Young yesterday. He didn't say anything about sending a lawyer."

Sutherlin replied, "Would you rather I leave?"

"No. No." Broderick took another sip of coffee. "It's just that—the Coyote Project is top secret. Mr. Young specifically told me not to say anything to anyone until he got here."

Buck stiffened, every muscle in his body concentrated on reading between the lines, silently willing Broderick to say more.

"I can assure you anything you tell me is confidential," Sutherlin said.

Broderick put down the cup and brought his forefinger to his upper lip, blotting a sheen of perspiration there.

"Look at Broderick's pupils," Jolene said softly.

Buck had almost forgotten she was there, watching over his shoulder. He did not take his eyes off the screen. "That stuff works fast," he said.

Broderick said, "I didn't kill Martin Anderson." He picked up the cup and took another gulp of coffee. There was a noticeable tremor in his hand when he set the cup down. "But I think I know who did."

Sutherlin made a note on his pad, but from the angle of the overhead camera it appeared to be nothing more than a meaningless doodle. "Go on," he said.

"Either he's got the worse handwriting I've ever seen," Buck murmured.

"Or he's not really taking notes," Jolene said.

"Because he already knows what Broderick is going to say?"

"Or he doesn't care."

Broderick stared at Sutherlin, seeming to struggle to focus. The dampness on his face was visible even to the black and white camera across the room. He said again, "I think I know who did."

Sutherlin said, "Mr. Broderick, are you feeling all right?"

Broderick said, "They threatened my little girl. They were going to hurt Celie."

Jolene's fingers tightened on the back of Buck's chair, reflecting the excitement he felt. Buck didn't dare take his eyes off the screen.

"And the dog," Broderick went on. He paused, his breathing slow and loud. "It was all about the dog. I had to get them both out of there. You understand that, don't you?"

"I do," said Sutherlin. "I do understand."

Broderick squeezed his eyes closed. "My head," he said. "My head is killing me."

"Shall I see if the deputy can get you an aspirin?"

Broderick said nothing.

"Dr. Broderick?"

"I can't do this now," Broderick said, with an effort. "I don't feel... don't feel well."

Sutherlin made no effort to rise. "Do you need a doctor?"

"I just…I need to lie down."

"Very well." Sutherlin took his time unclasping his briefcase, returning the legal pad to its depths, fastening it again. He stood. "I'll get the deputy to take you back to your cell."

He walked to the door with briefcase in hand, knocked on it, told Deke they were finished, and waited while Deke uncuffed Broderick from the table and escorted him from the room. Sutherlin followed them out in an unhurried manner, closing the door behind himself.

They watched all the way through to the point that Buck himself, angry and impatient, burst into the room, turned off the camera, and the screen went dark.

Buck leaned back in his chair. "Nothing," he said.

"The man was perfectly normal looking when he sat down," Jolene observed. "Two sips of coffee later and he's barely able to talk. Could the hospital lab have missed something?"

"They ran the test twice," Buck said. "They knew it was a police matter. They were also looking for other narcotics or toxins that may not have been identified in Broderick's blood. The coffee was absolutely clean."

"No wonder Mr. Sutherlin was so cooperative," Jolene said. "He somehow managed to walk into our jail, poison an inmate before our eyes, and walk out knowing we couldn't prove a damn thing."

Buck stared at the blank screen. "Broderick said he knows who the killer is. If the video of the murder is as fake as it looks and he was set up, Sutherlin couldn't take a chance on him making it back to Raleigh where he could talk to a real lawyer. Or even tell the FBI what he knew."

"Someone threatened his little girl before he left Raleigh," Jolene said. "What do you think the chances are that same person followed them here and kidnapped her?"

"And that son of a bitch Sutherlin knows who it is," Buck said. "I'd bet my badge on it."

He leaned forward and clicked Play again. They watched up to the point that Broderick sat down and took his first sip of coffee. Buck clicked Pause. "Was Sutherlin wearing a raincoat when he was brought in this afternoon?"

"He wasn't brought in," Jolene corrected, because it was her nature to be a little pedantic. "He followed the deputy back here at our request. But no, he wasn't wearing a coat. It had stopped raining by then."

Buck restarted the footage from the beginning.

"He never takes off his coat," Buck observed. "Look how he just stands there with his hands in his pockets. He knows he won't be there long, so he doesn't bother to take off his coat."

"Or his gloves," Jolene added.

"Wait a minute." Buck fast-forwarded the footage. "He does take them off."

He slowed the video to normal speed as the two men shook hands and Sutherlin started to take off his gloves, folding them neatly back into his pocket as he apologized, "Sorry about the gloves. It's bitter outside."

"It wasn't that cold," Buck muttered and rewound the scene a few seconds. There was something about the care with which Sutherlin removed his gloves...

He slowed down the speed and watched the last few frames again. "Wait," Jolene said abruptly, leaning forward. He stopped the playback and zoomed in on Sutherlin's hands as he removed the gloves.

"That's a nitrile glove inside his leather glove." She pointed with a neatly manicured fingernail to the faint strip of blue, fuzzy from magnification, which was visible as Sutherlin folded back the glove.

"Looks like it to me," Buck agreed. He sat back in the chair, eyes on the screen, and stretched his arm to click the mouse again. "Watch how careful he is not to touch the gloves when he puts them in his pocket."

"Fentanyl is absorbed through the skin," Jolene said. Her lips were compressed with restrained excitement. "That's how he did it!"

Buck nodded, starting the footage from the beginning. "He couldn't know whether the jail would even allow him to bring coffee past the security point, so he had to have something more foolproof. Not to mention virtually untraceable."

Jolene frowned. "But he handled the coffee cups with the gloves on. There should have been traces there."

"Not if the drug wasn't applied to the gloves until after he put the cups down," Buck said. "Look, he keeps his hands in his pockets from the time he puts his briefcase and the coffee on the table until he shakes hands with Broderick. My guess is there was some kind of container in his pocket, and he was using the time he was waiting for Broderick to saturate his glove with the drug. He didn't want to take a chance on the stuff soaking through the glove to his own skin, so he wore a chemical-resistant glove underneath."

"He'd be a fool to keep those gloves," Jolene said. "And without them, we have no evidence."

"Criminals have done dumber things," Buck observed, "but my guess is that he burned them. Sooo…" Buck got to his feet with an elaborate shrug. "Looks like there's nothing we can do but thank the good lawyer for his time and tell him he's free to go."

Jolene stared at him. "Sir?" She blinked, embarrassed, and blurted quickly, "I mean, I don't understand. We're just letting him go?"

Buck's expression was implacable as he said, "I think I left his paperwork on my desk. I'll be right back."

Jolene picked up the folder he had dropped on her desk. "Actually," she began, but she was talking to his back.

Buck left the building in long, easy strides and circled around to the visitor's parking lot. There were only six spaces, and even on a weekday they were rarely all filled. Today there was only one car; a white sedan with a rental car sticker on the bumper. As he approached it, Buck ducked down and scooped up a good-sized chunk of granite from the curb near where it was parked, and when he walked past, he drove the rock into the taillight of the sedan with a single powerful backward jab. He heard plastic crunch and saw a few shards of red sparkle on the gravel.

"Oops," he said.

He tossed the rock away, barely slowing his stride. He'd write an incident report later. If he got around to it.

Jolene was standing at the doorway to her office when Buck returned barely four minutes later, her arms crossed over her chest, Sutherlin's file in her hand. Buck took the file and looked at her for a moment thoughtfully. "Chief Smith," he said, "I know you don't work for me anymore, but in the interest of solving this crazy-ass case and finding that little girl, it would be a big help if you and Deputy Nike would station yourselves at the corner of Courthouse Square and Main. The chances are good that, within the next twenty minutes or so, you will observe a rental car from the Asheville airport go through that intersection with a busted taillight. Naturally, you'll make a routine traffic stop to inform the driver of the problem and possibly issue a warning. In the course of that stop, you might allow your highly trained drug detection dog out of the unit to stretch her legs. At that point, the investigation will simply have to take its course."

Her expression, which until that moment had been implacable, faded to curiosity, but it was curiosity strongly mitigated by doubt. "Do you really think he kept the gloves?"

"Probably not," Buck admitted. "But that coat is expensive, and not as easy to dispose of as a pair of gloves. It's worth a shot, right?"

"Except," she pointed out, "the deputy who pulled him over ninety minutes ago didn't make any mention of a broken taillight."

"Really?" He lifted his eyebrows in surprise. "Must've been some kind of hit-and-run in the courthouse parking lot then. Imagine that."

She drew breath as though to object but released it with words unspoken. Buck turned to go, but then he looked back, his expression serious. "There's one more thing, Chief Smith. I treated you unfairly before, and I'm sorry. I thought you were a good law officer when I hired you, and I still think so now. And you can call me Buck."

She looked at him for a long moment without reaction, then she nodded. "Yes, sir," she said. She nodded toward the crate where Bongo still lay with his head on his paws surveying his surroundings with droopy eyes. "I'll make sure somebody keeps an eye on the dog while I'm gone."

She started to leave, and then hesitated. "Buck," she said.

He looked at her in some surprise.

"The FBI is on the scene," she said. "They've got this. This is not the county's responsibility. We don't have to take this investigation any further."

He said, "I know."

She inquired simply, "Then why?"

He looked for a moment as though he wasn't sure of the answer himself, and then he gave a small, wry lift of one shoulder. "I guess I'm not done yet," he said, and he walked down the hall to tell David Sutherlin, who he was almost certain was guilty of attempted murder, that he was free to go.

TWENTY-FIVE

"It doesn't make any sense," I said, staring at my computer screen. "Why would the kidnapper call *here*? How did he even *know* to call here?"

"You have a business number," Miles said, gazing over my shoulder at the image on the screen. "It was easy to find. Also a public Facebook page where anyone can message you."

And that was exactly what someone had done. Using my Dog Daze business account—the one anyone could easily access by clicking the button next to "Got a question? Contact us!"—someone had posted a photograph of Celie. She was wearing her pink tennis shoes and a white sweater over a short green and white polka-dot skirt, and she was clutching her teddy bear. Her hair was tousled and she looked scared, but otherwise she seemed unharmed.

Miles reached around me and manipulated a few keys on the keyboard. "I'm sending you a screen shot of this," he told Grayson, who was standing along with Corny and Jamie in the crowded area behind the check-in desk. "Get it to the people at the photo-analytics lab and see what they can do with it. The

FBI is going to need all the help they can get with this one."

"Yes, sir," said Grayson and pulled out his phone.

Jamie, who was clearly intimidated by Miles, said, "Sir, that's evidence. I don't think…"

"Oh, for heaven's sake," I said, "it's a picture. Looking at it doesn't change anything. It's still a picture."

"Dispatch said a team is on the way," Jamie insisted stubbornly. "I don't think anybody should touch anything until they get here."

I looked over my shoulder at Corny, who was chewing his thumbnail and looking as anxious as I'd ever seen him. "Tell me again what he said."

"I should have recorded it," Corny fretted. "But how could I know? And, oh, Miss Stockton, I started to hang up! I thought it was some kind of prank call and I almost hung up!"

"It's okay," I assured him. "You did the right thing. I don't think you can even record a call from this telephone system. What did he say?"

"Maybe it was a he," Corny said. "It could have been a she. The voice was all distorted and mechanical, like with one of those trick voice boxes you buy at the magic shop, you know."

I did not know, but I nodded, encouraging him to go on.

"And all it said—the voice, that is—all it said was, 'Check your e-mail. I'll call in an hour. She stays alive until then.' And like I said, I thought it was a prank and I almost didn't even look, but there was that part about staying alive, so I checked the office e-mail and…I thought it might be her. I thought it might be that little girl." His voice shook a little with that last word and he folded his arms across his chest, gripping his elbows. "That's when I came to get you."

I tried to give him a supportive smile. I'm not sure how well I succeeded. "Thanks, Corny. It's a good thing you were here. Otherwise we might not even have gotten the message until it was too late."

Miles looked at Grayson again. "Any luck with that e-mail address?"

"I've got our people trying to trace it, sir. It'll take a while."

I said, a little shakily, to Miles, "You have people who can trace an e-mail address? I thought only law enforcement could do that." I kept thinking, *He called me. The kidnapper called me. Why did he do that?*

Miles tapped more keys on my keyboard. "For crying out loud, Raine, where do you think the government gets its technology? From the private sector." He looked at me and specified, "Me. I'm the private sector."

Of course I knew Miles was something of a techno-geek. He had a house that locked itself when you were inside and turned its windows from clear to opaque when the sun went down. His kitchen was so high tech it did everything except set the table by itself. He invested in tech companies because, he said, that's where the money was. Still, I was beginning to wonder if I knew as much about Miles as I thought I did.

Jamie said, "Um, Mr. Young, sir? I need you to step away from the computer, please."

Miles held up his hands in a show of good faith and straightened up, taking out his phone. He said, "Are you finished with my security chief?"

Jamie said, "I guess so. Everything came back clean."

Barely waiting for him to finish, Miles said to Grayson, "I need you to get out to the hospital and keep an eye on Broderick. Let me know the minute there's any change."

"Yes, sir." Grayson left the room, and I returned my attention to the photograph on my computer screen.

Celie was standing against a brown background that might have been wood, or it might have been a painted wall. The resolution was not that great, so I guessed it had been taken with a cell phone indoors. There were no shadows, nothing on the floor, no glimpses of anything in the background to give a clue about where she was.

Reading my mind, Miles said, "The experts can enhance the photograph and see things we can't. The texture of the walls, the floor, even the edges that are almost off screen. There could be a clue anywhere."

I looked at the clock overhead. If the caller kept his word, we had forty-five minutes before he called again.

I sank back against the chair, thinking hard. Why me? Why had the kidnapper called me? There had to be a reason. And I was afraid if I waited until he was ready to tell us, it would be too late.

Jason Broderick had fled the Research Triangle in the middle of the night with the two things he valued the most: his daughter and his dog. My aunt had been responsible for the one; I had been responsible for the other. There was a connection there, an invisible pattern of dots that I couldn't see. But I thought I knew who could.

I looked up at Miles, whose eyes were lowered to his phone, his face in shadows as he typed out a message. "Miles," I said, and waited until he looked at me. "Why did Jason Broderick come here to see you? What is the Coyote Project?"

A subtle change came over Miles's face as he looked at me. He put away his phone and shot a quick glance around the room at the others. Then he touched my shoulder, urging me to stand. "Walk with me," he said.

TWENTY-SIX

Down the linoleum-tiled corridor from the double glass doors that opened onto the sheriff's office was a frosted glass door with the words "Hanover County Prosecutor" inscribed in black on it. Behind those doors was a reception area with two secretaries, a good-sized office for Dan Howell, the county prosecutor, and another, slightly smaller one for the assistant prosecutor, a position that, due to low compensation and a high case load, turned over so often it didn't pay to paint a name on the door. Buck's office was not inside the prosecutor's office or the sheriff's office, but symbolically in between. It had a plaque on the door that read simply, "Buck Lawson," but the only time the plaque was visible was when the door was closed. And since the only time the door was closed was when Buck wasn't there, he found the plaque to be both redundant and pretentious. Anyone who wanted him knew where to find him.

Buck had left the door closed. Now, as he returned to his office to wait for Jolene to report in about Sutherlin—and to somehow find a way to explain the whole thing to the sheriff—he was surprised to find the door open and a man making himself comfortable in the one visitor's chair, checking his phone. Buck recognized him immediately.

"Special Agent Manahan," he said, extending his hand as he entered the room. "I didn't know you were here. Did I keep you waiting long?"

Manahan put the phone away and got to his feet, shaking his hand. "I just got in," he said. "Checked in with the sheriff, had a few things to wind up. I was getting ready to call you. They tell me you're the man to see about open cases these days."

Buck had worked with Special Agent Manahan before, on a case that still gave him nightmares; one that had, before it all played out, left his life in shambles. He hadn't expected to see him again outside the federal courtroom in which they would both be called upon to give state's evidence, and he said so as he gestured for Manahan to resume his seat.

"Last I knew, you were on the anti-terrorism task force," Buck said.

"And last I knew you were county sheriff," Manahan returned with a dry smile.

He was a big man whose broad shoulders had started to slump and whose barrel chest was now mostly fat. He had thinning silver hair and a look of weariness that came from too much dedication to the job. Buck looked at him and saw himself in twenty years.

Buck sat on the edge of his cluttered desk. He had a feeling neither one of them was going to be here long enough to get comfortable. "I guess you came to take this Broderick mess off our hands."

Manahan's expression sobered. "You're right about one thing. It's a mess. But the minute

Broderick ended up with an overdose in your jail, it became your mess. We've got the kidnapping, but when it comes to Broderick, the only thing I can do is lend as much support from the field office as we can."

Buck said, "You were awful damn anxious to take custody of Broderick yesterday."

"Yesterday we had a live suspect," Manahan replied mildly. "Today we have a victim who may or may not live through the night. And, by virtue of that very fact, he's no longer as much of a person of interest to the FBI as he might once have been."

Buck said, "You have some pretty convincing evidence of homicide."

Manahan smiled faintly. "My notes say your office requested a copy of the Hartwell Labs video. Have you seen it?"

Buck admitted that he had.

"What did you think?"

"Fake as a supermodel's boobs," Buck said.

"Any thirteen-year-old with a video editing app on his phone could've put that film together," Manahan agreed, "but I guess whoever did it was in a rush. What we do know is that approximately three minutes of the original video were scrubbed, and that crap was substituted. We've had a team working to reconstruct the original since 6:00 this morning."

Buck said, "So Jo was right—the third-floor cameras were on a separate circuit."

Manahan nodded. "Whoever disabled the entry-level cameras didn't get a chance to knock out the ones at the scene of the shooting, so they had to patch something in. They had to know it wouldn't fool the experts, but it was just enough that we had to mark it as evidence."

"Still," Buck speculated, "not everyone can knock together a video like that on short notice. That's got to narrow your suspects."

Manahan shrugged. "Not by much. In a place like Hartwell it would be hard to find somebody who couldn't do it."

Buck lifted an eyebrow. "So you're telling me Broderick's telling the truth? What about the gun, and the bloody clothes?"

"We've got an eyewitness and a neighbor's security camera suggesting that someone broke into Broderick's house close to 3:00 a.m., long after he was gone. His own security system—which was disabled around the time of the break-in—shows him returning home at 1:52 p.m. wearing an entirely different set of clothes than the ones that were found with blood on them, and carrying nothing but a set of keys." He shrugged. "A good defense attorney could make a case that the evidence was planted to delay an investigation into the real murderer. We never liked him for the homicide."

Buck nodded. "The sheriff said something about corporate espionage."

Manahan said, "Right. The last couple of years a new brand of techno-pirates hit our radar. These guys are slick, smart and virtually impossible to trace. They traffic information the way the Mexican cartel traffics drugs, only..." There was a slight, rueful quirk of his lips. "With a lot more style and a lot less blood. They've stolen billions of dollars worth of intellectual property and corporate secrets, easy enough to smuggle right out the front door on a microchip or thumb drive. Half the time a company's new top-secret product is already coming out of some factory in China before they even know it's missing. Like I say, billions of lost American dollars."

Buck nodded thoughtfully as the pieces began to come together. "Would I be wrong in thinking Broderick's dogs played a part in recovering some of those dollars?"

"Our solve rate doubled when we started using the dogs," Manahan said. "All electronic devices are coated with this chemical called TPPO, or triphenylphosphine oxide, during the manufacturing stage. That's what the dogs are trained to detect. They're the most efficient method anybody's come up with yet for stopping these guys."

"So far it sounds like Broderick should be on your payroll, not your wanted list."

"You'd think so," agreed Manahan. "Until, over the last year or so, we noticed a disproportionate amount of the stolen tech was coming out of Hartwell Labs. They do some high-level R&D there, a lot of it for the military, and it was slipping out of the country. More than once we had the perps dead to rights, but the dogs brought back a negative report."

Buck frowned. "So something was wrong with the dogs?"

Manahan shook his head grimly. "Somebody figured out a way to get past them. And it looks pretty clear that whoever it was worked at Hartwell."

Buck was about to ask the obvious question when his phone buzzed in his pocket. He took it out and read the message, pushing to his feet as he did.

"Looks like the ransom call came in," he said. "Let's go. You can finish briefing me on the way."

I shivered in the breeze that rattled the treetops and shook the last few remaining drops of moisture from the leaves—not so much because I was cold, even though I did wish I'd remembered to grab my jacket before leaving Aunt Mart's house—but because the effort to make sense of everything that had happened in the past twenty-four hours was starting to catch up with me. Microchips sprayed with TPPO, corporate espionage, military secrets at risk... it was a lot to absorb on top of everything else.

Miles put his arm around my shoulders for warmth, and I was glad of it. We had walked across the yard to bring the dogs down to the kennel from the porch. Cisco was striding along at the end of my leash while Pepper bounced and bounded at the end of Miles's. Mischief and Magic would have been insulted at the mere mention of a leash for such a short trip, so they trotted along a few feet ahead of us, sniffing at the mud puddles and taking in the sights.

I said, "So what went wrong? How was the stuff getting past the dogs? I thought their hit rate was almost one hundred percent."

Miles said, "It was pretty simple, really. All the thief had to do was spray the micro-tech with a substance called DBT before taking it past the dogs. It reacted with the TPPO in such a way as to disguise the scent from the dogs. The problem, for the pirates at least, is that DBT starts to deteriorate in a matter of hours, and can actually damage the very tech they were trying to steal. What they needed was a substance that could get past the dogs without the risks and disadvantages of DBT. So we gave them one."

I said uncertainly, "Wait a minute. You were helping the bad guys?"

"Once we figured we had a leak inside Hartwell, we had no choice," Miles said. "Sugar, you have no idea how much was at stake. In the past twenty years, the innovations that have come out of the Hartwell Group have changed the way we live, and they've got things under development now that, within the next fifty years, will change what it means to live on this planet. And," he added somewhat grimly, "if they fall into the wrong hands, not in a good way. Corporations pay hundreds of millions of dollars a year in sponsorship fees to have first pick of the inventions that come out of that think tank, and if it got out that we weren't reliable, all that goes away. We'd be out of business, and the world would be a much, much poorer place."

Sometimes when I'm with Miles, I feel a little awed—star struck, even—by who he is and what he's done with his life; what he cares about and what he's accomplished and, well, just everything. Fortunately, that doesn't happen often. But I have to admit, this was one of those times.

Pepper chose that moment to jump up and try to bite the leash, thus restoring the balance between us. I said sharply, "Pepper! Don't!" And to Miles, "Don't let her do that."

He passed Pepper's leash to me and took Cisco's from my hand. I tightened Pepper's leash and told her to heel, and she looked up at me with a proud grin on her face as she complied. Dogs, like people, appreciate boundaries.

I didn't want to take the dogs through the office, where, in the past few minutes, two more law officers had moved in, so I gestured the way around the side of the building, toward the play yard. I said a little stiffly, "You should have told me, Miles. You should have told me all this on the phone when I asked."

He lifted his hand to my neck, caressing the stiff muscles there lightly. "Baby, I wish I could have. Most of it, I've spent the past twenty-four hours trying to find out, and the rest I couldn't talk about on the phone. I never imagined you'd get involved in this, or your aunt. I never thought Dr. Broderick would involve his child. God, what a mess."

We walked in silence for a while, the mood heavy between us. Cisco, who had sneaked far too many dog biscuits from Miles to take him seriously as a disciplinarian, started weaving and sniffing the grass at the end of the leash. I didn't even bother to point out the lapse to Miles, or to Cisco.

I said after a moment, "I still don't get it. Why did you decide to help the very people who were stealing from you?"

"What you have to understand," he explained, "is that these weren't just a bunch of random hoodlums looking to get rich quick. The buying and selling of corporate secrets is big business, and most of it is controlled, in this country at least, by a highly organized group of thieves with big ambitions. It's one thing to score a few million on a scratch-resistant paint formula or a faster acting pain reliever, but when you're auctioning off information that can bring down an airliner…that's something else entirely. The fact that they were experimenting—more or less successfully—with DBT was pretty scary. They had to be stopped. The best way to catch a thief is to offer them a prize they can't refuse, and the big prize for them was a product that could fool both dogs and electronic scent analyzers without harming the underlying tech. So that's what we put our engineers to work on. We weren't helping the bad guys," he told me, "we were trapping them. Because Broderick was also training the only dog in the world who could detect this stuff. *That*'s the Coyote Project."

"Wow," I said softly. "So Bongo really is the most valuable dog in the world."

He nodded. "Of course we knew some of the lower level operatives would still be using DBT for awhile, but the object was to catch the big fish—the one who would go after the fool-proof formula. Bongo was key to that. You can see why it was so important to Dr. Broderick—and to me—to keep Bongo safe. Broderick had been training him for nine months—virtually since birth—for one job. Without him, we were back to square one."

"So why did Dr. Broderick steal him? Why take the risk?"

Miles shook his head. "Something went wrong. I don't know what." He hesitated, as though uncertain how much more to tell me. He hardly ever did that. Finally he said, "The latest information was that it was one of the team members on the Coyote Project who was selling information to the cartel. The evidence pointed to Dr. Broderick, and he was released from the project. Of course I knew he was innocent. I think that's why he came here to find me."

Now I was really confused. "But how did you know Dr. Broderick was innocent?"

"Because," Miles said, opening the gate to the play yard, "I'm the one who set him up."

Buck followed the sheriff's car into Raine's driveway. When he made the turn, he could see that two black SUVs were already there, blocking the turnaround, along with a couple of HCSO cruisers. Manahan was saying, "We got our first break a few months ago, when we noticed that a lot of the stolen material had to do with bio-tech and drug development. And that it appeared to be passing into the hands of a particular pharmaceutical company."

"Entretex," Buck said.

Manahan looked at him in surprise. "Not bad for a country sheriff."

"Former country sheriff," Buck reminded him. "I'm still not sure how it all ties together, though."

"It turns out that one of the partners in the Hartwell Group is also a major shareholder in Entretex," Manahan said. "He makes sure his company gets a jump on the competition and he doubles his profits—once from selling the research, once in dividends from the new product when Entretex gets it to market ahead of everyone else. Sweet deal all around."

Buck swung his SUV behind one of the cruisers in the Dog Daze parking lot, his expression grim. "So the partner would have a few million reasons to make sure his scheme was never discovered. And if Broderick found out what was going on, he would basically be a marked man."

Manahan opened his door and got out. "It's a theory," he agreed.

"So that's how Broderick ended up here," Buck speculated out loud as the two of them walked up the short path to the building. "He was probably looking to make some kind of deal and it backfired on him."

Manahan glanced at him. "I'm not sure I follow you."

Buck said, "That partner you were talking about. It wouldn't happen to Miles Young, would it?"

TWENTY-SEVEN

Buck barely had time to register Manahan's frown of confusion before the door to the kennel building opened, and Miles Young stepped out. "Tom," Miles said, clasping Manahan's hand warmly. "Thanks for coming."

Manahan replied, "Good to see you again." He glanced around the room as they stepped inside, and said to Buck. "You two know each other, right?"

Buck looked at Miles, his eyes cool. "So I was right. You're the one who brought the FBI in when you couldn't talk Marshall into keeping Broderick overnight."

"I thought he'd be safer in your jail until we figured out what was going on," Miles replied. "Turns out I was wrong."

Though there was no accusation in Miles's tone, Buck's jaw went tight.

Manahan's eyes were busy on the crowded room. "I need to check in with my team." He touched Miles's arm absently as he moved past him. "Why don't you two bring each other up to speed?"

Buck waited a moment after Manahan had crossed the room, then he said, "Where's Raine?"

"Outside with the dogs, on the phone to her aunt," Miles said. "She was worried that all the resources had been moved over here, and no one had stayed to protect Aunt Mart."

Buck did not like the way that rolled so easily off his tongue: *Aunt Mart*. He said, "We wouldn't do that." He added, in as neutral a tone as possible, "So what's your involvement with Broderick?"

"Dr. Broderick was part of a four-man team working on the Coyote Project," Miles said. "I guess you've been briefed on that."

Buck gave a single nod of his head.

"He was the one who first became suspicious of a leak inside the project, and it just so happened I was at the facility at the time. I wanted to meet him because of the dogs, you know. I thought Raine and Mel would get a kick out of it." His expression darkened. "The last thing I expected was that it would turn into something like this."

Miles went on, "Broderick came to me with his suspicions, and I called the FBI. We didn't want to spook the real thief, so I set it up to look like Broderick was the suspect, and we'd fired him. We took him off the project and gave the real thief a chance to show his hand. That was two weeks ago. Something must've happened to make Broderick think Bongo was in danger. That's why he went back to the lab to get him."

Buck said, "He didn't try to contact you to tell you what it was?"

Miles shook his head. "Not until he called from jail Saturday."

"Who else knew about the sting?"

"Besides the FBI? As far as I know, no one."

"Were you aware the FBI suspected one of the partners in the Hartwell Group was orchestrating this?"

Miles's expression altered subtly. "Is this an interrogation?"

"Right now," Buck replied, "no. But I can't help finding it interesting that since you moved to town you've been involved in more than half the cases I've investigated."

Miles gave a small shake of his head that was mostly puzzled amusement. "Excuse me," he said. "I need to check on Raine."

Buck's phone buzzed, and he took it out. Miles turned to go, but Buck held up a staying hand. He read the message.

K-9 alerted to black trench coat in backseat of vehicle during routine traffic stop. Plastic bag with traces of white power found in right outside pocket. Suspect David Sutherlin in custody, possession of Class 3 narcotics.

Buck's expression tightened in grim satisfaction. He typed back, *Book him.*

He put the phone away and looked up at Miles. "Do you know a man by the name of David Sutherlin?"

"No." Miles started to leave, and then stopped, looking back. His expression had gone from hard to thoughtful. "Wait," he said. "Maybe I do. He's an attorney, used to do some work for us at Hartwell. The son-in-law of one of the partners, Chaz Kramer. He left to take a job with Entretex Pharmaceuticals last year."

Son of a bitch, Buck thought, but he didn't break eye contact. "He's in custody," he said. "I think he's responsible for Broderick's overdose."

He could see the other man's mind working, then Miles gave a short nod. "He wouldn't have been working alone. He might have information about the little girl."

"We're checking that out."

Miles looked at him for another moment. In the background voices clattered and equipment rattled and buzzed. There was an ear-piercing screech as someone moved a filing cabinet across the tile floor. In the distance, muffled by concrete walls, dogs barked. Miles said in a pleasant, somewhat detached voice, "I'm not your enemy, Lawson, no matter what you think. If you want to blame me for treasuring what you threw away, that's your problem, not mine. But you need to remember I didn't take anything from you. You lost it. And we've both got bigger things to focus on right now, so maybe we could put personal feelings on the back burner for the time being and try to work together. What do you say?"

Buck's jaw tightened, and he felt a heat on the back of his neck. He said nothing.

Miles smiled, but there was no humor in it. "Right," he said, and walked away.

TWENTY-EIGHT

The phone rang at 3:49, eleven minutes before the ransom call was expected, but it was only a client, wanting to know when the start date of the next puppy class was. My throat was so dry I could barely answer her question, and I'm still not sure I told her the right date. I could see the shoulders of every man in the office visibly sag when I hung up.

"Okay, Raine," Marshall said with an encouraging smile, "good dress rehearsal."

Dale, the FBI agent who'd helped set up the monitoring equipment at Aunt Mart's house, glanced at the clock. "Remember, delay agreeing to his demands as long as possible. The more recording time we get, the better chance we'll have to analyze the background noises, maybe get a location."

"Ask for proof of life," put in the other agent tersely. "We do nothing without proof of life."

I glared at him. "Are you kidding me right now? I thought your *job* was to do everything possible to get that child back home safely. What do you mean, you do nothing?"

Miles put a calming hand on my shoulder. "It's just another way to keep him talking, Raine. These guys know what they're doing."

Buck was there, and Marshall was talking quietly to Special Agent Manahan, who had interviewed me last year after the hostage situation at Camp Bluebird. Corny stood huddled in a corner behind me, chewing what was left of his thumbnail. The door was open to the front gate and several deputies were standing around there; I wasn't sure why. We all waited.

On my computer screen was the picture of Celie, standing against that indistinguishable brown background, holding her teddy bear. I reached out with a nervous, involuntary gesture to touch the screen, and smiled a little when I noticed for the first time that she had pinned the sparkly palm tree from her Florida hat onto the bear's floppy bow tie. "Aunt Mart said she liked to dress up her bear," I said, apropos of nothing.

Miles kissed the top of my hair lightly and squeezed my shoulders. "Deep breath, sweetheart. All you have to do is answer the phone."

I nodded. We'd been over and over it, and the best explanation anyone could come up with for why the kidnapper would contact me was because of my connection to Miles. Likely they didn't know he had returned from Europe and thought I was the fastest way to get a message to him. After all, that's how Dr. Broderick had contacted him in the first place: through me. Miles had deep pockets; naturally they'd assume he would be the one to ransom the child of one of the top scientists at Hartwell.

Of course, the other explanation was that this was all just a distraction and that the real call would come to Aunt Mart. For that reason, the half of the police force that wasn't currently camped outside my door was guarding hers. Meanwhile, no one was looking for Celie.

The phone rang, and my eyes flew to the clock: 3:59. The room went as still as a photograph, with everyone looking at me. Instinctively my hand went to the receiver, but Agent Dale held up a staying hand.

"Remember," he said, holding my gaze. "Proof of life. Keep him talking."

I swallowed hard and nodded.

He leaned forward and pushed the button that switched the call to speaker. He pointed a finger at me. I took a breath.

"Dog Daze," I said. "This is Raine."

There was silence. I waited. "Hello?"

A rustling sound came from the other end of the line, and then a small voice. "Hello?"

My heart skipped a beat, and I leaned forward urgently. "Celie? Celie, is that you?"

"I want my daddy!" she cried. "Where is my daddy?"

"Celie, are you all right? Where are you?"

More rustling, and I gripped the corner of my desk so hard that my fingers hurt. "Celie!"

The mechanical voice came. "Raine Stockton."

Miles's hands tightened on my shoulders, a gentle, steadying pressure. Yes," I managed. "This is Raine."

"There's an abandoned gas station on Lake View Road. Bring the dog there in one hour. Come alone. No one but you. The girl for the dog."

I was so stupefied that I literally did not know what he meant. I blurted, "What dog?"

"The girl for the dog," the voice repeated deliberately. "One hour."

"But—but I don't have him!" I looked desperately around the room, leaning into the speaker. "He's not here! That's not enough time! I can't…"

But the light on the speakerphone went dead. He was gone.

The room sprang into action.

"Where's the dog?"

"Do you know the place?"

"Show me."

"How far?"

"Is it defensible?"

I spun around in my chair to look at Miles, panic racing through my veins with such speed that it was actually hard to breathe. "Wait," I said. "Wait—he wants to trade Bongo for Celie? Is that what he said?"

Miles's face was grim, but he was looking beyond me, at Manahan. He didn't reply.

"But—that's crazy!" I cried. "Who does that?"

Buck said, "You're not sending Raine in alone."

Marshall agreed, "We're not involving a civilian." He demanded of Manahan, "Do you have a female agent?"

"Not that we can get here in time." Manahan replied. "That's why the short deadline—he's making sure we don't have time to get teams in place." He turned to one of the agents with the laptop. "Get a map up. Let me see that place."

"Already done, sir."

While Marshall and Manahan bent over the map, Buck dialed his phone. Buck muttered, "That's what

Broderick meant when he said it was all about the dog. It was the dog they wanted all along." Then, "Chief Smith, the dog is the ransom. We need him out here, highest possible priority. That's right. We've got less than an hour to make the exchange."

But before he had even finished speaking, I pushed out of my chair. "Are you serious?" I turned to Miles, horrified and incredulous. "You're not really going to let them take Bongo, are you? How can you do that? You can't do that!"

Manahan looked up from the map. "What about another dog? Can we substitute another black Lab?"

Corny spoke up nervously. "Bongo has a tattoo in his ear. They'll know that."

Manahan spoke to Marshall. "We'll put her in a vest. If we can get men up there, we can protect her."

Manahan looked at me, his expression somber. "Miss Stockton," he said, "I'm not going to tell you that this undertaking is without risk. But almost one hundred percent of the time in a case like this all the kidnapper wants is the ransom. If you follow his instructions and don't do anything foolish, there's very little chance that he'll harm you."

I couldn't help notice the way he used terms like "almost" and "very little chance," but I didn't say anything. The truth was, I wasn't all that worried about myself. I had Miles and Buck and Marshall and the entire Hanover County Sheriff's Office, plus the FBI, to protect me. But Bongo...

Manahan went on, "He specifically asked for you. That means he's seen you, or knows enough about you to recognize you and to know that you're a civilian who'll be scared enough to do as you're told.

He probably thinks you still have the dog, and the fact is, if he could've gotten in here and stolen it, the little girl probably never would have been kidnapped. This has got to be his Plan B. So our job is to make it easy for him. Do you know the place he's talking about?"

I nodded dully. "It'll take about half an hour to get there from here. It's a dirt road, used to be the main access road to Powers Lake, but nobody uses it anymore. The gas station closed down in the thirties. There's nothing around for miles."

Manahan spun sway and started giving orders. Buck was on his phone. Marshall was dispatching deputies. Two of the agents were poring over a topographical map on their laptop. Everyone was moving. My tiny office looked like an ant hill someone had kicked over.

I heard Marshall say something about bringing a team up from the lake, and Buck said, pointing at a spot on the map, "Peters and Bradley are good woodsmen. If we can position them on this ridge here, they'll be ready to cut him off during the exchange."

Manahan said briefly, "If there is an exchange."

Buck's eyes met Marshall's and I saw an understanding pass between them that I refused to share. I gripped Miles's arm. "What does that mean?" When he didn't answer immediately, I whirled on Manahan. "What do you mean, if there is an exchange? He said he would exchange Bongo for Celie. That's the whole point!"

Manahan looked at me somberly. "Miss Stockton, our entire focus will be on extricating the child safely. But the only way we can do that is by giving the man what he wants. He wants the dog, but we've got to be prepared for the fact that he might not let you get close enough to turn him over."

I just stared at him, still not comprehending.

"Honey," Miles said gently, "they don't want the dog. They want to make sure no one else has him."

I felt something cold drain through my body. Across the room, Corny made a soft sound of horror, but when I looked at him he wouldn't meet my eyes. "They're going to kill him," I said. My voice was dull with shock. It made perfect sense. Bongo was the only one of his kind. Once he was gone, nothing stood in the bad guys' way. They didn't need him. They needed him dead.

"I won't do it," I said. I turned from Manahan to Miles and back again. "I won't turn him over." My hands tightened into fists and my voice rose a notch. "The man on the phone said I should bring him, no one but me, and I won't do it!"

Manahan came over to me. "Miss Stockton," he said quietly, "we can't force you to do this. Believe me, if there was more time we wouldn't even consider it. But this is our best chance to get that little girl back unharmed, and we need to take it."

I looked at Miles desperately. "Think of something," I pleaded. "There's got to be another way! Find it!"

But all I saw in his eyes was pain and regret. He lifted a hand to touch me, but I jerked away, wrapping my arms around myself, showing him my back.

Buck stood before me. His eyes were quiet, his expression set in the lines of a man who knows the outcome, and hates what he knows. "Raine," he said.

"No one wants you to do this. God knows I don't. But I'm asking you to do it anyway. Because if you don't, that little girl will probably die."

I stared at him, hardly able to believe the words I'd heard him speak. He actually expected me to put a leash on that beautiful, brilliant dog and lead him to his death. A life for a life. Bongo's for Celie's.

My throat convulsed and I thought for a moment I might throw up. Shaking, I pushed my way past them and out of the office, into the kennel. Dogs started barking when they heard the heavy fire door slam, and I broke into a jog, down the concrete corridor, into the playroom, out the back door and into the play yard. My four dogs were the only ones in the yard, and they spun around and raced toward me when I came out. I sank down on the steps and let them jump all over me with their muddy paws, licking my face, pushing me off balance. I hugged them, together and separately. I rubbed their ears and kissed their noses, and when they'd had enough affection, Pepper, Mischief and Magic scrambled down the steps to play three-way tug with a flying disc. Cisco, who never got enough affection, plopped his paws over my knees and stretched out across my legs, tongue lolling happily as he gazed up at me. I wrapped my arms around him and dropped my face to his neck, squeezing my eyes tightly closed, inhaling the scent of his sunny fur with wet, muffled breaths.

I didn't look up when the door opened behind me and Miles sat down next to me. He didn't try to comfort me, or say anything at all. He just stayed close.

I straightened up at last, wiping at my face with my fingers, smearing the tears and dog hair there. "They don't understand what they're asking." I said. "If I do this…" My voice was so tight it was barely audible. "Who will I be if I do this?"

Miles watched Pepper snatch the toy out of Mischief's grip and race gaily across the yard, golden tail waving, the two Aussies in hot pursuit. He answered quietly, "Who will you be if you don't?"

I tightened my fingers in Cisco's fur and pressed my cheek to his head. "I can't," I whispered, closing my eyes again. "I can't do it."

But in the end I did.

TWENTY-NINE

I remember thinking that this operation could probably be used as a teaching example in the police academy of how to improvise when you have no choice. The FBI dealt with hundreds of kidnapping cases every year, but even the Bureau didn't have a contingency plan for when the ransom price was a living being. All we could do was the best we could.

I wore a heavy armored vest underneath my sweatshirt and a wire with a microphone and an earpiece so that the FBI could communicate with me. "There's every indication this is going to be a straightforward exchange," Manahan told me. "He hasn't had time to set up anything elaborate, and we don't think he knows this area well enough to take chances. All he wants is the dog. We'll have eyes on you the whole time. Do exactly what he says. The minute you have the little girl, get her to the car and get out of there. That's all you have to do."

Jolene wanted to go in my place, but no one seriously considered it. The kidnapper had been specific, and there was no way she could be mistaken for me, even at a distance. Likewise rejected was the idea of hiding an officer in the back of my SUV. Bongo and I would be alone.

Jolene put Bongo in the crate that I kept in the back cargo area of the SUV, and I couldn't watch. I waited until she had closed the hatch before I went outside and got into the driver's seat. Corny stood in the doorway, holding Cisco's leash, and Miles stood beside him. Neither one of them said anything, but Cisco barked sharply, once, in annoyance at being left behind.

Ten minutes down the road, Buck's voice spoke in my ear. "You're going to be fine, Raine. Let us know when you get to the exchange spot."

All my senses went on high alert. I said, "I thought you'd be watching me."

The silence on the other end was chilling. He replied at last, tensely, "Just let us know."

I guess that's when I realized exactly what "improvise" meant.

Lake View Road was little more than a rutted path off another, wider dirt road that circled the lake. Fallen branches crunched under my tires and wild blackberry vines scraped the side of my car. Bongo shuffled in his crate as the car bounced over ruts, splashing mud as high as my windows. There was no sign of any other car ever having been this way, and I had a brief moment of panic, wondering if I had misheard the rendezvous instructions. But no. There it was, just as I remembered from when Cisco and I had hiked around the lake two springs ago: the old Texaco gasoline station.

The big sign was secured to its mast only on one side, so that it hung vertically. The letters were faded and half of the "E" was missing. Someone had long since scavenged the antique gasoline pumps, leaving only a cracked cement pad scattered with dead leaves and tiny sprouts of dandelions. A pine tree had crashed through the roof of the squat concrete block building some years back, and vines grew through the gaps where windows should have been. Surely no one was inside. I had tried to explore it once, and couldn't even get past the debris in the threshold. Why had he sent me here? If Celie was in there, she would be terrified. But I didn't think she was there.

I pulled up in front of the abandoned building and put the vehicle in park. The dashboard clock told me I was one minute early. I said into the microphone that was pinned inside the neck of my sweatshirt, "I'm here."

Another voice—it might have been Manahan's, or Dale's—said, "We see you."

I looked around, twisting in my seat, even though I knew the officers wouldn't be foolish enough to make themselves seen. "Where?"

A hesitation, then, "There's a drone in the treetops on the ridge to your west."

A *drone*? Drones didn't have guns. Drones couldn't surround and disable a perpetrator. Drones couldn't snatch a child out of the bad guy's hands and rush her to safety.

I ducked down and peered upward through my west-facing window. "I don't see it."

"You're not supposed to."

I straightened up, again searching the tangled terrain with my eyes. "What about Celie? Do you see her?"

"No."

"What do I do if he doesn't show? What if..."

The voice that interrupted startled me, then made my heart leap with a completely inappropriate, and wholly temporary, joy. "Hey, slugger," Miles said. "Take it easy. You've got this."

"Miles?" I looked around as though actually expecting to see him. "How did you—what are you doing here?"

"Never one to sit around the cook fire, darlin'," he said. "And you needed somebody to keep an eye on you."

I twisted in my seat, scanning my surroundings. "Where are you?"

"I've got the best seat in the house, watching the drone feed with a bunch of cops waiting to swoop in and save the day," he replied. "There are a lot of people keeping an eye on you, sugar. You're going to be fine."

"I can't believe they let you do a ride-along on something like this." Though I was still searching the sky for the drone and the surrounding terrain for any sign—any sign at all—of the approaching kidnapper, I felt less panicky than before. Something about the sound of Miles's voice had always been able to soothe me.

"Remember what I told you the first time I met you?" he said.

I almost smiled. "It pays to have friends in high places."

"Right." Then he said, "Do me a favor, okay? Don't do anything stupid."

I didn't answer.

"Because I know your instincts will be otherwise."

"You're the one who once ran into the path of gunfire to save my dog," I said.

"Yeah, well, that was me. Besides, I barely even know this dog, and I've gotten kind of used to having you around." His tone sobered. "There's a GPS transmitter in his collar," he reminded me. "We can track the dog. Don't do anything stupid."

But we both knew the transmitter had been an afterthought, just in case the kidnapper decided to take Bongo to a second location before killing him, or on the off-chance that he was working for someone else and had to deliver the dog before getting paid. The transmitter would help the FBI track the kidnapper. No one really expected to see Bongo alive again.

But it was good of Miles to pretend otherwise.

I looked at the clock. "It's time. He should be here."

Someone else's voice spoke in my ear, one of the agents. "He won't show until he's sure it's safe. Stay inside the car until we tell you."

I waited. The digital display on the dashboard clock changed numbers. Once. Twice. My mouth was dry. I fumbled in the console for a bottle of water but all I found was empties. I wondered if Bongo was thirsty, and then I couldn't think about it.

The kidnapper was five minutes late.

"What if he's watching me?" I said suddenly. "What if he's waiting for me to get out of the car?"

The voice in my ear said quietly, "Stop talking."

I caught my breath as I saw, out of the corner of my eye, a movement to my left. Bongo stood up in the back, rattling the crate. A man in a black sweatshirt and black ski mask came out of the woods, carrying Celie on his hip.

"Damn it," I whispered. I'd forgotten about the old apple shed twenty yards farther down the road. There had been an orchard there, back in the eighties, and the owners had sold fresh Golden Delicious in five-pound paper bags to tourists in the autumn. Its metal roof and three plank sides were still intact, though covered with vines this time of year. Anyone hiding inside would be invisible from the air and from the lake.

I watched him climb the short hill and cross to the center of the road. He walked toward me about ten feet and stopped.

"Get out of the car," the voice in my ear said. My hand was already on the door handle. "See what he has to say."

I got out and crossed in front of my car. I stood there, heart pounding.

"Where's the dog?" he called across the distance that separated us. Without the mechanical alteration, his voice sounded normal, not scary at all.

I replied, lifting my voice to be heard, "In the back."

He ordered, "Get him out."

"Do it," said the voice in my ear.

I called, "Put Celie down. Let me see her."

He hesitated, then lifted Celie to the ground in front of him, holding on to her shoulders. She clutched her bear and sucked her thumb. Her face was dirty and puffy from crying, and her white sweater was no longer entirely white. Neither was the bear.

I bent forward, trying to make my face look friendly. "Hi, Celie," I said. "Remember me?"

She looked for a moment too frightened to speak. Then she dropped her thumb from her mouth and demanded tremulously, "Where's my daddy?"

"I'm going to take you to him, okay?" I assured her. "It'll just be another minute."

The man transferred his grip from her shoulders to one of her upper arms. With his free hand he reached behind his back and brought out a gun. My heartbeat accelerated.

He said, "Get the dog out of the car and bring him here."

"Do it," said the voice in my ear.

"Celie," I called, trying very hard to keep the pounding of my heart from shaking my voice, "be very still, okay? I'm going to be right back. Just stay there."

I turned and walked to the back of the SUV. "He has a gun," I whispered into the microphone.

There was no reply.

I opened the tailgate. Bongo was standing inside the crate. His head was down due to the limited space and his eyes were on a level with mine. There was a moment when I couldn't look away. Then I clenched my teeth together and unfastened his leash from where Jolene had hooked it on the top of the wire crate. I shot the bolt, unlocking the door, and clipped the leash to his collar.

"Come on, Bongo," I said tightly, tugging on the leash. "Let's go."

Bongo sprang out of the crate and landed neatly on the ground. He walked eagerly by my side around to the front of the car.

I would be hard-pressed to say exactly how the sequence of events unfolded after that, although I would try, in one official interview after the other, to get it right. We reached the front of the SUV and walked a couple of steps forward, when Celie cried, "Bongo!" She tried to pull away from her captor. I remember thinking in a rush of blind hot panic, *Please don't, please don't, please don't shoot this little girl's dog in front of her...* While at the same moment Bongo suddenly tensed, staring at Celie with ears forward and tail up, like a pointer on alert or a guard dog ready to attack. Instinctively I reached down and grabbed his collar. It was a rookie move and I knew better, I swear I did. *Never* relinquish the leash to grab the collar unless it's a slip collar or martingale that tightens when you pull on it. I knew that. But in a moment of panic, people, like dogs, tend to forsake learned behavior and revert to impulse, a choice that is almost invariably the wrong one. With a twist and a leap, Bongo was out of my grip, shooting forward like a rocket and leaving me holding an empty collar. I screamed, "Bongo, don't!"

Bongo bore down on Celie, and the man holding her took a startled step backwards, raising the gun. I screamed again, "*Bongo!*" Celie wrenched away from her captor and ran toward Bongo. Bongo plowed into her and she lost her balance, shrieking as she fell to her knees. The teddy bear landed a few feet away and Bongo grabbed it, shaking it, pawing the ground in excitement.

A gunshot exploded.

By this time I had reached Celie. I scooped her up and dragged her back toward the car. She was screaming, her arm outstretched for Bongo. There was shouting. Three men with guns poured down from the ridge and two more ran up from the lake. The man in the ski mask was on the ground, facedown. I half pushed, half threw Celie into my car.

She screamed, "Bongo!"

I turned my head in the direction of her frantically pointing hand. The last I saw of Bongo was as he ran into the woods, carrying the teddy bear in his mouth.

THIRTY

All I could do was slam closed the car door and huddle over Celie, trying to keep her head below the level of the windows, bracing against whatever might come next. She screamed in my ear so loudly that I couldn't hear the sound of approaching sirens, if in fact there were any, and my eyes were squeezed so tightly closed that I didn't see the flash of lights or the approach of multiple cruisers. I knew all these things only in retrospect, after I heard a firm tapping on my window and I opened my eyes to see Buck looking in at us. I straightened up, bringing Celie with me, and saw that the entire clearing, and the road beyond, was filled with police cars.

I reached over and unlocked the car door. Celie seemed to have screamed herself out, but she still clung to me with arms that were like vines tightened around my neck. Buck opened the driver's side door and bent in toward us. "You okay?"

I managed a nod, but I could not for the life of me make my voice work. I ground my teeth together to keep them from chattering as a sudden delayed rush of adrenaline surged through my body.

Celie turned her head toward him and Buck leaned in farther, smiling at her. "Hey, sweetheart," he said. "Remember me?"

She started crying again, burying her hot, red face in my shoulder. "I-I w-wet my p-pants."

I patted her tangled hair uselessly, but it was Buck's voice that soothed her. "Hey, that's okay," he said. "We'll just call Miss Mart and tell her to bring you some clean clothes and maybe a ribbon for your hair, what do you say? So you'll look pretty for your dad."

She turned to look at him cautiously, the sobs lessening. "Where's my daddy? Are you going to take me to my daddy?"

He held out his arms for her. "I sure am. You know he's been a little sick, but the doctors and nurses at the hospital have been taking real good care of him. I'm going to take you to meet them now, and they're going to take good care of you too."

Celie hesitated, but her arms around my neck were not quite the death-grip they'd been before. Buck met my eyes. "Broderick is coming out of it," he told me. "We got word right after you left. It looks like he's going to be okay."

He smiled again at Celie. "Come on, hon. Have you ever ridden in a police car? It's really cool."

This seemed to intrigue her enough to relax her grip, and I passed her over to Buck. "Bongo stole my bear," she said, tearing up again as Buck lifted her out of the car.

"Well, it just so happens," Buck replied, "I know where to find another one. Do you like girl bears or boy bears?"

I blew out a long slow breath, sinking back against the passenger seat and quivering like a leaf in high wind as I watched Buck carry her away. I pulled the microphone and battery pack out of my clothes with shaking hands and dumped them clumsily into the cup holder. I couldn't tell what had happened to the man in the ski mask, or to his gun, although I knew Buck wouldn't have come for Celie until the suspect was secured and the crisis was over. All I could see in every direction were police cruisers, flashing lights and uniformed officers. All I could hear was the delayed pounding of my heart, booming like a drum in my ears. All I could think about were those last few minutes, Bongo pulling out of his collar, racing straight into danger, Celie screaming, the gunshot, Bongo tearing into the woods like a maniac, gripping the stuffed bear in his mouth.

When the passenger side door opened, I jumped, expecting Marshall or maybe even Manahan. Instead I was overcome by the sound of scrabbling paws and happy panting breaths; I was enveloped in golden fur and wet doggie kisses.

"Cisco!" I gasped. I wrapped my arms around him in a fierce hug even as I ducked my head to avoid his sloppy tongue. No matter what the crisis, it's hard not to smile when a golden retriever climbs in your lap and licks your face. "Cisco, what are you doing here?"

"I thought you might need a friendly face." Miles reached into the car for my hand, and Cisco and I tumbled out.

I walked straight into Miles's arms and he kissed me fiercely, holding me so tightly I thought my ribs would crack. I kissed him back and didn't let go until Cisco, panting excitedly, jumped up and rested his paws on my waist, looking for all the world as though he was hugging me too. That made me laugh a little, which was a lot better than crying.

When I stepped away, Cisco dropped all four paws to the ground and I caught his leash. That was when I noticed Bongo's collar and leash were still twisted around my fingers. I'd been holding them so tightly that red marks were etched into my palms. I looked up at Miles, and then quickly, frantically, around the clearing. "Bongo," I said. "He ran into woods. We've got to find him."

"Whoa, baby." Miles placed a staying hand on my shoulder. "Priorities, okay?"

I shook my head violently, pulling away from him. "It's my fault he's out there! It's my fault he's here at all! Besides…"

But I couldn't say the rest. I couldn't even put into words the picture that my random, strobing thoughts were beginning to form. The way he had broken from me, just the way he had lunged out of my grip in Aunt Mart's house. The way he had searched Celie's room, finally grabbing her hat and shaking it in frustration. His dejected demeanor when I led him away. I knew that behavior. I'd stake everything I knew about dogs on the fact that he was tracking something.

"I need to find him," I finished simply, and there was a measure of pleading mixed with the determination in my voice. But my plea was for understanding. I didn't need permission or approval;

I knew what I had to do. "He's a laboratory dog. He won't survive in the wild."

Miles's gaze flickered over my shoulder and Marshall came up behind me, saying, "Great job, Raine. We got the guy. No ID or motive yet, but the FBI is confident we'll have both before the hour's out. We owe you our thanks."

Miles said tersely, "The dog?"

Cisco wagged over to Marshall, and Marshall dropped his hand to his head absently. His face was grave. "We know how important the dog is. The military is sending specially equipped drones and search teams in, but they won't be here until morning. We can activate our own drones, but it'll take them a while to recharge, and it'll be dark in a couple of hours. Our thermal vision isn't sophisticated enough to tell the difference between a deer and a dog at night, so it'll be slow going. If you've got anything better, we're open to it."

I looked at Miles. "The military?"

His expression was at first reluctant, and then resigned. "That's who Bongo was scheduled to be sold to, and that's who funded his training. Our main goal with the Coyote Project has always been to keep military secrets, and industrial secrets that can be used for military purposes, from falling into the hands of foreign governments."

There was something about the way he said "our" that would later strike me as odd, but at the moment I was focused on something else. "So Bongo is a weapon," I said, slowly understanding.

Miles looked as though he wanted to argue, but couldn't find a valid point. "You could look at it like that," he admitted. "But sometimes weapons are the only things that keep the peace."

There's an old saying: the only problem with having the biggest gun is that somebody is always looking to build a bigger one. I think that's what you call a zero-sum game.

I looked down at the collar and leash I still gripped in my hand. Absently I turned the collar over and spotted the small GPS button attached to it. It was amazing how small they could make those things. I supposed that was why they called it micro-technology.

I pried the button loose and handed it to Marshall. I looked at Cisco, who returned my gaze with an amicable swish of his tail. I said, "Cisco can find him."

Marshall said firmly, "You've done your part for today, Raine. We'll search until it gets dark, and like I said, we'll get tech in the air at first light. Until then—"

"We can find him," I interrupted, with a deliberate ferocity to my voice that disguised my desperation, "as long as your so-called search teams don't destroy the trail. That dog is in flight or fight mode, and the more boots you have tramping around in those woods the more frightened he's going to get. Cisco and I are your best chance. Your only chance."

Miles said roughly, "No." That surprised me because he was usually more subtle with his objections. I realized only then how hard it must have been for him, knowing that I was walking into danger and knowing there was nothing he could do about it. He hated to feel helpless. He hated to risk anything, or anyone, that he loved.

"It's getting dark," he said. His tone was clipped. "The dog has a twenty-minute head start, and he's a dog, for God's sake, not a human. Who knows how far he could have gone? Forget it."

I walked to the back of my SUV and opened the cargo hatch. I looped Cisco's leash around the trailer hitch while I stripped down to my tee shirt and removed the body armor the police had loaned me, then pulled my sweatshirt back over my head. I took my backpack, all-weather jacket and Cisco's SAR vest from the storage bin where I kept them in the cargo area. Cisco began to pant and wiggle his rear end with excitement when he saw the tools of his trade. I shrugged into my jacket and walked around to the front of the car. "We've got two hours before dark," I told Marshall, handing him the bulletproof vest. "If I don't find him before then, you can send in your drones and your search teams. But we'll find him."

I pulled on the backpack and bent to strap on Cisco's vest. When I straightened up, Miles was staring down at me, his eyes dark and tumultuous. His nostrils flared with a breath and I thought he was about to say something stupid, but he changed it to a terse, "I'll get my jacket. I'm coming with you."

He swung away, but I caught his arm. "Miles," I said.

I waited until he turned to look at me and then I said simply, "It's what we *do*."

We looked at each other for a long moment, communicating without words in the way that people who care about each other have learned to do since the beginning of time. He understood, and hated it. I understood, and was sorry.

He looked away. I saw his chest rise and fall with his breath.

I said, "I have my phone. I'll stay in touch."

He looked back at me. "Two hours. If you're not back by dark, I swear to God—"

"You'll send out the militia," I finished for him. "Got it."

I snapped on Cisco's tracking lead and led him through the sea of uniforms and police cars and flashing lights and crackling radios to the edge of the woods, near the place I'd seen Bongo disappear. Across the tangle of scrub pine and blackberry vines, the shadows lay quiet and still, like an invitation from an old friend. The noise and the chaos faded behind us. There was only the steam of Cisco's breath on the cooling air, the slant of the sun glinting off newly budded leaves, the smell of the lake. I took out Bongo's collar from my pack and held it for Cisco to sniff.

"Track," I said.

THIRTY-ONE

The suspect's name was Amos Thompson Gerrard, although a quick search of his vehicle uncovered three other identities, each complete with credit cards and driver's licenses from three different states. Also onboard were an AK-47, two handguns with the serial numbers filed off, and a plain old sawed-off shotgun loaded with heavy lead slugs. There was also a silencer for a nine-millimeter handgun, but, oddly enough, the gun itself was not located. A twenty-minute search of the database showed six arrests with no convictions. One of the arrests had been for homicide; the eyewitness in that case had unexpectedly died of a fentanyl overdose two weeks before trial.

"He's what you call an enforcer," Manahan told Buck as they arrived back at the sheriff's office a little after 6:00 p.m. "Mostly works a triangle between Raleigh, Charleston and Atlanta. We've had him on our radar a year or two but haven't been able to tie him to anything significant until now. It's just a matter of tugging on a few more threads until we find the one that leads back to the person who hired him for this job."

"In that case," Buck said, "I might just be able to save you a little thread-pulling." At Manahan's curious glance he explained, "David Sutherlin happens to be a guest of the county detention facility right now, courtesy of his sloppy habits when handling and transporting fentanyl. I might have mentioned he's an attorney for Entretex Pharmaceuticals and the son-in-law of Charles—also known as Chaz—Kramer. That would be the same Kramer who heads up Kramer Worldwide Enterprises and is a founding partner of the Hartwell Group. I thought you might like to say hello."

Manahan lifted an appreciative eyebrow. "As a matter of fact, I would."

The deputy on duty who brought Sutherlin to the interview room was not Deke, and Buck felt a little bad about that. However, the CCTV camera was on and recording when Sutherlin, cuffed but unruffled even in jailhouse khaki, sat down at the interview table.

He gave Buck a cool smile. "You know you're wasting your time and the taxpayers' money. In the first place, your charge will never stick. I work for a pharmaceutical company. I walk off the factory floor with enough Class 3 residue on my clothes to set off every drug dog in the country. In the second place, I'm not sure your so-called traffic stop was even legal. In the third place..." His smile, faint and relaxed, suggested he was enjoying himself. "You have genuinely messed with the wrong lawyer. I've made a career out of making sure that people like me never serve a day in prison. I'll be out of here by morning."

Buck nodded, giving his words due consideration. "You might find this hard to believe," he said somberly, "but I've heard that before." He glanced at Manahan. "Mr. Sutherlin, I don't believe you know Special Agent in Charge Thomas Manahan."

Manahan pulled out a chair, wooden legs scraping on the linoleum floor. "I'd shake your hand," he said pleasantly, "but the last person who did that ended up in a coma."

Sutherlin's expression remained unperturbed, although his smile may have flickered just the slightest. "FBI? For a minor possession charge?"

Manahan leaned back in his chair, flipping open a file folder. "Thanks for reminding me. It looks like I'm going to have to ask the county to drop that charge so that the federal government can prosecute a few more serious ones."

Still, Sutherlin looked unimpressed. "Such as?"

"Such as first-degree murder, theft by taking, kidnapping, fraud, unlawful manipulation of the stock market—also known as insider trading—conspiracy against the United States Government, and that's just off the top of my head." He flipped a page in the folder. "Mr. Sutherlin, do you know a man by the name of Amos Gerrard?"

Buck stayed and listened for a while, but this wasn't his case any longer. By the time he left, Sutherlin was no longer smiling.

Just as Buck was turning for the door, Manahan glanced up and said, "In case I don't see you again, Lawson, it was good working with you. And I sent you an e-mail. I thought it might help tie up your paperwork on the Broderick case."

Buck crossed the breezeway to the courthouse as the sun was setting, bone tired and knowing his day was only half-done. He'd left little Celie in the custody of Jenny and Mart, and with an ER doc checking her for damage, but he hadn't been able to interview Broderick. The charge nurse told him the breathing tube was out, but he wouldn't be strong enough to talk until morning. Buck had made her promise to let the little girl into Broderick's room long enough to kiss her daddy good night, and with a reluctant, admonishing smile, she'd agreed. That was the best he could do for Celie, but he still had three or four hours of desk work, sorting out jurisdictional reports on Sutherlin and Gerrard, not to mention bringing Broderick's file up to date.

He stopped in the sheriff's office to fill his coffee mug from the pot in the break room and was surprised to find Jolene still there. She was sitting in one of the folding chairs that were gathered around the round wooden table, eating vending machine peanuts from a cellophane bag and flipping through a *People* magazine. Nike lay beneath the table at her feet, snoring softly. Second shift was only fifteen minutes old, and no one else was there. Buck took his cup and sat across from her.

"You know," he said, "when I had your job I went home at end of shift."

She looked up at him briefly. "No, you didn't."

"Manahan is interviewing Sutherlin," he said. "He wants us to drop our charges so the FBI can have him."

"My pleasure," replied Jolene, and turned a page.

He took out his phone. "Bad guys are in jail, good guys live to tell the tale. We did good work today, and both of us deserve more than peanuts for dinner."

She didn't reply, and he started checking his e-mail. When he found the one from Manahan, he clicked on the attachment. "Holy crap," he said. He beckoned to Jolene. "Come look at this. The FBI reconstructed the security video from the shooting at Hartwell."

When Jolene heard the familiar words, "Martin? What are you doing here?" coming from the tinny phone speakers, she got up to look over Buck's shoulder at the images on his screen.

Martin Anderson took a surprised step back, looking frightened. "Dr. Broderick. You shouldn't be here."

Here there was a flicker of digital decomposition, and the next words were Broderick's, picked up in mid-sentence. "...isn't it? You've been stealing tech from the project and selling it..."

The video pixilated, and when it resolved again, Martin was objecting, "Crazy! You're the one they fired! You're the one..."

"I should have figured it out sooner," Broderick said. "You had access to everything—all the computer codes, the development labs, the storage facilities...and once you proved you could be bought, you were transferred to the Coyote Project. My God, Martin, do you have any idea what kind of dangerous game you're playing? If I figured it out, do you really think the FBI is that far behind?"

Martin cast an alarmed glance around, as though looking for a place to bolt. He licked his lips. "It's not like that," he said. "You don't understand. Okay, I was being paid, yes, to copy the formulas before they went to market, but by Mr. Kramer. It's his company! That's not illegal."

"You idiot," Broderick said. "You don't know the kind of people you're dealing with. They were grooming you. Let me guess. The last thing Kramer asked you for was the formula from the Coyote Project."

Martin looked terrified, then defeated. "I managed to smuggle out one of the test samples," he admitted, almost in a whisper. "But, Dr. Broderick, you know how many firewalls are guarding the actual formula! I can't get past those. It's all encrypted in a dozen different ways. There's no way I could... and when I said so, he threatened to turn me in. He gave me twenty-four hours or he said he'd turn over enough evidence on me to put me in prison for the rest of my life. He can do it too." He took a breath. "That's when I knew I had to protect myself."

Broderick said, a little incredulously, "So you came here tonight to try to break into the lab? Is that why you turned off the cameras downstairs?"

Martin stared at him. "I didn't turn them off," he said.

There was more distortion, and then Martin Anderson grabbed Broderick's hand with both of his as he said urgently, "We've got to get out of here. If I didn't turn the cameras off downstairs someone else did, and he's in here now. I can't be caught with this.

You've got to get it to the police. It has all the evidence you need."

Broderick said, "I can't—"

"Go!"

With a frantic, distressed glance over his shoulder, Broderick continued at a fast pace past Martin Anderson, down the hallway. Martin moved off screen. In another moment, the dog stopped barking. Martin reappeared on the camera, looking terrified, his hands lifted halfway to his shoulders in a placating gesture. He looked as though he was about to say something, and then there was the soft off-camera *Pouf! Pouf!* of a silenced gun and Martin collapsed, his head blooming red.

"Well." Jolene straightened up slowly when the video went dark. "That explains a lot."

Buck said, "It sounded to me like Anderson was about to turn whistleblower, which is what got him killed. He passed something to Broderick when he took his hand."

"Which would explain why Sutherlin came all the way down here to shut him up."

Buck said thoughtfully, "They found a silencer in with the arsenal in Gerrard's vehicle."

"So they did." Jolene sat back down and picked up her magazine again. "I'm sure the FBI took note of that."

"A lot of unanswered questions," Buck remarked. When she said nothing, he added, "Like what it was Martin Anderson handed off to Broderick just before he was killed. And what Broderick did with it."

She shrugged. "It's out of our hands now."

"Yeah, I guess." He stood to go.

She turned a page in her magazine. "Let me know what you find out."

He said, "What makes you think I'm going to find out anything? Like you said, it's out of our hands. I'm going to go home and get some dinner."

She just chuckled and shook her head, offering the remains of the bag of peanuts to him as she turned another page of the magazine. "Right," she said.

THIRTY-TWO

I found Bongo about twenty minutes into the search, tangled in a thorny blackberry copse at the edge of the lake, looking helpless and scared. He still had the stuffed bear clenched between his teeth. Cisco had practically made a beeline for him, nose to the ground, for there's nothing easier for a dog to track than another dog, as I knew very well. Cisco bounded up to the trapped Labrador, sat and barked his alert, tail swishing as he waited for his reward. I took Cisco's rope toy from my pack and tossed it to him, declaring, "Good find! Good find, Cisco!"

He danced around with the toy in his mouth while I got down on my knees and tried to part the thorns that trapped Bongo. "Hey, dude," I said softly, wincing as a blackberry vine slapped back across my face. "Got yourself in a little mess, didn't you?"

I wiggled farther into the thicket, thorns tearing at my hands and my exposed skin, until I was on level with Bongo. "Hey, buddy," I whispered, reaching out to stroke his head. "Hey, sweet boy. Everything's going to be okay. I promise."

I tried to pry the teddy bear from his mouth so that I could get his collar on, but he held firm. I tried,

"Okay, boy, release." And, "Bongo, drop." He stared at me, his teeth clenched. I tried to wrest the toy from his mouth, and he actually growled at me. I pulled back.

I remembered how he had torn the leash out of my hand to search Celie's room, grabbing her hat, shaking it, dropping it in disappointment. When he'd slipped his collar this afternoon and wrenched out of my grip, I thought he was rushing to Celie, but what if it had been something else?

Sonny had said he was worried about bears.

My heart started to pound. I held Bongo's gaze, and he stared back at me. "Bongo," I said firmly, "good find. Good find, Bongo."

He dropped the teddy bear into my outstretched hand. I scrambled in my back pocket for a handful of liver treats, and fed them to him one by one while I slipped the collar over his head. I painstakingly unwound the blackberry vines from his legs and torso, cutting them with my Swiss army knife when I had to, and carefully backed out of the thicket, tugging Bongo with me and holding the teddy bear under one arm. When we were free, I sat down on the ground and wrapped an arm around Bongo, who was panting from stress but otherwise seemed unharmed. "Good dog, Bongo," I whispered, pressing my cheek briefly against his neck. "Good, good dog. I'm sorry. You deserved better than this. So much better."

Cisco nudged his sweet golden head under my arm, and I hugged him too. "You too, Cisco," I said. "You too."

I wrapped both leashes around one hand and took out my phone, scrolling down until I found the number. I hesitated just one moment, because I knew that what I was about to do could not be undone. Then I pushed the button.

"Sonny," I said, when she answered. "I need a huge favor."

It was almost sunset when Miles pulled his Range Rover onto the side of the highway where Cisco and I waited. He took one look at my scratched face and hands and said, "Tough going, huh? You okay?"

I swallowed hard and couldn't quite meet his eyes. "I'm sorry," I said. "We tried but... it was getting dark, and I knew it was pointless to keep going."

Miles moved behind me to ease the straps of my backpack off my shoulders. "You did the right thing," he said. "If you hadn't called when you did, we would have had to send a search party in after you, and that would've pissed everybody off." He gave me a reassuring smile and opened the back door. Cisco jumped in, and he placed the backpack on the floor beside him.

I showed Miles the teddy bear. "Bongo dropped this," I said. "I think it's why he ran away. The only other time he ever acted like that was this afternoon when he pulled away from me to run into Celie's room. He was looking for something, and he grabbed her hat, but what he was looking for wasn't there." I unpinned the sequined palm tree from the teddy bear's tie. "Because it was here."

Frowning, Miles took the palm tree pin and turned it over in his hand, examining it in the fading light. After a moment he took a pen knife from his pocket and pried something away from the back side of the pin. He placed the small disk in his open palm, showing me.

"What is it?" I asked.

"A micro-disc," he replied. "It holds a couple of terabytes of data, and if you're right about Bongo, it's probably coated with the theft-proof formula that only he can read."

"Which means it's important," I prompted.

He kissed my hair lightly. "Which means you did good, sweetheart." He reached inside the car and ruffled Cisco's ears. "You too, big guy."

Faint praise, for one of the biggest finds of Cisco's life. But it would have to do.

I was too tired on the drive home to speculate on what the micro-disc might hold, and Miles did not share his thoughts. I allowed myself to be hypnotized by the pink and orange glow of a sun setting into the lavender valley of the Smoky Mountains, and was only roused when Miles said, "One point five million dollars."

I glanced at him.

"That's what the military was going to pay for Bongo," he explained. "With an additional amount to lease the formula annually. Not to mention ongoing subsidies that could run into multiple tens of millions."

I turned my gaze to the passenger window, setting my teeth. "I wonder how much those techno-pirates, or whatever you call them, would pay to have Bongo out of the picture. Just because they failed this time doesn't mean it's over."

"True," Miles agreed. "He would've never been safe."

That was when I realized he was already speaking of Bongo in the past tense. I said quickly, "Marshall and the FBI will get their drones out in the morning. Search teams, too."

"Sure they will," Miles said. He signaled the left turn to my road. "But somehow I don't think they're going to find anything."

I turned to look at him.

"And you know something?" He made the turn and reached out to rest his hand on my knee, squeezing gently. "I'm okay with that."

I settled back against the seat, the dusk hiding my smile. I don't think I've ever loved him more.

THIRTY-THREE

Miles and I got to the hospital the next morning just as the police were finishing their interview with Jason Broderick. He was downstairs in the family visiting room because Celie wasn't allowed upstairs and because, under the circumstances, he did not want to spend one unnecessary moment separated from his daughter.

Aunt Mart had called first thing that morning to tell me that Uncle Ro had arrived in time for breakfast, and that she was taking Celie by to visit her father that morning. Jason Broderick was scheduled to be discharged from the hospital that afternoon and would most likely be released on his own recognizance. Miles had a lawyer—a real one this time—working with the Raleigh prosecutor's office to get the charges against him dropped before Broderick was released from the hospital. One thing was certain: he would not be returning to the Hanover County jail.

I was not looking forward to telling him—or Celie—that I'd lost his dog, and when Miles asked if I wanted to come with him to visit Dr. Broderick in the hospital, I almost chickened out. When we arrived and I saw that Buck was among the people gathered around the small table with coffee and donuts in the sunny private visitor's lounge, I wished I had. Things are never particularly comfortable when Miles and Buck are forced to be in the same room together.

I brought Cisco with me, both because I felt bad about not being able to bring Bongo, and because I thought he would be able to keep Celie entertained while we talked to her father. As a certified therapy dog, he had been to the hospital many times, and he knew his job. But first, of course, he had to make an absolute fool of himself greeting Buck, who encouraged him with hearty ear-tugs and shoulder-rubs.

In addition to Buck, Marshall, Agent Manahan and the lawyer Miles had brought up from Atlanta were sitting at the table with Dr. Broderick. For the trip downstairs, Broderick had exchanged his hospital gown for a sweat suit that didn't quite fit—courtesy, I suspected, of the lawyer—which made him look thinner and paler than when I'd last seen him. Aunt Mart sat on the floor with Celie across the room, helping her to put together an oversized puzzle. When I arrived with Cisco, the scene deteriorated into chaos, with Celie running to greet him and Cisco bouncing like a puppy while the adults at the table tried to protect the food. Celie clutched a new teddy bear, this one sporting a blue bow, and when I returned the original, pink-bowed bear to her—as filthy and stiff with dog slobber as it was—she squealed with delight and ran to show her father. This gave me a chance to get Cisco back under control, at least marginally.

"Look, Daddy!" she cried. "Bongo brought back my bear!"

Broderick scooped her up and kissed her and admired the battered bear, but I could tell by the way his eyes met mine that he knew Bongo had not brought back the bear.

Celie wiggled out of her daddy's lap and told me solemnly, "Bongo ranned away. But my daddy says I'm getting a new puppy, and he's going to live at my house and never go to work and be my puppy forever and ever. I'm going to name him Waffles."

I told her I thought that was a great name and asked her if she would like to practice having a new puppy by taking care of Cisco for a while, to which she enthusiastically agreed.

The other men at the table might reasonably have assumed that I would join Aunt Mart, Cisco and Celie on the floor with the toys, but they didn't know me. I turned Cisco over to Aunt Mart, who knew enough about how to get him to perform his tricks to keep Celie occupied for a good long time, and returned to the table. Buck stood up to offer me his chair, but Miles waved him off, bringing up two chairs from the other side of the room for us both.

"I know we're interrupting," he said. "If you'd rather we come back later, no problem."

It sounded like a formality, and as his gaze moved from Manahan to Marshall to Broderick, the response in their eyes gave casual consent. Of course, it's not procedure to conduct a police interview in the company of bystanders, but Miles never had been and never would be simply a bystander. Everyone understood that... except perhaps Buck.

Manahan said, "I was just saying that Gerrard confessed to the killing of Martin Anderson, as well, of course, to the kidnapping. He says he was working for David Sutherlin, but Sutherlin is a tougher nut to crack. It would really help us to know, Dr. Broderick, why you went to the lab that night and, in your own words, what happened when you encountered Anderson."

But Broderick was looking at me. "You're the woman who saved my daughter," he said.

I shifted uneasily in my seat. "I'm sorry I lost your dog."

He looked at me as though he didn't know what I was talking about.

Marshall put in, "We'll continue the search for another twenty-four hours, but frankly, in this terrain, the chances are not good." He darted a quick glance at me for confirmation, and I barely nodded my head. "Of course, we'll post his picture on our website and around town, and notify all the vets and animal shelters in the tri-county area. If you want my opinion…if we find him, it will be because some citizen turned him in."

Broderick shook his head. "It was my fault. I should have factored in redundancy. You *always* have a backup. But the time schedule was so tight, and Bongo was so smart…" Again he shook his head. "My fault."

He folded his hands atop the table and directed his attention to Manahan. "My daughter has a rare blood cancer. Entretex Pharmaceuticals developed a new treatment that looked like a miracle cure, and because of my relationship with Hartwell, I had a chance to get Celie in the clinical trial. We went to Orlando, met with the doctor heading up the trial, did all the tests, and she was a perfect candidate. She was supposed to start regular infusion therapy next week. Then, out of nowhere, I got a notice that she had been pulled from the trial. I couldn't believe it. This was my daughter's *life* we were talking about."

He pressed his lips together for a moment, fixing his gaze on the far corner, composing himself before he went on. "I was frantic. I called everyone I knew. No one could give me an answer about why she had been kicked out of the study. Finally, a couple of days ago, someone from Entretex returned my call. She said she worked for the selection committee and that she wanted to help me get Celie back in the trial. She started going on with some long story about how Entretex wanted to bid on the Coyote Project but questioned some of the data, and that she could virtually guarantee Celie would be put back into the trial if I could help them out by letting their own research department test Bongo on a sample of the formula, which they claimed to already have. The problem was..." He looked at Miles. "They only thought they had the formula. It was part of the trap we'd set up to find out who was buying the stolen tech."

Miles explained, "The FBI suspected Kramer was funneling a lot of the stolen IP to Entretex, but we needed evidence. We knew the big prize, the thing that would make them billions on the black market, was the masking formula, and that the thief wouldn't be able to resist a chance to take it. So we gave him one."

"We knew that whoever had the formula—or what they thought was the formula—would need Bongo to verify it," Broderick went on. "And since I was already discredited—not to mention fired—they figured I would be an easy target." He shrugged uneasily. "When they came to me I didn't have a choice, really. I knew if I turned them down, they'd be suspicious—who would trade his daughter's life for a dog? So I agreed."

I swallowed hard, and Miles, whose arm rested casually along the back of my chair, stroked my shoulder in quiet reassurance.

Manahan said, "Why didn't they just have Martin Anderson deliver the dog? He's the one who gave them the test sample."

Broderick shook his head. "One of the safeguards I'd always used with my dogs is that they were trained to perform on command with a key word. It was a well-known fact. Until I taught the key word to the dog's new owner, the dog was useless. They didn't just need Bongo, they needed me to activate him, so to speak."

"But that's not true," I objected. "Bongo was tracking the scent of the micro-tech in Celie's room, and he went straight for the bear—all without a release word."

Broderick smiled faintly. "Exactly. Bongo was trained differently. I needed one hundred percent reliability, and I needed it fast, so I trained him completely on instinct. There was never a command key. But no one knew that but me."

Manahan nodded. "So you broke into the lab that night to retrieve the dog and deliver him to Entretex.

Had you already arranged a time and place to turn him over?"

"Monday morning," Broderick said. "Today. I was supposed to show up at the lab and claim I had a court order to take possession of Bongo. But I was never going to turn him over. I broke into the lab to get Bongo out of there and keep him safe until I could report what had happened to someone I trusted." He glanced at Miles, and then away.

Manahan nodded. "So what happened when you met Martin Anderson in the hallway? We have part of it on video, enough to tell most of the story, anyway, but we weren't able to recover all of it."

Broderick gave a slow, sad shake of his head. "I should've known it was him. He had access to everything, but he was such a quiet, unassuming guy no one would suspect him... he started going on about Chaz Kramer paying him to sneak tech out of the building, but when Kramer threatened to turn him in unless he delivered the masking formula from the Coyote Project, he got scared. Said he wasn't going to jail for something that stupid, that he had enough money to light out for Mexico and he wasn't coming back until he was cleared of the charges. He gave me a micro-disc that he said had a record of all the transactions he had made to remove IP from Hartwell, and the computer codes he'd used to do it. He told me he was going to use it to blow the whistle on Kramer, but now it was up to me."

Buck spoke up. "What happened to the disc?"

Miles reached into his pocket and produced a zip-lock kitchen bag, passing it across the table to Manahan. Inside was a flat round button so small it might have been overlooked if you didn't know it was there. "Let me guess," he said to Dr. Broderick. "You hid it inside the back of a pin on your daughter's hat."

Broderick shrugged. "I didn't have a lot of time. After talking to Martin, I knew things were a lot more complicated than I'd thought, and that they were about to blow up. I had to get Bongo and get out of town right then." He looked at Miles, seeming momentarily abashed. "Intrigue is not really my thing. You gave me your card, but I never put your number in my phone and all I could remember was that you had a house here in Hansonville. I never expected…" He blew out a breath and finished simply, "I never expected."

Miles said, "Don't worry about the clinical trial, Dr. Broderick. We'll make sure Celie is reinstated immediately. As for Chaz Kramer…" He looked across the table at Manahan.

Manahan answered his unspoken question. "His bank records and computers are being seized as we speak." He nodded at the small disk in the plastic bag. "And if this contains what Martin Anderson claimed, our job is going to be a lot easier."

I looked at Miles, confused. "So it was one of your partners, this Chaz Kramer, who was behind all this?"

Miles nodded. "It looks that way. His son-in-law, David Sutherlin, was his fixer. I suspect the whole reason Sutherlin moved to Entretex was to oversee this theft operation. So much of what was misappropriated from Hartwell these past couple of years was in the biotech and pharmaceutical fields."

I knew it wasn't my place to ask questions, but that had never stopped me before. "I don't get it. If he was a partner in the company, why didn't he just take what he wanted?"

"Because it's illegal, for one thing," Miles said. "And for another, he didn't have access to the kind of material that was being stolen. No one does except the people actually working on the project."

"So what it looks like," Manahan said, "is that Sutherlin—or maybe Kramer—got wind of the fact that Martin Anderson was about to turn on them and had him killed. It was just a stroke of luck that you happened to be at the lab that night, Dr. Broderick, and they could frame you for the murder. Lucky, that is, until they got ready to scrub the security footage and heard what Martin told you. That's when Sutherlin himself came down to take care of you."

Marshall said uncomfortably, "On behalf of the county, Dr. Broderick, we're sorry. About everything."

Dr. Broderick shook his head wearily. "I'm not going to sue."

The lawyer looked as though he wanted to object to that, but a small shake of Miles's head stopped him. Broderick's gaze rested on Celie, who was giggling as she tickled Cisco's white-feathered tummy. He lay on his back, splay-legged, his tongue lolling, looking like a perfect goof-ball.

I pushed back my chair and stood. "I'm going to take Cisco outside," I said.

I promised Celie we'd be back, and couldn't help noticing Aunt Mart's look of relief as I called him to heel. While she adored Majesty, she more or less tolerated all other dogs, and Celie and Cisco at the same time were probably a bit much for her.

I took Cisco out into the cool morning sunshine, across the parking lot and into a grassy area, where he made use of the bushes there. I let him sniff and wander aimlessly for a while, not really paying much attention to anything other than my tangled thoughts. When his ears went up and he swiveled his head excitedly toward someone approaching from my left, instinct kicked in and I brought him sharply back to my side. "Enough," I told him. "Heel."

"So," Buck said, falling into step beside us. "Can't tell the players without a scorecard, huh?"

"I guess."

Buck dropped a hand to scratch Cisco under the chin, and I frowned at him. "Don't do that. He's heeling."

He straightened up. "Tough break about Bongo."

"Yeah." This was something I really didn't want to talk about. "Tough break."

I released Cisco from his heel and he went back to sniffing and exploring. We walked in silence for a while, skirting the fenced dumpsters around the back of the hospital, past the employee parking lot. Cisco paused to scratch a hole in the pine mulch of a recently planted bed of pansies, and I quickly kicked the mulch back into place with my toe.

Buck said, "I wanted to tell you…"

He hesitated for so long that I turned to look at him. His eyes were narrowed in the sun, looking beyond my shoulder at the mountains in the distance. The lines of strain on his face were from more than fatigue.

"Wyn and I have decided to call it quits," he said.

"Oh, Buck." I wanted to reach out and touch him, to pat his arm or smooth his hair, but I knew that wouldn't be appropriate. "I'm so sorry."

"It was mutual." Then he met my eyes and gave a small, sad shake of his head. "It wasn't mutual," he admitted.

He started walking again, his hands tucked into the pockets of his windbreaker. I tried to think of something to say, but couldn't.

He said, "In the last twenty-four hours, I've broken the law twice."

I looked at him in surprise and he added, "For a good reason. It's always for a good reason."

I could tell he was working up to something, and I could tell I wasn't going to like it. I returned my attention to Cisco.

He went on, "You know, in most cases like this, the FBI would shut down the whole company while they completed the investigation. No one would be above suspicion. But I guess not this time."

"The Hartwell Group does a lot of important work," I said. "Besides, they have their suspect in custody."

"Right."

We watched for a moment as Cisco stalked a bumblebee around the pansy bed. I smiled. Buck didn't.

He said, "It doesn't bother you that Young was in partnership with this guy and claims to have no idea what was going on?"

"Miles did have an idea," I pointed out, perhaps a bit sharply. "And as soon as he did, he went to the FBI."

Buck nodded. "That's true." Cisco lost interest in the bee and we started walking again. "But it doesn't say much about his judgment when it comes to picking business partners."

I tried not to bristle. I tried to keep my tone conversational. "Miles told me once that if he only did business with nice people, he'd be in business by himself."

"I guess."

We rounded the corner of the building toward the parking lot. Miles was standing on the steps, talking to Agent Manahan and the lawyer.

Buck said, "I'm curious about why he went to Belgium. In the middle of everything that was going on at Hartwell, knowing that a major government program was about to be compromised, with one of the top scientists on the project in the middle of a sting operation that he set up... He just left the country. What could be so important?"

I felt an uneasiness tingle the back of my neck. "He has business there. Hotels and stuff."

That sounded stupid, even to my ears. We walked for a while with only the sound of Cisco's happy panting between us. Miles noticed us, finished his conversation by clapping Agent Manahan on the shoulder, and started down the steps toward us.

"Raine," Buck said quietly, "don't marry that guy."

I turned slowly, looking at him in disbelief. He gazed back unwavering, tired eyes filled with unspoken regrets. This was the man who had betrayed his marriage vows to me not once, not twice, but three times. Who had left me for Wyn and who now had left Wyn for…what? Who? The man I'd loved since I was fifteen years old and who I would never, ever trust again. There was a lot I could have said to him then, a lot I wanted to say. But all I said was, cooly, "I'll see you around, Buck."

I tugged Cisco lightly into place and walked toward Miles.

"Ask him," Buck said behind me. "Ask him why he went to Belgium."

I did not look back.

THIRTY-FOUR

The night before Melanie was to return from Montana, I got an e-mail from Sonny. I might have mentioned she runs an animal sanctuary up on the mountain, and she has contacts with rescue agencies all over the country. The e-mail was a photograph of a good-looking young couple with their two tow-headed boys, probably eight and ten years old, with a very handsome, very happy-looking black Lab. The caption said, "Jon, Rachel, Timothy and Cade Ivers of Van Nuys, California, and their newest family member."

I beamed and dropped a hand down toward Cisco, who was stretched out at my feet. He immediately sat up for his petting. "Good work, Cisco," I said, scratching his ear. "No one may ever know it but us, but you did good work."

He grinned and swished his tail along the floor, looking as though he not only understood me, but was in perfect agreement.

I heard Miles coming in from the kitchen and quickly closed the laptop. He handed me a mug of coffee, so thick with sweetened cream that it was more of a dessert than a beverage, and gestured with his own mug toward the front porch. "Nice night," he said. "Want to sit outside?"

All four of the dogs bounded outside with us. I pulled the portable gate across the front steps to keep them confined, and Miles and I sat on the swing, watching the stars appear and recede as we glided back and forth. The air was mild, smelling faintly of wet grass and lilacs and, inevitably, of dogs. I sipped my coffee.

"I was thinking," I said. "Maybe we shouldn't say anything to Melanie about the whole Bongo thing. I don't think she would understand."

Miles rested his arm across my shoulders. "You did one of the bravest things I've ever seen anyone do. You saved a child's life. You have nothing to be ashamed of. I think you need to give her more credit."

I shook my head, dropping my gaze to my mug. "I was ready to turn him over to a killer. Melanie wouldn't understand. I don't think even I understand."

His fingers stroked my neck in a light, comforting gesture, then he turned to put his mug on the wicker table beside the swing. He said, "I brought you something from Belgium. I was waiting for the right time to give it to you, but I'm not sure there is one."

I love presents, I really do. But when I turned with barely repressed excitement to see what he'd taken from his pocket, I caught my breath. It was a velvet ring box.

"I know you're not a diamond ring kind of girl," he said, "but this is yours." He opened the lid, revealing what was possibly the most exquisite ring I had ever seen nestled inside. The center diamond was a brilliant marquis-cut stone that was so clear it looked like water. In the light from the living room window behind us, it didn't sparkle; it glowed. The setting was a complex twist of platinum that didn't so much hold the stone as embrace it, and—this was the most striking part—the center stone was surrounded by a bunch of smaller, darker stones that looked like frozen chocolate. The contrast was breathtaking.

"The dark stones are actually industrial diamonds," Miles said, "the workhorse of the diamond world. Solid, dependable, but not worth much until some clever marketer decided to polish them up and call them 'chocolate.' The center diamond is only a carat, because I knew you wouldn't wear anything bigger, but it's flawless." He smiled. "That's a category of clarity, in case you want to tell your friends."

He took the ring out of the box, his expression sobering. "I had it designed for you, Raine, to remind you that I love all the parts of you... the practical and hard-headed, the dark and the light, and that there's value in the parts that you take for granted, maybe that you don't even like. Because the dark only amplifies the light, and what they form together is beautiful. That's why I want to marry you," he added quietly, "and I don't think I ever told you that before. Because when I'm with you I remember how all the pieces fit together, and that you don't have to be flawless to be perfect."

I don't think anyone, ever in the history of the world, has ever received a more beautiful proposal.

His expression turned a little dry. "Like I said, I know you're not a diamond ring person. But this is yours. It's *you*. Wear it when you're ready."

He started to return to ring to its box, but I held out my left hand to him, palm down, fingers outstretched. He slipped the ring on my third finger. Perfect fit.

What do you know about that? Turns out I am a diamond ring kind of girl after all.

A long time and many kisses later, when I had almost—but not quite—grown tired of admiring the way sparks of light and dark danced on my finger, I snuggled up against Miles's shoulder and said, "Is this why you really went to Belgium? For the ring?"

He hesitated just long enough to make me look up at him. His face was half-shadowed, and grew even more obscured when he lifted his cup to his lips. "Partly," he admitted.

I straightened a little, trying to read his expression. "And the other part?"

He didn't answer.

I ventured cautiously, "Because you knew something big was about to break at Hartwell, and that Bongo—and even Dr. Broderick—could be in danger. Whatever you had to do in Europe must've been really important for you to leave them like that."

I waited and got silence. I prompted, "It didn't really have anything to do with hotels, did it?"

A long time ago, Miles made me a promise: he would never lie to me. As far as I know, he's never broken that promise. But truth can be a dangerous weapon, and to avoid its sharpest edges I've learned not to ask questions I don't want to know the answers to. He has learned that sometimes the best thing to do is not to answer at all.

Because, when you get right down to it, the truth is either you trust someone, or you don't.

He kissed me lightly and rose to go in the house. "Coffee's getting cold. Want another?"

I hesitated a moment, then smiled. "Sure."

I knew then that he would never answer my question about why he went to Belgium. And you know something?

I was okay with that.

ABOUT THE AUTHOR

Donna Ball is the author of over a hundred novels under several different pseudonyms in a variety of genres that include romance, mystery, suspense, paranormal, western adventure, historical and women's fiction. Recent popular series include the Ladybug Farm series, The Hummingbird House series, The Dogleg Island Mystery series, and the Raine Stockton Dog Mystery series. Donna is an avid dog lover and her dogs have won numerous titles for agility, obedience and canine musical freestyle. She lives in a restored Victorian Barn in the heart of the Blue Ridge Mountains with a variety of four-footed companions. You can contact her at

www.donnaball.net.